"Coincidence? Uncle Sherlock claimed that was impossible, but for once, I wasn't certain."

*E*valine Stoker and Mina Holmes never meant to get into the family business, but after the Affair of the Clockwork Scarab, they are eager to help Princess Alix with a new case close to her heart. Seventeen-year-old Willa Ashton is obsessed with spiritual mediums, and is convinced she is speaking with her mother from beyond. While Mina is determined to prove Miss Ashton is the hapless victim of fraud, Evaline senses there is something more sinister—or otherworldly—at work. The list of clues piles up—an unexpected murder, the return of vampires to London, and a mysterious spiritglass—but are these things connected? As Uncle Sherlock would say, "there are no coincidences." It will take all of Mina's wit and Evaline's muscle to keep London's sinister underground at bay.

# MORE PRAISE FOR THE STOKER & HOLMES NOVELS

## *The Clockwork Scarab*

"With its fog-shrouded setting, its heart-racing and clever plot and, most of all, its two completely delightful, kick-butt heroines, *The Clockwork Scarab* is pure, delicious fun from beginning to end."

—Rachel Hawkins, *New York Times* bestselling author of the
Hex Hall series

"Thank you, Colleen Gleason, for giving the world the teenage female equivalent of Sherlock Holmes! Where has she been all these years?"

—Sophie Jordan, author of the Forgotten Princesses and the
Firelight series

"Two strong, intelligent heroines, who establish themselves as worthy of the legends that surround each of their families, come together to solve a most dangerous mystery. Gleason's writing is witty, humorous, tense, and beautifully Victorian."

—Kady Cross, author of *The Girl in the Steel Corset*

## *The Spiritglass Charade*

"If Buffy the Vampire Slayer and Sherlock Holmes ever met, this book would be the result. If you loved 'Nancy Drew' or 'The Hardy Boys' as a kid, you're going to love this sci-fi/fantasy mystery series."

—*SLJ Teen*

"Well written, fun, and a clever mix of new story with historical and contemporary references that just kept the pages turning."

—*Nerd Girl*

# The
# Spiritglass
# Charade

A STOKER & HOLMES NOVEL

# THE SPIRITGLASS CHARADE

COLLEEN GLEASON

CHRONICLE BOOKS

SAN FRANCISCO

*To*
the tireless and creative
Maura Kye-Casella
Congratulations on winning the title game!

First Chronicle Books LLC paperback edition, published in 2015.
Originally published in hardcover in 2014 by Chronicle Books LLC.
Copyright © 2014 by Colleen Gleason.

ISBN 978-1-4521-2885-6

The Library of Congress has cataloged the original edition as follows:
Gleason, Colleen, author.
  The spiritglass charade: a Stoker & Holmes novel / Colleen Gleason.
     pages cm.–(A Stoker & Holmes novel ; book 2)
  Summary: In 1889 Evaline Stoker, Mina Holmes, and their time traveler friend Dylan are asked by the Princess of Wales to find out what happened to Robby Ashton, who may have drowned–but the reappearance of vampires in the heart of London threatens to become a more urgent problem.
  ISBN 978-1-4521-1071-4 (alk. paper)
  1. Vampires–Juvenile fiction. 2. Time travel–Juvenile fiction. 3. Missing persons–Juvenile fiction. 4. Spiritualism–Juvenile fiction. 5. Detective and mystery stories. 6. London (England)–History–19th century–Fiction. [1. Mystery and detective stories. 2. Vampires–Fiction. 3. Time travel–Fiction. 4. Missing persons–Fiction. 5. Spiritualism–Fiction. 6. London (England)–History–19th century–Fiction. 7. Great Britain–History–Victoria, 1837-1901–Fiction.] I. Title.

PZ7.G481449Sp 2014
813.6–dc23

                              2013030945

Manufactured in China.

Design by Jennifer Tolo Pierce.
Cover photograph by Alex Farnum.
Typeset by Happenstance Type-O-Rama.
Typeset in John Baskerville.

10 9 8 7 6 5 4 3 2 1

Chronicle Books LLC
680 Second Street, San Francisco, California 94107

Chronicle Books–we see things differently. Become part of our community at www.chroniclebooks.com/teen.

# LONDON, 1889

# MISS HOLMES

## Miss Adler Is Tardy

I reside in the very modernized London of the fifty-second year of Her Majesty Queen Victoria's reign. Our Prime Minister is Lord Salisbury, and Parliament is led by the esteemed Lord Cosgrove-Pitt.

My nation is besotted with science, evolution, and invention. If a device can be conceived, someone somewhere is determined that it should be built (which is the only explanation I have for the unfortunate Hystand's Mechanized Eyelash-Combe).

This proliferation of invention and scientific practice is why I found it both amazing and disappointing that no one had yet invented a working time machine. And the reason I felt this disappointment looked up at me with deep blue eyes.

"Good morning, Dylan," I said as I closed Miss Irene Adler's office door behind me.

Though I'd expected to find the attractive dark-haired woman sitting at a large desk in her Darjeeling-scented chamber,

I confess I wasn't at all disappointed to find the young man instead. In fact, to my chagrin, my cheeks heated and my insides gave a little flutter the instant I saw him.

Such a base reaction can be excused by the fact that, aside from being charming and kind, Dylan Eckhert was one of the most handsome young men I'd ever seen. Not much older than I, Dylan had thick hair in every shade of blond. It was unstylishly long, falling into his eyes and covering his ears, and winging up a little at the tips. He had a strong square chin and jaw, perfectly straight, white teeth, and a clear blue gaze that turned pleasantly warm when he was happy or amused. Unfortunately, more often than not, that cerulean gaze was tinged with sadness or despair—a condition which I meant to help eradicate.

If I could help him find a way back home.

"Hi, Mina." He was holding a curious device. It was a slender, sleek object, slightly larger than my palm. Silvery and mirrorlike, the rectangular item was capable of making loud, erratic noises, lighting up at unexpected moments, and showing amazingly tiny moving pictures.

According to Dylan, it was a telephone. And apparently, this sort of mechanism was very common where he came from . . . more than one hundred and twenty years in the future.

Hence the requirement of a time-traveling machine.

"I expected Miss Adler to be here," I said, sitting in one of the chairs on the other side of the desk. "Her message said ten o'clock sharp." My impatience could be excused, for I had been waiting for nearly a month to be summoned to this chamber again.

My mentor's office was deep inside the British Museum, for Irene Adler was, among other things, the current Keeper of Antiquities at the institution. Or, at least, that was what she told curious-minded people. But there was more to her current occupation than simply unpacking and cataloguing long-forgotten treasures from Egypt and the Far East.

One couldn't tell it from her work area, however. The chamber wasn't particularly large, but it was well-organized and elegantly furnished, with a circular table in the center and the large desk at one end. Bookshelves lined the walls and a Tome-Selector had halted in the process of using its slender mechanical fingers to replace—or remove; one couldn't necessarily tell—a copy of *The Domesday Book*. A stack of newspapers sat at the corner of the desk, and one of them was mounted in a Proffitt's Dandy Paper-Peruser.

Behind Dylan was a credenza, on which I observed a new addition to the chamber: a charming copper teapot. It appeared to be a self-heating one, for it sat on a small cogwork dais from which I heard the emission of soft clicks and whirs.

Mingled with the scent of Miss Adler's favorite tea (the aforementioned Darjeeling), as well as a hint of her preferred perfume (gardenia), was also the faint odor of antiquity and even a little mustiness, though my mentor was meticulous about keeping her office dusted and swept. At the moment, the set of tall, narrow windows that looked out onto a small patch of grass on the north side of the Museum were unshuttered. The openings revealed the usual dull, grayish London weather at midmorning, and in the distance, I could see the shiny black spire of the Oligary Building.

Before Dylan could respond to my query, the door flew open. The pile of newspapers fluttered, the teapot's top rattled, and I actually felt a breeze announcing the late arrival.

"Good morning, Mina. Hello, Dylan," said Miss Evaline Stoker. The energetic young woman was my reluctant partner and occasional companion. Presumably, she'd been summoned as well. I wouldn't go so far as to call her an intimate friend, but I suppose since I'd saved her from being electrofied and she'd dragged me out of a fire, we'd progressed beyond mere acquaintances. "Miss Adler isn't here? Where is she?"

"Dylan was about to tell me before you—er—bounded into the chamber," I told her, watching as she settled gracefully, but no less quietly or slowly, into a chair across from me.

Miss Stoker was an attractive woman of seventeen with thick, curling black hair, lively hazel eyes, and perfect features. Unlike myself, she was petite and elegant—and also unlike myself, she was social, capricious, and a member of the peerage.

And while I, a member of the famous Holmes family (the niece of Sherlock and the daughter of Mycroft), was blessed with brilliant deductive and observational skills (not to mention the prominent Holmesian nose), Miss Stoker had been endowed by a very different family legacy. According to legend, she was supposedly a vampire hunter.

Or at least she would be if there were actually any vampires to hunt.

"I don't know where she is," Dylan replied, picking up his silvery telephone-device again. "Evaline, didn't you say you knew somewhere I could get electricity?"

"*Dylan.*" I glanced at the door, which was still tightly closed.

"Yeah, I know. Electricity is illegal here. But Evaline said she knew someone who might be able to help me charge my phone."

"Right. Yes. I . . . believe I do." Miss Stoker held out her gloved hand matter-of-factly, but of course I noticed the heightened color in her cheeks. "I'll take it to—uh—I'll get it charged for you."

He hesitated handing it over, and I was certain I knew why.

Even though Dylan had accidentally traveled here from London in 2016, somehow that singular device occasionally— *very* occasionally—was able to connect him back to that time if he stood in a particular area of the Museum. I suspected he was afraid of allowing out of his possession the one thing that might help him return—or at least communicate with—home.

Dylan had uncertainty written all over his face. "I don't know if I told you this, but there have been a few times when

I've been in the room where I first appeared that my cell phone seemed to connect to the Intern—I mean, to my time."

"I believe it happened once while I was present." I found the small mechanism fascinating and yet eerie.

"Last night, I was down there in that basement room and it connected for a *long time*. Almost three minutes. I texted—I mean, I sent a message to my parents to let them know I was okay. They're back home in Illinois, and as far as they know, I'm still at school here in London."

He drew in a deep breath, as if to collect his thoughts. "I also had the chance to do some quick research on time travel, to see if there was anything science had discovered from my time that might help. There's this thing called string theory, which says that space and place are always constant, always the same. But time is different—like strings hanging in one space. So we're each on a string that hangs or floats or whatever, in our time. It seems like I might have gotten bumped over to your string, which brought me from my time to this time, but kept me in the exact same place."

I nodded, understanding the elements of what he was saying (unlike Miss Stoker, whose blank expression indicated how little she comprehended). "And the question is . . . how did you move from your string to ours?"

"Exactly. If we figure that out, maybe that's a way to send me back. Scientists in my time say time travel is impossible. But . . . well, here I am. Proof that it isn't. Unless it's all just a bad dream." His expression sobered and the light faded from his eyes. "It has to be some sort of mathematical calculation, I think. That causes a vibration or something that makes the time-string move. . . . I don't know. I don't understand much of it. And I know you're working on it, Mina," he said earnestly. But that sadness lingered in his eyes.

I bit my lip. "But perhaps not as hard as I should be. Instead of studying face powders and—"

"Don't feel bad." He reached over to pat my arm. "If the greatest scientists of my time can't figure it out, I don't know how *you* could expect to in only a few weeks. But that's why this is really important to me, and why I need this thing charged." He turned to Miss Stoker.

"I'll take good care of it. But I can't let you come with me. It's too dangerous—not only because it's in Whitechapel, but also because I have to protect my . . . um. . . ." Her cheeks turned a shade pinker.

"Your source?" Dylan supplied.

"Right. My *source*. I like that word." Evaline smiled and held out her hand once more. "I'll protect it with my life. I promise."

I had misgivings about Miss Stoker's ability to keep the device safe, for she's an impetuous young woman who doesn't often think before she acts. Not only that, but she had more than once given me the impression she would rather seek out danger than find a more thoughtful, logical, *safer* way to solve a problem. But I didn't see how our friend had any choice other than to entrust her with it. After all, the device would no longer be useful to Dylan if he didn't get more electricity for it. And since the use or generation of that dangerous commodity had been criminalized by the Moseley-Haft Steam Promotion Act, such a source of energy was illicit and highly illegal.

Just as Dylan allowed the object to slide slowly into Miss Stoker's palm, the door opened once more. This time, it was the expected, elegantly garbed woman who entered.

Irene Adler is an attractive American woman of stage talent (mostly song). She is more famously known, at least to myself and my family, as the only woman to ever outsmart Uncle Sherlock. Thus, he calls her *the* woman.

To commemorate the occasion, he keeps a picture of her on his mantel—along with several other mementos of previous adventures. The photograph was the only compensation he accepted for the case, which had involved a scandal with the King of Bohemia.

Miss Adler subsequently married Godfrey Norton, at least according to what was published in the papers. However, during the time I knew her, she was always Miss Adler rather than Mrs. Norton, and she never referred to her husband. I suspected there might have been a divorce . . . or perhaps he never even existed. Regardless, for unknown reasons, the vivacious Miss Adler left the European stage (where she had quite a following) to take on the role of the Keeper of Antiquities for the Museum.

"My apologies for being late," Miss Adler said as she swept briskly around to the seat behind the desk. Dylan had vacated the chair as soon as she appeared, and now he stood, leaning against the wall. "One of the cog-carts blew a gasket and stopped traffic in the Strand. And now we are behind schedule."

"Do you have a new assignment for us?" Evaline asked before the poor woman had even settled into her seat. I glowered at my counterpart, but she didn't seem to notice.

"Perhaps," Miss Adler replied, seeming not at all nonplussed by my companion's impatience. She turned her arm to check the wide-banded wrist-clock she always wore. "But we must leave immediately. It's later than I thought." She hadn't taken a seat at the desk, but instead reached behind it to pull out a small reticule and an umbrella, then marched back around toward the door.

"Where are we going?"

"You might join us as well, Dylan." Miss Adler slung the umbrella's curled handle over her pristinely gloved wrist and eyed him critically. "You're dressed well enough to be presented to Her Royal Highness, now that you've put on the new clothing I bought you."

"Her Royal Highness?" A prickle of interest and excitement swept over me. "Are we going to Marlborough House?"

During our first meeting, Miss Adler confessed to Evaline and me that, although she was employed by the

Museum as prescribed, she was also using her contacts and expertise in Europe to work for Alexandra, the Princess of Wales and daughter-in-law of the Queen, on a variety of tasks related to royal and national security.

That was how Evaline and I came to be called into service for our country as well. Miss Stoker and I had been approached because of our family legacies, and because we were young women. In short, no one would ever suspect *us* of working as secret agents for the Crown. Young women, claimed Society's conventional wisdom, lacked the intelligence or the skills for anything other than marrying and raising children.

That school of thought was a delicious joke, in my opinion. After all, weren't England's two greatest monarchs— Queen Elizabeth and now Queen Victoria—women?

A faint smile curved Miss Adler's lips, but I observed weariness and shadow in her normally bright eyes. "Indeed. The Princess of Wales wishes to meet you and Miss Stoker, and I suspect she may have something else about which she wishes to speak to you. And as we have an eleven o'clock appointment, we are in danger of being late, so we must be off. One cannot keep a princess of the realm waiting."

"No, of course not." I rose, aware of a sense of relief and anticipation that Princess Alexandra wanted to see us.

My first (and only) assignment with Miss Stoker had been thrilling and dangerous—and it had been completed more than a month ago. When neither Evaline nor I were contacted by Miss Adler in the weeks that followed, I couldn't help but wonder whether the near-disaster that occurred during the

Affair of the Clockwork Scarab (as I'd begun to call it) had soured our royal sponsor on the concept of pressing extraordinary young women like us into service. I'd tried to ignore the crushing disappointment—the fear that I'd bungled my first assignment and would be relegated to working alone in my laboratory and poring over books day after day in my father's silent study.

Miss Stoker elbowed me as we followed Miss Adler out of the office. "All that worrying for nothing," she muttered. "We're going to meet the princess so she can thank us herself."

When we left the Museum, we were obliged to employ umbrellas—a not uncommon occurrence in our dreary London. However, today the dampness in the air was hardly more than a drizzle, and I could almost feel my thick chestnut-brown hair begin to tighten and kink beneath my hat like the bric-a-brac that trimmed my gloves. I patted the tight coil at the nape of my neck, hoping it wouldn't appear too disastrous by the time we arrived at Marlborough House.

I sat next to Dylan, in the carriage, and he seemed to take up quite a bit more room on the seat than I expected, for he was very close to me, and our arms brushed companionably. If it weren't for the layers of petticoat beneath my narrow skirt, surely I would have been able to feel heat from the side of his leg pressing against mine. I confess, I didn't mind his proximity in the least—although when I noticed Miss Stoker watching me with knowing eyes, that dratted flush warmed my cheeks again.

"London can be so dark and gloomy, even in the middle of the day," Dylan observed. Despite the drizzle, he'd unlatched the carriage window and nearly had his head poking out the opening as he watched the sights. "It's like dusk all the time, with the buildings so tall and close together and it being rainy and foggy almost every day. What's that tall black one over there, with the spikes on top?"

I knew which structure had prompted his comment. "The Oligary Building. Mr. Oligary's factories are the premier manufacturers of steam-cogs and gears. He manages his business from the offices in that building. Incidentally, Miss Adler—did you hear the news about Mr. Babbage's Analytic Engine? There's to be a small exhibition in the lobby of the Oligary, displaying all of Mr. Babbage's notes and prototypes."

"I would find that quite fascinating," replied my mentor. "When is it to open?"

"The article in the *Times* said it opened today. Perhaps we can make a detour and stop there on our return."

Miss Adler nodded, but once again I noted her tight, drawn expression. She appeared pale beneath her expertly applied rouge and was more subdued than usual. I wondered if she was ill or merely tired.

"That's a creepy-looking building, if you ask me," Dylan commented. "It looks like something out of Mordor. Tall, black, and shiny."

I was used to Dylan's references to unfamiliar places and people, as well as his odd vernacular. "I find the structure rather interesting in appearance. It's very different from the rest of London, with our flat-faced, rectangular brick buildings lined up in a row like uneven teeth, gears and chimneys protruding from their roofs."

Dylan turned from the window and grinned at me—an event that, I'm ashamed to admit, made my insides go soft. "And you didn't even ask me what Mordor was," he said in a low, teasing voice. "Surely you haven't lost your sense of curiosity, Miss Holmes?"

My insides squished more. I hastily turned my attention back to the cityscape, studiously avoiding Miss Stoker's gaze.

"Of course not," I managed to say calmly. "For if I asked what you meant every time you made a reference I didn't understand, we'd never finish a conversation. And look— there's one of the new vendor-balloons. They make it easier for the merchants to travel without clogging up the streetwalks."

Thus distracted, Dylan gazed out the window at the neat elliptical balloon with its small cart beneath. His thick blond hair ruffled in the breeze as drizzle splattered the windowsill, and I couldn't help but admire his handsome features.

Unlike with Evaline Stoker, young men never teased me. They rarely even spoke to me, and certainly not with such familiarity and ease. Nor did I feel comfortable enough around them to do more than converse in a stilted fashion— or, worse, launch into some babbling lecture.

Despite the fact I rather enjoyed feeling Dylan's solid arm jolting against me as we traveled through the clogged streets, I was impatient to arrive at Marlborough House and be apprised of the princess's intentions.

We finally alighted from the carriage. Once ushered into the palatial home, we were directed to the princess's private parlor. This entailed taking three steps from the threshold of the grand foyer, then stepping onto a slow-moving circular platform. When we came around to the proper direction, we stepped off the dais and onto one of three moving walkways that led to different wings of the palace. A page stood at the junction of each walkway and the circular platform, offering the assistance of a gloved hand to make the transition easier for each visitor.

The boy who handed our group off onto the walkway was wearing yellow livery, down to his gloves and shoes. Through simple observation, I noticed the young man had a fondness for caramels, had recently had his hair cut, and was left-handed.

"Notice," I murmured to Dylan as the walkway rumbled along beneath our feet, "the pages here are dressed in yellow because they attend Prince Bertie and Princess Alexandra. The personal servants of the Queen always wear red, white, and blue."

"Queen Victoria." Dylan's tones weren't quite as circumspect as mine had been, but such wonder blazed in his eyes I didn't have the heart to admonish him for it. "The *real* Queen Victoria. Do you think there's any chance we might actually see her?"

"Not here. She is currently in residence at Buckingham Palace, and I can think of few reasons for her to come here. She is a grand lady, and very imposing, as one would expect. But she hardly ever leaves the palace anymore."

"And . . . uh . . . who exactly is Princess Alexandra?" Dylan asked, this time in a more subdued voice.

"She is the Princess of Wales and her father is the King of Denmark. She's married to the Queen's son, Prince Albert Edward, informally known as Prince Bertie. Everyone loves Bertie and Alix, as she's often called. They're much more popular than the Queen—the princess especially."

The end of the moving walkway approached, and I took Dylan's arm (for he hardly ever remembered to offer it, claiming that simple courtesy was hardly ever done in 2016) as we stepped off. A yellow-gloved page was there to assist on this end of the journey as well.

A tall set of double doors confronted us. The page pulled an ornate copper lever and the entrance parted like a theater curtain, revealing a surprisingly small and cozy parlor. Because of the dampness and the princess's propensity for taking chill, a small fire burned at the hearth.

Surprisingly—or perhaps not, due to the nature of our visit—there was only one occupant in the chamber. Her Royal Highness was sitting on a dark red settee with thick velvet cushions. Its brass frame was fashioned like a tree trunk, with elegant branches arching into sidearms on either end. A mechanical bird perched on one gleaming branch, singing softly.

Princess Alexandra was forty-five years of age—making her at least a decade older than Miss Adler—and still a slender, extremely handsome woman. She had dark hair swept into a complicated mass of braids and coils, leaving a fringe of tight dark curls just above her brows. Her almond-shaped eyes were dark and lively, framed by thick lashes. She wore a bodice with a high, lacy neck meant, I knew, to hide a small scar from her childhood. Leaning against the settee within easy reach was a gold-knobbed walking stick encrusted with emeralds and topazes. I observed the princess had recently had her fingernails buffed and used a hair dye to keep her tresses ink-black.

"Irene." She gestured for us to approach. Her voice was warm and melodious, and she seemed much less stilted than her mother-in-law, to whom I'd been presented several times due to my father's work. "Come in and introduce me to these most amazing young ladies. And this handsome young man."

"I apologize for being tardy," said Miss Adler with a curtsy. She spoke a trifle louder and slower than usual due to the princess's partial deafness. "But you know how London traffic is."

"Not at all," our hostess replied with a tinkling laugh. "You know how terribly unpunctual I am! Now, please. I feel certain I've met this young lady when she was presented at Court. Evaline Stoker. You're a Grantworth as well, if I recall. And you must be the Holmes girl. Mina, is it? Your father has been instrumental in assisting the Home Office with a variety of situations. And your uncle! Miraculous in his solving of crimes, if I do say so. Make yourselves comfortable, ladies. This is an informal meeting. But who are you, young man?"

Evaline and I had taken our turns curtsying during Princess Alexandra's breathless speech, but now that the princess's attention had fallen on Dylan, Miss Adler gestured for us to sit as she introduced him. "He is helping me with a variety of tasks at the Museum, but Mr. Eckhert was also instrumental in assisting Miss Holmes and Miss Stoker in their last assignment."

"Well, then I must include Mr. Eckhert along with you two young ladies in my gratitude for investigating the business with the clockwork scarabs and discovering who was killing those poor girls. Thank you, most sincerely, from the bottom of my heart for stopping the Ankh before she hurt anyone else."

While I flushed with pleasure under her open regard and appreciation, it also made me slightly nauseated. For while Princess Alexandra was correct that Evaline and I had foiled the androgynous character known as the Ankh, I alone remained unconvinced that the female body that had been recovered and identified as the murderer's was in fact the villainous person we'd been chasing. Everyone else—including Scotland Yard—believed the case was closed.

I, on the other hand, had nearly accused Lady Isabella Cosgrove-Pitt, wife of the Parliamentary leader, of being the Ankh.

That had not been my finest hour. Particularly since it had been witnessed by one Inspector Ambrose Grayling of Scotland Yard.

"Thank you for giving us the opportunity to serve you and our country." Miss Stoker inclined her head in graceful acceptance of the princess's gratitude. "I speak for both Mina and myself when I say we are looking forward to our next assignment."

"Indeed." I was irritated for not having responded before Evaline did so.

"Excellent. Then I shall tell you why I have called you to attend me. But whilst I do so, if you don't mind, Irene, would you make certain your companions sample the truffles? As you know, they are not to be missed." The princess smiled, and a charming dimple appeared at the corner of her mouth.

"Most assuredly," Miss Adler replied, picking up the tray on the small table next to her. "Her Highness does not exaggerate. The chocolate truffles made by her Danish pastry chef are so delicious, even the Queen makes excuses to visit in order to have one."

Dylan and I exchanged covert glances and he waggled his eyebrows. I merely smiled and shook my head. It was simply inconceivable he'd meet the Queen any time soon.

Miss Stoker was already examining the tray of chocolates. They were each the size of a large cherry, and in a variety of unusual colors: pastel pink, robin's egg, daffodil, mint, and iced orange. Each was enclosed in a loose, springy swirl of spun sugar that glittered in the light, giving the truffle the appearance of being in motion. I could not conceive how the chef had placed the spheric chocolates inside each delicate coil without fracturing them.

"Now," said our royal hostess. "On to the matter I wish you to investigate. There is a young woman by the name of Willa Ashton. Her mother, Marta, and I were very close friends until Marta died, for she was one of the few ladies who came from Denmark with me. She married Ferdinand Ashton, the son of Baron Fruntmire. When I was ill with the rheumatic fever—goodness, twenty years ago that was—Marta sat with me nearly every day, and I came to love her dearly. Willa is just as charming and empathetic as her mother was, and I have summoned you today because I am greatly concerned for her mental and physical well-being."

When the princess paused to take a sip from the tea in her delicate china cup, I took the opportunity to slip one of the bite-sized truffles into my mouth. The sugary coil melted on my tongue, and the tinted exterior turned out to be a thin shell with an essence of citrus (I had selected one of the yellow ones). But inside. . . . It was nearly impossible for me to hold back a sigh of delight, for the interior of the sweet was like nothing I'd ever tasted. Light and fluffy, chocolaty without being too rich, buttery and decadent with a hint of crunch.

"Do you not agree they are the best chocolates you've ever tasted?" asked the princess, obviously noticing my reaction.

As my mouth was still filled with the ambrosia, I could only nod vehemently.

"Marta died five years ago," continued our hostess. "Before that, she and Willa often accompanied me on my visits to London Hospital. Willa has continued to do so, and she's grown into such a sweet, lovely young woman. She spends much of her time in the children's ward, telling them stories. The boys in particular ask for her every day, or so the nurses tell me.

"But then her younger brother, Robby, disappeared, a little less than two months ago. It's believed he fell into a canal and drowned, but his body was never recovered. Willa isn't convinced he's dead, and has become obsessed with finding him. She's become enamored with Spiritualism, and believes it can help her solve the puzzle."

"Spiritualism? Do you mean to say Miss Ashton attends séances—or that she is acting as a medium herself?" I asked, firmly redirecting my attention from the tray of truffles, which, thanks to Dylan and Evaline, had been pared down to a meager trio of chocolates.

"She is attending them—quite regularly, in fact. And, I suspect, is paying quite a bit of money to the mediums she uses. Willa insists her mother is speaking to her from beyond— and although that may very well be true," the princess added hastily, surely thinking of her own mother-in-law's attraction to spirit-talking with the Queen's dead husband, Albert, "I fear there is some other unpleasant purpose at work here. For I am concerned . . . well, I suspect either someone is attempting to fleece her fortune out from under her, or—worse—that someone is attempting to drive her mad."

# Miss Stoker

## *An Unexpected Maneuver*

I had taken the last of the chocolates—right beneath Mina Holmes's bladelike nose—when Princess Alexandra made her announcement about Willa Ashton.

"Fleece her fortune? Drive her mad?" I repeated, my enthusiasm deflating. That sounded beyond boring. No abductions? No chases through the streets? No visits to opium dens? I popped the chocolate in my mouth and tried not to appear uninterested.

Mina, on the other hand, looked as if she'd been given a jeweled cuff on a golden platter. No surprise there, for this was the type of problem she was good at: putting pieces of a puzzle together.

Me? Give me a dark street to patrol. A disreputable neighborhood in which to look for trouble—or at least a vampire to slay. I surreptitiously felt inside my pocket. Dylan's sleek telephone-device was still there, waiting for me to take it to a particular seedy pub in Whitechapel.

At least I'd have *something* interesting to do tonight.

"What sorts of things have been happening to make you believe Miss Ashton is the target of some villainy?" my so-called partner asked.

"It's Willa's insistence that her brother is still alive. It's . . . unnatural. She claims her mother has been visiting her and sending her messages from beyond. Poor Willa is filled with grief, distracted and utterly moddle-headed—I'm simply concerned she's being taken advantage of."

"Visits from her dead mother?" There was skepticism in Mina's voice.

The princess shook her head. "I believe it would be best if you met Willa, and perhaps attended a séance with her. Then you can experience it—"

An urgent knock at the door had us all turning.

"Yes?"

The door opened and a wide-eyed butler appeared. "The *Queen*. Is *here*, Your Highness."

"The *Queen*? How unexpected." The princess's brows rose up into the fringe of black curls on her forehead. "Well, don't keep her wait—"

But she didn't finish, for the butler's face turned pink, then white, and he yanked the door open to reveal none other than Queen Victoria.

We all leapt to our feet, curtsying and, in Dylan's case, bowing, as she rolled—literally—into the chamber. At seventy years of age, the Queen was large, gray-haired, and stately. She was wearing a plain, simple gown of taffeta in several shades of gray, along with a lacy white veil. Her only jewels glinted at the cuffs of her dress and in a brooch pinned to its collar. Accompanying her was a retinue of footmen, ladies, and a small copper-colored dog.

The Queen was riding upon a small platform with two dinner-plate-sized wheels, one on each side. Her veil and the hem of her skirt fluttered as she trundled across the floor, using something similar to bicycle handlebars to navigate. The small dog sat in a bucket attached to the side.

"Madam," said the princess as she rose from her brief curtsy. "What a pleasant surprise. You've arrived just in time to join us for some of the chocolate truffles you enjoy so much." She gestured to the gaping butler, who fled the chamber.

"Be seated," said the Queen to the room as she alighted carefully from her vehicle. She made her way to the largest sofa. Two footmen assisted her in settling her bulky self, yards of skirts and petticoats, and the long lacy veil onto the cushions. The ladies who accompanied her found seats where they could—including in the ones Mina and I had just vacated.

I glanced at my companion, who, for once, had nothing to say. I noticed Dylan was standing very close to Mina, and he seemed to be poking her with his elbow. Was he *laughing*?

"And who is this?" the Queen demanded, and Dylan sobered.

Princess Alix introduced us, but didn't mention the reason for our visit. The Queen didn't ask. Nor did she indicate any reason for her unexpected appearance. Instead, she seemed to be watching the parlor entrance, and we all sat in an awkward silence. The only noise came from Queen Victoria's small, fluffy dog, who was snuffling about on the floor around the hems of everyone's gowns. I hoped he wasn't about to lift his leg.

Then I realized with a start that among the attendants— all of whom were ladies of the realm—was none other than Lady Cosgrove-Pitt. I smiled a greeting at her. The wife of our Parliamentary leader was an attractive woman in her early thirties, dressed expensively and in the height of fashion. She was like a bird of paradise next to our drab, pigeonlike monarch.

"Ah," the Queen said at last when a maid and two footmen appeared. The young men were carrying tiered trays piled high with truffles.

Apparently the Queen really *did* like the chocolates.

"Tressa, have a large box of them packaged up for Her Majesty." There was a subtle layer of amusement in Princess Alix's voice. As her mother-in-law devoured several truffles almost as quickly as Dylan had, the tension in the chamber eased. Small bits of conversation sprang up.

"Why, Irene Adler. What a pleasure it is to see you . . . and not even onstage," said Lady Cosgrove-Pitt, inclining her head toward my companion. She didn't rise from her seat.

"Lady Isabella." Miss Adler adjusted her wrist-clock. Her tones were unusually cool and very polite. "You're looking quite well."

"As are you," replied Lady Cosgrove-Pitt after a noticeable pause. "I understand you're working at the British Museum now?" Her tone was pitying. Not surprising, coming from a woman who hadn't worked a day in her life.

At that moment, the princess turned her attention back to Mina and me. "Very well then, ladies. I've told you all I can at this time. I suggest you visit Willa Ashton yourself and—er—get to know her. She'll be expecting your visit."

This was clearly a dismissal, so the four of us curtsied (and bowed).

"Your Majesty, we beg your leave," Miss Adler said to the Queen.

"Of course." The Queen smiled and was reaching for another truffle when she noticed her dog scrabbling at something beneath the settee. "Marco!" she scolded as she slipped the cherry-sized chocolate into her mouth. "You bad boy!"

He poked his head out from beneath the skirt of the settee with a scrap of lace hanging from his mouth like a long, pink mustache. The poor thing looked completely bewildered at being caught out that everyone erupted in raucous laughter, including his mistress.

But Queen Victoria's laugh stopped abruptly. Her eyes widened. She began to clutch at her throat, her mouth open.

"She's choking!" exclaimed one of the footmen.

"Do something!" cried Lady Cosgrove-Pitt.

But no one seemed to know what to do.

It was horrid: a noiseless, gaping Queen, her eyes goggling and terrified, her face turning pale. Not a sound came from her throat, for the round chocolate was fully lodged there.

We all stared—frozen and helpless. Time seemed to stop.

The chamber had gone sickly quiet. We watched in horror as the Queen continued her silent struggle. Her face was turning gray and her hands eased from her throat.

There was nothing that could be done.

We were watching the Queen of England *die*.

"*Do something*! Why is no one doing anything?" Dylan shouted as he looked around frantically.

"Try pounding her on the back," cried Miss Adler, starting to move to do it herself.

One of the footmen reached the Queen first, and, after a brief hesitation, began pounding on the choking woman's back. But the Queen continued to collapse, horribly silent and still. Grayer. Weaker.

"*Move*." Dylan rushed over. "Let me."

He pushed the footman aside so hard he bumped into Miss Adler. When Dylan put his arms around the Queen from behind, I heard a soft gasp from one of the ladies.

The Queen is a large woman, but Dylan was strong enough to . . . "My *gad*, what is he doing?" I whispered to Mina as our friend seemed to embrace Victoria, his hands wrapping around her center.

"I haven't the faintest idea."

Dylan clasped his hands together in the middle of the Queen's torso and slammed this joined fist sharply into her, once, twice, thrice.

Someone gasped and one of the footmen shouted, "What are you doing to her? Stop him!"

"I'm . . . saving . . . her . . . life," Dylan said, struggling with the heavy woman. By now, the Queen, still eerily silent, was half sagging over his strong arms, and as we watched, he delivered four sharp blows to her back, then did that odd embracing-thrust again.

He cursed under his breath, his expression desperate and determined as he slammed a hand into her upper back for a third time, one, two, three. . . . Two of the footmen lunged for Dylan, but he wrapped his arms around the Queen and thrust his fists once more into her torso. All at once the chocolate flew out of her mouth.

"Oh!" gasped one of the ladies. Another screamed. Marco the dog lunged for the candy, but a footman snatched it away in the nick of time.

The Queen dragged in a loud, desperate drag of air and began to gasp and pant. But she was breathing! Dylan gently released her onto the settee as the chamber erupted in exclamations, applause, and solicitous activity around the Queen.

Dylan tottered over to Mina, pale and bewildered. "Did I just save the Queen of England's life?"

"Yes," she replied, gawking at him. "That was . . . I've never seen anything like it. *Extraordinary.*"

"How did you know what to do?" I looked at Dylan with new admiration. "And she's not light of weight." *I* could have lifted her, but then again, *I* was an unusually strong vampire hunter.

"It's called the Heimlich Maneuver." A smile played about his lips. "I guess you don't know about it yet."

Mina shook her head. "We do now."

"Young man!" A querulous, scratchy voice caught our attention.

Dylan stiffened and turned to face the Queen, his smile fading. I could tell he was worried whether he was going to be reprimanded for touching her so roughly. *I* was worried that he was going to be reprimanded for touching her at all.

"You. Come here."

He walked over to face the Queen, back straight, head held high. With a glance at each other, Mina and I edged in behind him.

"Your Majesty," Dylan said, then gave a deep bow. "I hope I didn't . . . um . . . hurt you."

"You dared to put your hands on me," Queen Victoria said. Her voice was rough and raspy, but normal color had returned to her face. Dylan stiffened at her words and began to speak but she interrupted. "And in so doing, you saved my life. And though I miss my Albert terribly, I am not quite ready to join him yet. So I will always be grateful, young man."

She fiddled with something at her cuff, then handed a small shiny object to Dylan. "Keep this. It's one of Albert's onyx and diamond cuff links, one of my most prized possessions. You'll see his seal is on it. If you ever are in need of anything, Mr. Dylan Eckhert, you need only show this as a sign of my favor and gratitude."

"Thank you, ma'am. Your Majesty," he corrected himself. "It was nothing."

"I beg to disagree, young man. It was quite something to me. And," the Queen said, turning sharp eyes onto Princess Alix, "you will tell your chef that he must henceforth make those truffles much smaller, or much larger. They are quite a hazard at their current size."

# Miss Stoker

*In Which Evaline Reveals Her Cognog Side*

Although Mina was straining at the bit to visit Miss Willa Ashton and begin our investigation, Miss Adler insisted on returning to the Museum following the incident with the Queen. In fact, she urged us to wait until first thing the next morning to call on Miss Ashton, when we would more likely find her at home.

I had no complaints about this. The princess's assignment seemed dull and uninteresting compared to my plans for the evening. Dylan's silvery device was burning a hole in my pocket.

The only person I knew who might be able to put electricity into the mechanism lived in Whitechapel, the most dangerous area of London. The one time I'd been to his hideout, I had seen electric lightbulbs instead of gas lamps. A shadowy, disreputable character, Pix was fond of showing up at the most unexpected places.

Thus, I had preparations to make for a trip to the stews—and the most pressing one turned out to be shaking my beloved sister-in-law from my tail.

"But you haven't had a new gown in *ages*," Florence lectured me over luncheon. I had returned from the royal visit just after one o'clock. My brother Bram had already left for his job managing the famous Lyceum Theatre and their son, Noel, was visiting Florence's sister in the country. Which left me at the mercy of my sister-in-law. "And there's a new fabric merchant on Clements-lane who has brought in the latest styles from Vienna."

"Ages" in Florence terms was merely weeks in reality. "I don't need anything new. My wardrobe is overflowing with the gowns we got for the Season."

But my interest was piqued by the mention of clothing from Vienna, which was coming close to surpassing Paris as the fashion center of Europe. It had something to do with its proximity to the small nation of Betrovia, known for its fine fabrics.

"Bram expects us to wear something spectacular for the Opening Night soiree." Florence's blue eyes sparkled. "It's the new play by Mr. Gilbert! The crème de la crème of Society will be there, and you know how much Bram loves to arrive with two beautiful women on his arm."

And I knew how much Florence loved to shop. She looked so pretty and enthusiastic, it was hard to tell her no.

Except when she was trying to play matchmaker between me and an eligible bachelor. Vampire hunters didn't marry, but since Florence had no idea about my secret life, she didn't understand why I wasn't as excited as she was about attending balls and going to the opera in order to be seen by bachelors on the hunt for wives.

"The soiree isn't for more than a week," I reminded her. "We have plenty of time to find something."

"But it's such a nice day . . . ," she said, then, as we both glanced toward the windows, she gave a little laugh and flapped her hand. "Well, a little drizzle won't hurt either of us. And I think you should wear something ice-blue with sapphire underlays for the soiree."

I had picked up a piece of toast and paused with it halfway to my mouth. "Oh, yes. I *really* like that idea."

At the same time, I realized a shopping trip this afternoon could help me in other ways. It could provide me an excuse for not going anywhere this evening—for I would be weary and have a headache by the time we returned. That way I could sneak out. I could milk Florence for any gossip about Miss Ashton and her poor brother. And I truly enjoyed Florence's company, though she could be overbearing and controlling at times.

Hm. She rather reminded me of Mina Holmes.

I felt guilty about hiding my secret vocation from Florence, and even guiltier about any dishonesty I was forced to use in order to fulfill my responsibilities. I made it a habit to never lie directly to her, but sometimes it was difficult not to. She was a combination of mother and sister to me. It was she who insisted I live with her and Bram when my elderly parents became too old to provide for me. They still lived in Ireland, where I'd been born, and they were now cared for by our other siblings.

"Splendid!" Florence said, and our shopping trip was settled. "Now to review the latest batch of invitations." Her expression grew a little frosty, due to the occasion a few weeks ago when I'd purposely kept her from attending the most premier ball of the Season. Mina and I had been working on the Scarab case and had to attend. That was the only reason I went, but when Florence discovered I'd gone without her, she was not happy.

Thus, she insisted our housekeeper, Mrs. Gernum, intercept all of the invitations that arrived so we could "review" them together. It was a delicate balancing act for me to keep Florence happy by accepting enough of my own invitations that her social calendar was more varied than if she relied on her own—while declining as many as I could. I hated Society events. I despised the formality of them, the inane conversation, and the silly men who talked about their horses or clubs while trying to look down my bodice. Many of them had horrible breath or dirty gloves.

Although, lately, the events at which a certain Mr. Richard Dancy was present had become slightly more interesting. *He* actually knew how to carry on a conversation, and occasionally even listened to what I might say.

As the day turned out, after our shopping trip I no longer needed an excuse to stay in that evening. Florence was the one who went to bed early with the megrims, as she called it, after urging me to go to the card party at the Royce-Bailey house.

"Mr. Dancy's sister is supposed to attend," she told me, holding a cool cloth to her forehead. "It's a splendid opportunity for you to get to know her better."

"Right," I said, thinking not of whist or bridge, but of what to wear tonight. I knew how to dress when I was going to the theater or to a musicale or a ball . . . but what should I wear to the darkest, dingiest, most dangerous pub in all of London?

The pub in question, Fenmen's End, was located at the corner of Flower- and Dean-streets in the Spitalfields neighborhood. The most disreputable area of Whitechapel, it was famous as the location of the Jack the Ripper murders.

Any female would be beyond mad to wander the web-like culs-de-sac of the rookery at any time of day, let alone night. It was easy to get lost or trapped in the warren of dead-end streets, covered by low, overhanging roofs and darkened by tightly packed buildings. Thieves, murderers, and smugglers frequented the shadows, carrying out their business and removing anyone who got in their way.

But I was an exception. If Jack the Ripper appeared and showed me his wicked knife, I would be eager to introduce him to my own weaponry. In fact, I would relish the chance to do so. If I couldn't get to a vampire, a serial murderer was a fitting substitute.

I walked boldly into Fenmen's End and every eye in the place turned toward me. I was one of only four females in the establishment, and, I daresay, the cleanest of the lot. It was my plan to attract attention, for I knew word would get to Pix once I showed myself.

As for my attire . . . I wanted to be noticed, but I wasn't mad enough to wear a ball gown. Or even men's clothing, as I'd done the first time I came to the pub. Instead, my clothing was a walking dress in what was called Street-Fashion. Though I was much less of a cognoggin than Mina Holmes, I had come to appreciate elements of that style—especially the exterior corset. Actually wearing your undergarment for all to see! It was shocking. Yet the corsets made to be seen were often gorgeous pieces of fashion, and more decorative than practical.

Tonight, my ensemble jingled with decorative cogs and gears instead of the normal lace and embroidery. I wore long fingerless gloves made from soft, buttery leather. Tiny watchworks and jet beads were stitched all along the tops of them, and they laced tightly from palm to elbow, over my shirtsleeves.

I'd chosen a pale yellow shirtwaist, and the corset I wore over it was made of brown leather, plaited up the side so I could do it myself. My maid, Pepper, had helped me dress. She had assisted me in assembling the outfit—for Florence would never darken the door of a shop that sold Street-Fashion.

Pepper had also done my long, dark hair curled up into a tight, intricate coiffure. She insisted on secreting small vampire-hunting stakes in the mass of hair. She refused to let me leave the house at night without at least one somewhere on my person, in case I encountered a vampire. But that was highly unlikely, for there hadn't been any vampires in London for decades other than a random few over the years. And instead of a bonnet, I wore a gently curved topper positioned above my left temple. Its feathers and fringe gave it a rakish appearance.

But in spite of the visible corset, the most daring part of my attire—and what I liked the most—was the skirt. Its hem was in the shape of an inverted *U*. This meant it came to my knees in front, then draped down and around to a more proper length in back. Layers of ruffles and gathers of the emerald brocade created a fashionable bustle at the base of my spine. And for my footwear? Tall brown boots that laced up on the inside from ankle to knee—completely, shockingly visible due to the short skirt in front.

If Florence saw me, she would be overcome with vapors. But in truth, I hardly looked any more daring than some of the barmaids, who hiked up their skirts while serving.

"Good evening, Bilbo," I greeted the bartender. I'd only met him once, when in my disguise as a young boy. He

THE SPIRITGLASS CHARADE

gawked at me, overfilling a mug of ale or some other liquid that splashed onto the counter.

I sailed through the crowded place with ease, due to my short skirt and the fact that most of the patrons stepped back as they ogled me. My movements were as free as the rare times I wore trousers. I appreciated the way the chunky heels of my boots made firm, powerful clumps across the wooden floor.

I was halfway to a table when two bulky men appeared, blocking my way. Based on their dingy smiles, I was sure they'd never even heard of tooth powder, let alone used it. One of them might have shaved last month, but I doubted the other had used a razor since he sprouted his first chin hair. And maybe they'd bathed at Christmas.

"Weeeel . . . wot a peachy blowen we gots 'ere," said the one who might have once used a razor.

"Shore ain't no slavey, eh, Garf?" They laughed in apparent agreement. "Look'en 'ow nobby this one is. I'd like t'see wot's under dem daisy roots she gawt there."

"'Ow kind o' ye t'join us, fresh jenny," said Garf as he grabbed my arm. I gasped and reared back in pretend fright.

"Don't touch me," I said, struggling a little.

"Now, now, li'l loidy. We e'en 'ave a place t'sit," the nameless one said as I was propelled roughly toward a table in a dingy corner. He leered at me, his face coming much too close. The stench made my eyes sting.

The numbfists must have thought I was light-headed because of their charming personalities, for they laughed and

40

congratulated each other as I was shoved onto a chair. They took a seat on either side of me; the rest of the patrons were watching without appearing to be watching.

"No, thank you," I said, attempting to stand. But a heavy hand shoved me back in my chair.

"'Ave a seat, missy. Yer 'avin' a drink wi' us. And then later . . . we'll 'ave a bit more fun. If'n ye know'at I mean."

I hid a smile. Idiots were going to get the surprise of their lives if they tried anything with me.

My so-called companions hollered for a round of whiskey, and three small glasses were delivered to the table.

"Drink'm up, jenny," ordered Garf as his friend gulped down the spirits. Great. Rotting whiskey breath. "Things'll be much mo' fun if ye do. Loosen t'ings up a bit, eh? Like them laces on yer side, eh?" He poked at them.

"No, thank you. Do you have any lemonade, Bilbo?" I called to the bartender. "With a bit of ice in it, perhaps?"

This suggestion caused great guffaws of laughter and some backslapping from my so-called escorts, as well as some snickering from the other patrons. Bilbo seemed as shocked as if I'd asked for a new parasol, and Garf gave a long, aromatic belch that probably rattled his teeth. I gagged.

I'd attracted enough attention and if Pix was around, he'd know I was here. I placed my hands on the table to push my chair back. Bad choice. I should have known it would be sticky, and now I'd gotten it on my gloves and fingers. I thought about wiping them on my seatmates' shoulders, but decided that'd probably make things worse.

"It's been quite a pleasure, gentlemen." I stood. "But I fear your conversation is boring and your table manners leave much to be desired. Have a—"

"Where d'ye think ye're goin'?" The nameless one clamped a hand on my shoulder and slammed me roughly into my seat.

"Remove your hand from my person," I said in a voice Mina Holmes would have used. "Now."

"Now wh' would I wanna do 'at?" he asked, tightening his fingers around the top of my arm. "Ye ain' goin' nowheres, little jenny, wi'out me and Garf 'ere. We gots a goo' time planned fer ye. Jus' t'tree o' us. And dem laces o' yers. We're gonna r'lieve ye of them tight laces, ain't we, Garf?" His laugh was unpleasant.

"If you don't remove your hand from my arm by the time I count to four, I'll break your finger. Can you count that high?"

Oh, he didn't like that. At all. His eyes, already squirrelly and beady, narrowed. A glint of malevolence showed there for the first time, and I was quite glad of it. I didn't want to break his finger if he was just a drunken sot acting silly.

But this man was mean. How many times did a woman have to tell him to take his hands off her?

"One," I said.

He tightened his fingers and grinned. I could feel them digging into the soft flesh at the front of my shoulder. His filthy nails cut through the flimsy linen of my shirtwaist. "Ye don' tell Big Marv what 'e kin and kinnat touch. Ain't no one 'oo does 'at."

"Two."

The obnoxious beast's nasty grin turned nastier, and he reached over and yanked at the edge of my corset, causing me to jolt. "Oh yeah?" His words were tainted with whiskey and rotting teeth. Then he moved his hand down and rested it flat on my leg, curling those fingers tightly *over my thigh*.

My breath caught. I'd never been touched so intimately in my life. I wasn't ashamed. I was furious. Definitely a finger was going to get broken. No, two.

"Ye kin stop countin' now, jenny. Ye're gonna 'ave some oth—"

"Three." My voice was steady and I allowed the fury to show in my gaze. Other than that, I didn't flicker an eyelash. One would think the numbfist would be wondering why I wasn't writhing on the floor in agony, for his indecent grip was tight as a vise.

Instead, Big Marv chuckled and nodded for another drink from Bilbo as if he hadn't a care in the world.

"Four," I said, then reached up with my free hand, grabbed one of the sausage-sized fingers digging into my shoulder, and twisted.

He squealed like a train coming into the station. Before he could react, I snatched up his other hand from my thigh and smashed it into the edge of the table. Marv gave another roar of pain and rage and swung out at me, teeth bared, eyes burning with fury. I ducked half under the table and, with one slick, smooth move, used my hand and foot to yank the leg of his chair out from under him. The dinkus landed on his arse on the floor with a loud, satisfying thud.

"I told you not to touch me." I don't think he heard me over his howls.

Then I stood, shoving the chair away from the table. When Garf made a halfhearted move to stop me, I looked at him. "You can't be that stupid. At least you know how to shave."

Sinking back down onto his seat, he picked up Marv's new whiskey and glugged it down.

Every eye in the place was on me, of course. "I'm finished here." I dusted off my hands then smoothed my hair. Not one curl out of place, my hat still intact.

"'Oo *are* ye?" whispered Bilbo.

"A tempest in a bloody teapot is wot she is."

I turned. Pix was leaning against the wall beyond the countertop where Bilbo reigned. I had no idea how long he'd been standing there or where he'd come from, but it didn't matter. I'd accomplished what I set out to do.

Tonight he wore a long dark overcoat that covered everything but his hands (ungloved) and his lower legs and feet (booted). He was hatless, revealing a dark head of thick and mussed hair and long sideburns, which likely were fake. He also needed to shave the rest of his face. Other than that, he wasn't in disguise—at least, as far as I could tell. But then again, I wasn't sure I'd ever seen him when he *wasn't* somehow altering his appearance or hiding in the shadows.

"Ah. Just the man I was looking for."

"I should'a known ye'd be makin' an appearance." He moved with easy strides across the room. His dark eyes gleamed beneath heavy brows and I saw a hint of exasperation in them as he came closer. "Per'aps next time, ye migh' gi' the bloke to a count o'*five*, ye ken? Marv 'ere . . . 'e don't remember 'is numbers too well."

A low ripple of laughter trundled through the pub. Marv growled, but remained where I'd left him, nursing his hand.

"I gave him fair warning. If he'd listened, I wouldn't have had to count in the first place."

Pix shook his head and I saw his jaw move. Then he turned to Bilbo and said, "A gatter for me and the lady. In the back."

"But she prefers lemonade," the bartender ventured. "Wit' ice."

"I don' care wot she prefers." Pix gave the bartender a steely grin, then swept the same look over the rest of the pub. Then he took my arm with a firm grip. "This way."

With that, the patrons seemed to lose interest and they returned to their cards, arm wrestling, dice, and conversation.

I lifted a brow at Pix. "I've already broken two bones tonight because a bloody facemark thought he could man-handle me. Do you really want to attempt the same?"

"Now, luv, y' know it wouldn' be only an *attempt*," he said, his voice pitched only for my ears. His hold on me didn't ease, but I allowed him to lead me away. He was aware I could shake his grip if I wanted. "Ye came 'ere t'see me, and ye know it."

"I have no other way of contacting you, and you know *that*."

"Aye. I jus' didn' expect ye to 'ear 'bout it so quick," he muttered.

I hid my surprise. Hear what? What did he mean?

By now we'd reached the pub's back wall, which was covered with heavy walnut paneling—an expensive addition to such a lowly place.

Pix must have pushed a button or stepped on some release, for the paneling slid open as we approached. We walked through and it closed silently behind us, leaving us in near-darkness.

My heart thumped as I wondered if he meant to try and kiss me, which he'd done once before. Instead, he directed me farther into the dim space. I drew back in surprise when I felt a cobweb brush against my face, then drift over my shoulders . . . only to realize it was a heavy curtain. Pix lifted the drapes away, revealing a brick passageway lit with a cool, crisp, white illumination.

*Electric lights.*

The glass bulbs with their glowing interior wires were contraband in London since electricity had been banned by the Moseley-Haft Act.

"Will this lead us to your lair, Mr. Spider?"

"I didn' think ye'd be that eager t'visit me crib again, luv," he said, releasing my arm and gesturing for me to precede him down a well-lit stairway. "But if ye insist . . ."

The steps were clean and well constructed. Brightly illuminated by glass bulbs, their naked wires dangling along the brick walls, the stairwell curved into a gentle spiral. I saw no sign of rats, sewage, or any other refuse as we descended.

At the bottom, Pix gestured to the left. We went only another short distance before the arched corridor ended in a brick wall . . . or so it seemed.

He pulled back the sleeve of his overcoat, revealing a curious device strapped to his wrist. A small glow emitted from it, and he moved something on the mechanism. I heard gears whirring and a soft sizzle. Even a little flash of light zapped through the air.

Then . . . a click, a low, long groan, and the brick wall parted.

# Miss Stoker

## Of Daisy Roots and Gatter

Pix bowed with a grand flourish. "After ye."

I stepped into his private living quarters. I had been here once before, though via a much less direct route. We'd been running through a warren of streets and alleyways while trying to elude dangerous pursuers.

The chamber I entered was as comfortable as any parlor in St. James's. Settees and low tables were arranged in a neat group. Silk drapery covered two of the walls, fine rugs from India covered the floor, and a small dining area was nestled off to one side. A fireplace tall enough for me to stand in covered half of one wall and was currently empty of a blaze. Four large logs sat inside and two tall-backed brocade chairs were arranged in front of it. "So this is how you travel so easily to the pub. But it seems rather inconvenient for Bilbo to deliver your . . . what was it you ordered? A gatter? It sounds unpleasant."

"Nay, 'tis simply ale. An' Bilbo pours a mean'n." He gestured to one of the settees. "As I recall, ye took a bit o' likin' to the sip of a gatter ye 'ad before."

"I'm not drinking anything from you," I told him flatly, settling on the larger sofa. "Did you think I've forgotten what happened last time?" The tea he gave me as a soother had ended up being a literal one: He'd put a sleeping powder in it so I'd be unconscious as he delivered me home.

"Ah, aye. I thought ye might be still brushed up o'er 'at." The grin flashed, then disappeared. "Bu' after what ye did t'Marv, I should be feedin' ye a *lecture*. Did ye 'ave t'break *two* fingers—an' one on each 'and? Now the bloke'll be useless t'me fer an 'ole month!"

Right. "Perhaps you need to reconsider the type of man you have working for you. I can't imagine he's useful for much other than terrorizing women."

"Marv is a dangerous cove. Ye were foolish t'bait 'im as ye did." His expression turned sober.

"Me bait *him*? He was the one who put his hand on my—who forced me to sit with him. And wouldn't let me leave. I warned him what would happen if he didn't release me." My voice rose. Did Pix really think I couldn't handle myself? Did he really think I should have allowed that man to put his hands on me and do nothing? Blooming facemark!

"An' now ye've made an enemy o' Marv, 'ere in the rook'ry. As if ye weren't in danger enough as 'tis."

"He has two broken fingers. What sort of threat do you imagine he might be? Especially to *me*?" I countered, still furious at his assumption that *I* had caused the altercation. Tempest in a teapot, my *arse*.

A soft chime interrupted whatever Pix might have replied, and I looked over as my host slid open a small door in the wall. Inside the neat cubbyhole sat two large tankards.

Right, then. That was how Bilbo managed the bar *and* delivered down here.

Pix set the tankards on the table in front of me and settled on the settee next to mine. The bitter scent of ale wafted to my nose. As I examined the mug filled with creamy foam, he nudged one toward me.

Not a bloody chance I'd get even close enough to wet my lips. Especially since I had other reasons for being here. Though I had no idea what he meant earlier when he said he hadn't expected me to "hear about it," I intended to find out exactly what he meant—and what he believed had brought me here.

"Now that you've gone through all the trouble to get me here," I said, my voice cool, "giving me the chance to see yet again where you hide all your loot, you can tell me what you know."

"Wot about, luv?"

"You know why I'm here," I countered. "No sense in playing games, Pix. Talk."

"Wot d'ye want t'know? I ain't seen any m'self, but th' signs're there. They're back, is all I know."

A cold shock rushed over me. *They're back.* "The UnDead?" I said without thinking. *Vampires are back in London?*

"Ye didn' know? Devil it!"

"I would have known . . . eventually. And I *should* have known. I'm a vampire hunter . . . which, hmm, you knew the first time we met." I narrowed my eyes, fixing on him darkly. "Now would be a good time to tell me how you came upon *that* bit of information."

Pix lounged back in his seat. He'd removed his overcoat and left it lying over the back of the sofa. His shirt was made of fine, cream-colored linen. Much too fine for a resident of Spitalfields.

He gave a nonchalant shrug, which shifted his sleeve, giving me another glimpse of the device strapped to his wrist. "I know ever'thin' that 'appens 'ere in the Underground Worl' . . . not to be confused wi' the Underground trains, ye savvy. Information gets t'me faster'n the pox gets spread in 'aymarket. I buy it, sell it, trade fer it—"

"Kill for it?"

That dark gaze flashed to mine. "Per'aps that's one question ye don' wan' t'be askin' o'me, Evaline."

Despite the warning, warmth fluttered through my insides when he said my name, lingering over the syllables like a caress. He seemed to be trying to read my response. My heart thudded hard, for I found it difficult to pull my eyes from his.

Then sense rang in my head, and I turned away. I'd forgotten how improper and foolish it was for me to be alone with him. Or any man.

I had nothing to fear from Pix. The only thing I risked by being here was my reputation. When I looked up again, he was still smiling—cool, and yet charming enough to make my bloody fickle heart skip a beat.

But the most important thing was . . . the UnDead were back in London. A thrill of excitement rushed through me. Then a flicker of apprehension. I'd have the chance to prove myself worthy of the Venator title by slaying my first vampire.

If I could do it.

Of course I could do it. I *had* to do it.

"Aren't ye thirsty? 'Ave a drink, 'ere, darlin'." Pix gestured to the tankards of ale. "Ye can be sure I ain't mollied with 'em, fer ye can choose which one t'drink. I'll take either."

"No thank you."

"Please yerself, then, luv. And might I say, them daisy roots ye 'ave are some nobby nacks."

"Daisy roots?"

He grinned, gesturing toward me with one of the tankards. "Daisy roots—daisies. *Boots.* Yer boots're some nobby nacks, if I say. I find 'em quite . . . mem'rable."

I stood, aware of his attention trailing along my leather-clad calves. Maybe it hadn't been such a good idea to wear something so . . . daring. "I'll be going, then. Apparently, despite your claim to know everything that happens in the Underground, you have no information about the vampires."

He didn't move, but his expression changed from easy to sober. "Ver' well. So much fer th' sweet talkin'. It's business on yer mind, and nuthin' more, then."

He remained seated, even though I'd risen. That would have been a terrible breach of etiquette had we been in polite company. But social niceties were of no interest to Pix. I learned that the first time we met—when he pulled me up against him in a dark shadow. So that we not be seen—or so he'd claimed.

And then there was the time he'd *kissed* me. My cheeks warmed. I drew in a deep breath and held it. Florence had taught me that little trick would quickly dissipate a blush.

"It's always business on my mind, Pix. I've an important job to do—something the likes of you can't understand."

A flash of something dark crossed his face, then was gone. "Right then . . . but a'fore I talk, ye tell me this, luv— if ye didn't know about the vampires, wot's brought ye 'ere t'Spitalfields, then?"

Oh. Right. I dug in my skirt pocket and pulled out the sleek silver telephone-device and a white cord Dylan had also given me. "Do you know how to put electricity into this?"

"Wot the bloody 'ell is it?" He appeared unabashedly fascinated by the object.

I wasn't quite ready to hand it over. And I wasn't ready to tell him it had come from the future, either. "You have your secrets, and I have mine. Can you put electricity into it or not?"

Pix fixed me with an expression I'd never seen before. "That's illegal, Evaline."

I held his gaze as my pulse raced faster. I understood all of what he was saying with that simple statement. "It's important," I said, sitting back down.

He held out a hand and I let the device slip into his palm. I was placing a great bit of trust in this disreputable young man. *Gad. Don't let me be making a mistake.*

"Brilliant," he muttered, turning it over and over in his hands.

"I'm told the electricity goes in through this." I indicated the cord and its two-pronged end.

Pix nodded, fingering the cord. "Ye'll need to leave it wi' me."

I hesitated. "What are you going to do? How long?"

"If I narked ye that, I'd jeopardize more'n meself, luv. Don't ye trust me, Evaline?" His voice was wry.

"Do I have reason to trust you?"

"Ye came t'me, luv. I didn't seek ye out."

"This time."

He gave a short laugh, then turned back to the device. "I'll no' let it out from me possession."

I drew in a deep breath. I had no other option if I was to help Dylan. "Very well. But please take good care of it. And now that I've shown you a bit of trust, perhaps you could return the favor. What makes you believe vampires are back in London if you haven't seen one? Or have you?"

"I ain't seen one m'self—at least, 'ere in London—but there be plenty o' rumblings." He lifted his tankard again, watching me over the rim. "An' a coupla blokes was nattering about *La société* . . . pernishun. . . ."

My breath caught. "*La société de la perdition?*"

He nodded. "Aye. 'T could be. Ye've 'eard o' it, then."

Certainly I'd heard of it. Any self-respecting vampire hunter must know about the Society of Iniquity, for the mortal members of that group were nearly as dangerous as the UnDead themselves. Those who called themselves participants of *La société* enjoyed the company of vampires, seeking them out for various illicit reasons.

I glanced at Pix. Did he know about the Society? And what should—or shouldn't—I tell him?

He watched me with a strange expression, as if he wanted to say something more. Instead, he rubbed his stubbly chin and I heard the soft scrape of finger over bristling hair. He seemed suddenly introspective in comparison to the glib charm he usually adopted.

"What are you not telling me?" I demanded.

"Nawt. Nawt but to have a care, luv."

I opened my mouth to tell him *yet again* I knew how to protect myself, then stopped. There was something in his eyes . . . something different. "Of course I will," I said tartly, covering up my sudden uncertainty. I watched him. There was something more.

I sat upright, my heart thudding. "*La société*. They love the UnDead, they know all about them . . . and *you're* a member, aren't you?"

It all made sense: how he had so much power and control here in Whitechapel among stronger, meaner, older men than him . . . how he knew about me, including that I was a vampire hunter. . . .

His eyes widened a fraction, then narrowed, lit with wry humor. "But nay. Ye already know I don' bear the mark of *La société*, don't ye now, luv?"

"Wha—" I stopped myself as I realized exactly what he meant. The last time I'd seen Pix, he'd been wearing an open vest . . . over a shockingly bare torso. His biceps were smooth and muscular and unmarked . . . with not a sign of the spindly-legged spider image that labeled one a member of *La société*.

My face went steaming hot, and I felt parched. Yet I resisted picking up one of the tankards to drink. I still didn't trust him not to have "mollied with" the ale.

I gathered my wits. "You didn't have the mark on your arms, but it could be on the back of the shoulder. It wouldn't surprise me if you were a member—that's how you knew I was a Venator."

A slow grin eased over his face. "Ver' well, then, luv . . . if yer to trust m'word, I s'pose I'm forced t'prove it to ye."

He reached up to his collar, and before I could blink, *began to unbutton his shirt.*

"Don't." I held out a hand to stop him as I put the other over my face. *Not* a good idea. Not at all. It would break so many Societal rules. Florence would faint dead away if she ever found out. My reputation would be in shambles. It would mortify me to no end. Blast . . . and it would fascinate me, too.

"And 'ere I thought ye was fearless, me bold vampire-rozzer." There was laughter and something low and deep in Pix's voice that brushed my spine like a gentle finger.

Then I peeked through my hand. He'd stopped with only the top two buttons of his shirt unfastened. That was more than enough for me to see his strong throat and the shadowy *V* that opened onto his chest. Which, unfortunately, I remembered all too well from that open vest he'd worn at the opium den. I swallowed hard. "I believe you. For now. I don't know why I do, but I do."

His face still bright with levity, Pix reached for one of the tankards. "*La société* . . . nay, luv, their way 'as no appeal for me." He lifted the mug, drank several gulps, then returned it to the table.

"Nor to me." The very thought of wanting to be with a vampire, to have one feed on me, piercing me with its fangs and drawing out my lifeblood . . . I shuddered. "It's the chance for immortality that attracts them. And some say there is a sort of pleasure involved."

Siri had educated me about *La société*. At the time, it seemed she spent more effort on the secret cult than on the vampires themselves. I wanted to learn to fight, and she wanted to teach me history. Both had been burned into my brain.

"There are some people who like to be fed on by the UnDead. They pine for it and become addicted to it. Like opium-eaters. And the vampires can feed without killing a person . . . without draining all of their blood," I said.

"An' if they drain all o' the blood," Pix said, his voice steady and quiet, "the mortal can drink from the vampire's veins . . . and become UnDead 'imself." He looked up, his eyes hard and glittering. "I'll no' lie t'ye on this, Evaline. It's been offered t'me. In th' past. But as ye must know . . . I'm still as mortal as ye are."

"That's good." I really wanted to drink from the tankard. My mouth was dry as a wad of cotton. "For if you weren't, I'd have to kill you. And then how would I find my way out of this place?"

Pix laughed, and the dark spell was broken. "Drink up, luv. Then I'll take ye 'ome, like a proper cove. An' this time, I'll let ye stay awake."

# MISS HOLMES

## *Miss Holmes Is Skeptical*

"Vampires are back in London?" I lifted a brow at Miss Stoker, who sat across from me in Miss Adler's office.

It was the day following our visit with Princess Alexandra, and I was beyond anxious to begin the Ashton investigation. I would have arrived at Miss Ashton's front door at eight o'clock in the morning, but my companion refused to allow me to call so early. Despite my argument that Uncle Sherlock never allowed societal rules to dictate *his* investigations, Miss Stoker was adamant that we delay until a more proper time for making a call. Such as eleven o'clock.

"Did you actually *see* an UnDead?" I was still irritated with my companion's vehemence over the delay.

Miss Stoker was sitting—or, more accurately, lounging— in an armchair. Miss Adler wasn't present at the moment, or I'm certain she would have supported my disapproval for such an unladylike position. "Not exactly. But there have been signs of them. A mutilated body was found in Whitechapel, and it looked as if a creature with fangs had torn into it. According to my—my *source*, two drunk men tried to lift a bloke's wallet outside the Pickled Nurse and were frightened off when the mark's eyes turned red. And they both swore he showed fangs."

Bloke? Apparently Miss Stoker had been spending some time in the stews—likely with that disreputable young man called Pix. As if I wouldn't know who'd been feeding her information. "The Pickled Nurse?"

"A pub in Holborn. And there have also been rumors of activity from *La société de la perdition*." Evaline gave me what could only be described as a challenging look.

Perhaps she thought I would be uninformed about *La société*. If so, she would be greatly mistaken. I had, of course, read my father's copy of the rare book by Mr. Starcasset, *The Venators*, which was about Miss Stoker's family legacy. I venture to say I was just as informed about vampires and vampire hunting as was my companion. Particularly since I didn't believe she'd ever actually staked an UnDead.

I wasn't even completely convinced of the existence of vampires. Reanimated corpses who were sensitive to sunlight and wandered around drinking blood from people? I could hardly fathom such a thing. The very idea defied logic and science. As far as I was concerned, *The Venators* was just as likely a work of fiction—albeit a convincing one—as it was a treatise on the Gardella-Stoker family legacy. The legend that vampires had been chased out of London sixty years ago could be merely that, and nothing more.

I couldn't deny Evaline seemed unusually strong for a young woman, but that factor could be attributed to any variety of things—genetics, for example.

"*La société de la perdition* can be loosely translated as the Society Where One Loses One's Soul," I informed Evaline. "And it is aptly named. For, as I understand it, the group's purpose was solely for the pleasure of drinking blood or having one's blood drunk, vampires notwithstanding. Rather like an opium den, the purlieu is often hidden, dark and, quite literally, underground.

"The group was an illicit, secretive fraternity that identifies itself with the image of a spindly-legged spider with seven legs instead of eight. *La société* reached its peak of popularity in the early 1830s in Paris among those who enjoy that type of diversion. This was shortly after the UnDead were driven out of London by the famous Victoria Gardella. The vampires recongregated in Paris. My understanding is *La société* is a splinter cult which broke off from the more formal group known as the Tutela, a League for the Protection of Vampires. Although the popularity of *La société* waned in the 1860s, there was a resurgence of interest in the group in Paris in the late 1870s, but it was short-lived."

"That's correct," Evaline said. She appeared to have tasted something sour, if the puckered expression on her face was any indication.

"Is there anything else? I presume you came by this information during your visit to Spitalfields last night."

"I don't have any other details." Her tone was stiff, indicating some sort of displeasure.

"Has anyone actually *seen* a vampire, other than two drunkards trying to steal a wallet?"

"No."

I sniffed. "Very well. Then I shall wait to sharpen my wooden stakes and encircle my neck with a silver cross until someone does."

I turned my attention to the stack of newspapers on the desk next to me. One of them was mounted vertically on a Proffitt's Dandy Paper-Peruser. I had the intervals set to two minutes (I am a speedy reader) and as I watched, the delicate magnetic clamp slid along to turn the page, then snapped neatly back in place with a gentle click.

Like my uncle, I read a variety of publications daily. But even the newspapers had nothing of interest in them as of late. A carriage accident in Haymarket, a missing boy from Bloomsbury, a fire on Bond-street, a new sundries shop in St. James's, announcements of betrothals and descriptions of balls and masquerades—including the imminent reopening of an entertainment garden called New Vauxhall.

Parliamentary laws were passed, repealed, argued, or voted upon. There was even an editorial about how to protect one's belongings from a new and particularly adept gang of pickpockets running wild through London. The only thing remotely interesting was the brief notation about Mr. Babbage's Analytical Engine. I made a note of the visiting hours for the display of its prototype in the Oligary Building.

"Shall we leave now?" Evaline picked up her hat to pin it in place. "It'll take thirty minutes to get to Mayfair from here, and I thought we might make a stop on Bond-street."

"On Bond-street? Whatever for?" I removed the *Times* from the Paper-Peruser then flipped off the lever. The mechanism sighed and collapsed in on itself with a little hiss, becoming the size of a folded fan. I turned the dial on the desk drawer and it slid open with a gentle whoosh.

Evaline shrugged, but her smile was crafty. "I do love that bakery on the corner of . . . where is it? Ah yes, Tyrell-street. Their apple-cheddar tarts are divine."

Tyrell near Bond-street . . . that wasn't far from the fatal fire Scotland Yard was investigating. The thought of a chance encounter with Inspector Ambrose Grayling made my cheeks heat and my insides jittery. Considering the fact that I had nearly accused the esteemed Lady Cosgrove-Pitt (a distant relative of Grayling's) of being the mysterious Ankh, and that the last time I'd seen him, he'd had to haul me back from falling out of a second-story window . . . I decided it was best if I avoided him for the foreseeable future.

Possibly forever.

"I've already had breakfast, and from the dried jam on your chin and the faint scent of spilled coffee emitting from your handkerchief, I can see you have done as well. We should be arriving at Miss Ashton's in time for elevenses. Perhaps you can visit the bakery at another time?"

"Oh, very well then, Mina. But I was certain you'd want to find some excuse to visit Bond-street today. Perhaps you could direct Inspector Grayling about in his latest investigation. Isn't he working on the fatal fire case?"

I gave an aggravated sniff and shoved the Proffitt's into the waiting drawer.

We left the Museum, riding in Evaline's horsedrawn carriage. It was driven by a taciturn individual named Middy, who was fond of dogs, if the amount of hair clinging to his trousers was any indication. Being members of the peerage, my companion and her brother Bram had the resources to employ a full staff, unlike Father and I.

However, I didn't begrudge Miss Stoker the large Grantworth residence filled with upper maids and lower maids, cooks, housekeepers, groomsmen, and butlers. That number of people milling about my home, snooping through—or worse, *organizing*—my laboratory and generally being underfoot would make me itchy and twitchy.

I suspected there were times Evaline felt the same way, which was probably why she preferred to climb out her bedroom window when embarking on her so-called vampire-hunting excursions, instead of using the more conventional front door.

As noted, it was a thirty-minute drive to the pleasant, wealthy neighborhood of Mayfair. I had checked in *Kimball's*

*British Peerage,* volume 25, fourth edition, and learned Miss Ashton resided in a modest but expensive home with her spinster aunt, Geraldine Kluger.

Evaline and I gained admittance to Miss Ashton's home when my companion offered the butler her calling card—a charmingly handmakerish one made of sturdy stock, with nary a gear or spring or even a bolt for adornment. It didn't even have a clasp to fasten it closed. After being shown to the parlor, we removed our gloves and settled on the settee. Moments later, the door opened and a young woman bustled in.

"Miss Stoker? Miss Holmes?" Miss Ashton greeted us with a combination of warmth and hesitation. "How kind of you to come so quickly. Her Royal Highness sent word I should expect you, but I didn't dream you'd be able to visit so soon."

Our hostess was seventeen—the same age as Evaline and I. Miss Ashton had honey-blond hair and a pretty, oval face. Her eyes were pale blue and one of her top teeth was charmingly crooked. A tiny dimple appeared in her chin when she spoke and I wondered if more would appear when she smiled. She seemed a pleasant young woman with good manners, despite her absurd attraction to spirit-sitting. Since she came from a titled family and, according to *Kimball's,* had some significant wealth, she'd be a reasonably good catch for a young bachelor.

At least she didn't have to contend with a too-prominent nose or long, gangly limbs.

During our introductions, I noted a variety of details that would be lost on the average person.

Nails bitten to the quick, hangnails and small sores at the cuticles—*nervous and unhappy*.

Dark circles under the eyes, sallow skin, bloodshot corneas—*sleepless nights*.

Delicate needle-pricks and stretched threads on the lower half of her overskirt—*possesses a cat which craves attention or is agitated*.

Slippers worn and edged with dirt, each toe outlined—*recent lack of care for her appearance, walks out of doors in her indoor footwear that is growing worn and too small*.

"It's our pleasure to be here." Evaline shook her hand warmly. Then, still holding Miss Ashton's fingers, she said, "I was very sorry to hear about your brother."

Our hostess blinked rapidly and the tip of her nose turned pink. "It's been terrible. Everyone says he's dead. That he must have fallen into a canal—or even *jumped*. Which is ludicrous. I don't believe them. There's been no body found. My cousin Herrell has searched and searched, talking to everyone he can, looking for any clues. Every day he visits Scotland Yard, asking if a body has been found."

"I'm sure it's very difficult," Evaline murmured, patting the young woman's hand.

"Robby's not dead. I'm certain of it."

I was ready to delve into the puzzle, for the raw pain in Miss Ashton's voice caused an uncomfortably empathetic twinge inside me. I well understood the grief and confusion caused by the unexplained, unexpected departure of a loved one—although I would never allow such emotion to surface as blatantly as our hostess. My mother had left Father and me of her own free will, and she'd even sent a letter afterward so I would know it. "The princess didn't give us many details about your experiences as of late."

"Her Highness has been very concerned about my well-being. I think she's being a bit overprotective, but she is royalty. One cannot say no to the princess when she insists on interfering." Miss Ashton gave a wan smile. "She's skeptical about the messages I've been receiving from my mother."

"Messages from your *dead* mother?" I would have said more, but a sharp kick in the ankle turned my intended question into a smothered gasp.

Miss Stoker gave me a glare. "Miss Ashton, you say your mother is sending you messages?"

"She has been. I've no doubt of it. And you've come at an excellent time." Our hostess gestured toward the parlor door. "Mrs. Yingling is here, about to conduct a séance. Then you can see for yourself how my mother has been contacting me."

My abused ankle still smarted but I resisted the urge to rub it. I wouldn't give Evaline the satisfaction. "I presume Mrs. Yingling is the medium."

"Yes indeed. She has been very helpful in communicating with Mother. I learned of her quite by accident, after my acquaintance Miss Norton—who should be arriving any moment—attended one of Mrs. Yingling's séances."

I had numerous questions stacking up in my mind, but before I had the opportunity to launch into a full interrogation, the parlor door opened.

"Willa, darling, what on earth is that woman doing in—oh, my. I'm so sorry for interrupting." A woman, whom I presumed was the aunt, appeared in the doorway. "I didn't realize your friends had arrived already."

"Aunt Geraldine, may I introduce Miss Evaline Stoker and Miss Mina Holmes. They've come to . . . er . . ."

"We've come to attend one of Miss Ashton's séances," I said smoothly.

The aunt was relatively attractive and quite fashionably attired. If I were going to be a spinster—which of course I was—I intended to be as elegant and youthful as she appeared, even into that advanced age. She had soft brown hair without a hint of gray, a long, narrow face, and eyes so pale blue they seemed almost transparent. She'd recently been walking in the garden and was obviously in need of a new pot of face powder. And the absence of cat hair along her hem indicated a disdain for felines. "Miss Holmes? Are you any relation to—"

"Yes. I am Sherlock's niece and Mycroft's daughter," I replied as I always did.

"Indeed." Aunt Geraldine seemed impressed—though I cannot say for certain whether it was because of my family pedigree.

"Will you join us in the séance today, Auntie?"

"I should say *not*." The older woman stiffened. "I've told you it's foolish to be dabbling with such things. Opening the door to the spirit world can cause all sorts of evil to escape. I don't know why your cousin encourages you in these activities."

Miss Ashton's cheeks had gone slightly pink. "Herrell has an open mind, just as I do. *He* believes Robby is alive, and hasn't given up on finding him. And if Mother can help me, then I must do whatever is necessary."

What could have been an awkward moment was interrupted when the parlor door opened once more. Miss Ashton shot to her feet as a diminutive figure tottered into the chamber. The tiny woman was elderly and frail and looked as if she'd blow over in a good wind. She had thin, fly-away, obviously dyed hair of red-gold, bright blue eyes that peered out from behind eyeglasses that magnified them into bulbous coin-sized orbs, and skin so wrinkled it appeared as if someone had imprinted a screen on her face.

Although it was common for mediums and spirit-speakers to be young women of our age, my assumption was this elderly woman was, in fact, Mrs. Yingling. This was confirmed when our hostess greeted her. Introductions ensued, followed by more introductions when two other young women arrived. One of them turned out to be the aforementioned Miss Amanda Norton, who had "discovered" our esteemed medium. The other was a wide-eyed young woman named Miss Rolstone.

I immediately observed several indications that Mrs. Yingling was a fraud, but declined to point them out until I could examine her in action. A quiver of disappointment shuttled through me as I realized our new assignment from Princess Alexandra might be reconciled as soon as this afternoon.

What a shame.

Mrs. Yingling pulled carefully to her feet. "Shall we commence to the prepared chamber?" Her voice was querulous, and I wondered how such a flimsy woman could have the strength to lift the séance table during the so-called session.

As the astute reader will have guessed, I was in no way a believer in the Spiritualism mania. I was also quite familiar with the tricks employed by mediums seeking to prove their veracity in order to fleece their clients of money—which was likely what was happening to Miss Ashton. Princess Alexandra was right to be concerned that the young woman was being taken advantage of, spending a lot of money in order to receive messages purporting to be from her mother.

There were many techniques a fraudulent medium might use to make her clients believe she was talking to their deceased loved ones. Rapping on tables, seemingly from some disembodied spirit. The sudden gust of breeze that would send a candle flame guttering into darkness. The shifting or levitating table around which the séance participants would sit.

"Are you coming, Mina?" Evaline poked me in the ribs, her eyes dancing with mischief.

Rubbing my side, I followed the small cluster of females

out of the parlor and down a neat, clean corridor lined with paintings of pastoral scenes and flowers. I admired the fresh vase of gardenias, which smelled heavenly, and observed the wainscoting had recently been painted.

We came upon the cat as we rounded a corner. He was playing with a cricket, which I found quite curious. I noticed there was another of the same uncommon insect lying feet-up on the floor farther down the hall. I found that an anomaly in an otherwise perfectly neat and clean corridor and wondered from where the creatures had come.

Moments later, we entered the prepared chamber.

I'd hardly a chance to take in the room before Miss Norton squealed. "The oracle! It's here."

This drew everyone's attention to the device sitting on the table. The object would just fit in my open hand. Its sides, made of hinged bronze and copper pieces, were unfolded to reveal a centerpiece that looked like a glass sphere with ribbons of colors swirling inside. Approximately the size of an orange, the opaque blue-green orb—presumably the oracle?—was nestled in an intricate setting of gears and cogworks. I wasn't close enough to determine whether the orb itself was ancient, but its nest appeared to be a pleasing combination of ancient art and modern gadgetry. When its sides were folded up into place, the item would resemble a slender pentagonal box.

"What does it do?" asked Aunt Geraldine, who had unexpectedly followed us. I noted with approval the skepticism in her tone and demeanor.

"Why, the oracle opens the door wide between our world and that of the Spirit World. Merely having such an object present during the séance will be invaluable in our efforts to contact your mother, Miss Ashton."

"Truly?" Willa's whisper was heartbreaking in its desperation. "It will help me to communicate with her?"

"I'm certain of it."

And I was certain Mrs. Yingling's fee would have to increase in order to cover the additional expertise needed to "read" the "oracle."

The medium continued, "I shall have to do some more research and study in order to determine the best way to utilize the oracle—"

"That is an excellent idea," I interrupted. "Particularly since your continued reference to that object as an *oracle* isn't quite accurate. It might be an oracle's *glass*, but it is not an oracle per se."

Miss Stoker rolled her eyes while I continued my explanation with great patience. "An oracle is a *person*—or group of people who—supposedly—speak divinely; that is, through a deity, in order to answer questions or give guidance. Any type of device may *assist* the oracle in determining the answer to the query at hand—including a glass sphere such as this one, tea leaves, or small imprinted stones called runes. But the sphere itself *isn't* the oracle." I looked around the chamber to make certain everyone understood the distinction. "In this case, I believe a more accurate term for this object would be 'spiritglass.' "

"Very well then," said Mrs. Yingling in a vague manner. "Shall we begin?"

"Can't you keep your mouth closed for once?" Miss Stoker hissed, jabbing me in the side as we took our seats. "If you're rude, we might be off this case before we even get started."

Lifting my nose, I muttered, "I see no reason to allow a person to spout inaccuracies or misinformation, particularly to young, naive women. Recall, if you will, the danger that befell the foolish women involved in the Society of Sekhmet because they believed the ridiculous ravings of the individual known as the Ankh."

Miss Stoker returned my stare but said nothing—for of course I was correct. And if there was anything I could do to keep another naive young woman from being conned by a nefarious villain, I would do it.

# MISS STOKER

*In Which Our Heroines Encounter Raps and Jolts*

I barely managed to keep from stomping on Mina's toes as she paraded past me to take her seat. Not that her knowledge and deductive abilities didn't come in handy. But couldn't she learn when to keep her thoughts to herself? I smoothed my skirt and petticoats as I took a chair next to her. At least if I was sitting beside Mina, I could elbow her into silence.

I'd never been to a séance before, but I knew what to expect. The six of us gathered around a small circular table in a stuffy room with closed and curtained windows. The only light was a group of three small candles in wide, squat holders at the center of the table. They surrounded the oracle—no, *spiritglass*. The surface was bare and there were no furnishings other than walls of bookshelves. Long shadows danced across the table and ceiling, and the corners of the room were dark and gloomy. Could there be any more perfect place for a séance?

"*Hush.*" Mrs. Yingling's command halted Mina as she leaned toward me, obviously about to make some pithy observation. Maybe she'd noticed a loose hair on the table and was about to give an entire history of its owner.

"Everyone must remain silent or the spirits will not visit." Mrs. Yingling looked pointedly at Mina, then me, and then around the table. I was surprised Aunt Geraldine had taken a seat as well. Maybe she thought it was best to see exactly what her niece was up to.

"Join hands, please, ladies. You must remove your gloves." She pointed at Miss Rolstone. "It is imperative that we are flesh to flesh, for the energy will be that much more vibrant, and the connection with the spirits will be that much stronger. I can feel them gathering in preparation for our call." She looked up as if to see the spirits hovering on the ceiling.

Mina shifted next to me. I wasn't surprised to feel the skepticism rolling off her. Naturally, as a vampire hunter I was more inclined to believe in Para-Natural occurrences than most people. When you come face to face with a red-eyed demonic creature with fangs, your skepticism vanishes pretty quickly.

And sometimes, so did your wits.

The single time I'd encountered an UnDead, I *couldn't remember what happened.* The violent scene had become blanked from my memory. I don't know what I did after I took up the stake.

"Now," Mrs. Yingling said. "We join hands not only to make a bond of energy, but also to create a welcoming circle for our spirit friends in hopes they will visit us."

Despite the medium's warning, Mina muttered, "And to ensure everyone's hands remain in view."

Mrs. Yingling had removed her glasses, placing them on the table. Her eyes were closed and her face lifted toward the ceiling. "Come, now, spirits of our loved ones! We are here, and we beg you to join us. We welcome you and ask you to give a sign of your presence."

The chamber became quiet. I could hear Mina's soft, even breathing on one side of me, and on the other, the more labored breaths of Miss Ashton. She had a drowning-man grip on my hand as she gawked, looking about the chamber.

The candle flames burned straight and steady. Silence reigned. As the stillness went on, I felt a prickle of anticipation instead of my normal impatience.

Something was going to happen.

"There are nonbelievers here." Mrs. Yingling broke the silence in her soft, quavery voice.

Mina shifted, her fingers tightening over mine. I listened to her lecture all the way over here about the mediums who'd been exposed as frauds. Even the celebrated Fox sisters from America confessed their entire career had been a sham, according to the know-it-all Miss Holmes.

"I know it is difficult for you, O Spirits, to visit when you must breach a wall of unbelief . . . but I implore you to be strong and to come to us. Make yourselves known. Make the nonbelievers into believers. Give us a sign of your presence."

This time, Mrs. Yingling's voice had hardly died away when there was a sharp *rap*.

My tingle of anticipation became a full-fledged flutter as our medium responded, "Ah! You are here. Thank you for making yourselves known to us. Is there anything you wish to say?"

*Rap, rap. Rap.*

Beside me, Miss Ashton was very still. On my other side, I felt Mina quivering with interest. She muttered something inaudible. No one's hands had moved from the table during the rapping. Nor had anyone shifted in their position in order to, say, kick at the table. And the rap sounded more like bare knuckles than a slippered foot, anyway.

Did ghosts even *have* bare knuckles? How *did* they make that noise—assuming they were real?

"The spirits wish to speak," Mrs. Yingling announced. "They have messages for us."

Miss Ashton shifted next to me, her grip on my fingers even tighter. "Mother? Are you there? Please speak to me, Mother."

"You must remain silent," Mrs. Yingling said swiftly. "Only I may talk, or the spirits will wither away, dissolving back to the Other Side."

Mina gave a derisive snort, but before I could jab her in the ribs again, the table moved.

I mean, *it moved*.

The whole thing jolted, as if someone large had lumbered up and bumped into it in the middle of the night.

Someone gave a little shriek and I heard a mutter from next to me: "Trick wires." The candles hadn't tipped because of their solid holders, but the flames danced wildly. Everything became quiet once more.

"Thus the spirits acknowledge the nonbelievers. And yet, they remain, for their messages are of utmost importance. I implore you to remain silent, and to allow me to commune with them."

I swallowed, more than willing to allow the spirits to commune. There was no way the table had moved the way it did with any assistance on anyone's part. That much force would have required even myself, with my unusual strength, to move violently . . . and someone would have noticed it.

"Is Marta, mother of Willa, here? Marta, if you are here, make yourself known!"

*Rap!*

Miss Ashton jolted and her grip tightened even more. "Mother."

"Marta, do you wish to speak to us?"

*Rap-rap!*

"Ask if she is . . . if she knows where Robby is," Miss Ashton begged.

Perhaps realizing she was fighting a losing battle requesting silence, Mrs. Yingling didn't reprimand her. "Marta . . . do you know where your son is?"

*R-r-rap.*

A little shiver ran up my spine. That was a weaker knock, and even I could tell it wasn't an optimistic response.

"Mother!" Miss Ashton released my fingers and rose, crying toward the nothingness of the ceiling. "I miss you so much, and I cannot believe Robby is gone—"

"Please! Miss Ashton, you are disturbing the spirits! Calm yourself, and take up your friends' hands once more," Mrs. Yingling said.

Our hostess sat back down, and I could hear her shuddering as she tried to control sobs. I found her fingers and squeezed gently, trying to offer some comfort. Even Mina seemed affected, for she hadn't said a word.

"O, Spirits, please do not leave us," said the medium. "We wish to communicate with you. Please do not leave us. Please give us a sign of your presence."

Suddenly, I felt a change in the air. A vibration of sorts . . . or an energy. As if it sang or reverberated. The hair on my arms lifted. Something sharp prickled over my scalp. I turned to see Mrs. Yingling and was shocked that she was trembling violently. Her expression had gone blank and her eyes bulged even more than they had behind her magnifying lenses.

In the drassy illumination, the candle flames caused shadows to flicker eerily over the medium's face, making it appear drawn and gaunt, even gray. Her lips pulled back from her teeth in a grotesque fashion.

"I am . . . here. . . ."

My body went cold and numb. The words were coming from the medium's mouth, but the voice was not hers. It was loud, deep, and stentorous. The air in the room cooled and the tip of my nose turned icy.

The voice continued: "I am here . . . Linny-Lou."

I couldn't control a gasp and Mina pivoted to me. My fingers opened and my hands fell away from the ones I held. My heart was pounding.

I swallowed hard, giving myself a good, sharp shake to clear my head and ears. *It couldn't be.* I'd heard wrong.

"Linny-Lou . . . it is I, old Patrick O'Gallegh. . . . I am here, little colleen. . . . I have a message for you. . . ."

The dark, deep voice continued to roll from Mrs. Yingling's contorted mouth. And there was no mistake: he . . . she . . . it? . . . was speaking to *me*.

"Y-yes," I managed to say, even as the horrific image of Mr. O'Gallegh's bloody torso rose in my memory.

Blood . . . everywhere. Stark white bone gleaming through ravaged flesh and ragged clothing. Two telltale puncture marks on his neck . . . and a demon with glowing red eyes staring at me. With challenge and derision.

"You could not have been a-saving me, sweet colleen," rumbled the grating voice. Even in the warped, deep tones, I heard the old man's familiar Irish lilt. "But ye must be saving the others. Judas's minions have returned . . . ye must—"

Amanda Norton erupted from her chair, violently beating at herself as if to brush something away. "It *touched* me!" she shrieked, flinging herself away from the table and dancing about. "Something touched me!"

An ugly sound burbled from the other end of the table. I whirled to see Mrs. Yingling, her face twisting wildly. She seemed to be about to vomit. Mina leapt up, but by the time she got out from between the heavy chair and table, the medium had collapsed back in her own seat.

I was on my feet as well, dashing over to turn on the gas lamp. Our guide's face returned to normal, and although her mouth gaped open and her eyes were closed, she now breathed normally.

"Mrs. Yingling." Mina gently shook the elderly woman. "Are you quite all right?"

The medium blinked, then her attention darted about. "What are you doing out of your seats? Why have you broken the circle? Why have you turned the lights on? The spirits cannot cross over into our world in such bright light!"

Mina and I exchanged glances, then my companion continued to lean over the old woman. "You appeared to be in distress, madam."

I could hear the skepticism in her voice. Mina took the opportunity of her proximity to feel around the woman's chair and beneath the table in front of her. Searching for trick wires, no doubt.

Then, realizing my knees were a trifle wobbly and my palms a bit damp, I turned to see how the others were faring. Miss Norton appeared to have gotten herself under control with the assistance of Miss Rolstone and Aunt Geraldine. But Miss Ashton didn't seem to have moved from her place at the table.

In fact, she was staring at something high above. Her lips moved silently, and I could make out the word "Mother."

In the shadows of the inset ceiling, I saw the faintest wisp of a gaseous shape . . . glowing, faintly sparkling, like a soft green cloud.

And then it was gone.

"Mother! Please come back!"

# Miss Stoker

*In Which Our Heroines See Different
Sides of the Same Coin*

"Diversion, Miss Stoker," said my companion crisply as we rode away from Miss Ashton's home. It was nearly two o'clock, and heavy rain clouds rolled in.

Mina had her long nose lifted slightly, which was the sure sign of a coming lecture. "Performances such as the one we were subjected to are all a matter of diversion and timing. Trip wires, mirrors, tricks of light, special shoe-pads to make the rapping sounds, and other mechanisms your medievalist brain cannot conceive. When one is distracted by a noise or sight, another play is set in motion. Spiritualism is nothing more than sophisticated sleight of hand."

I was in no mood to listen to her. What had happened in Miss Ashton's parlor left me unsettled and jumpy. I wasn't going to let my companion dismiss it with a wave of her gloved hand and her so-called deductions. "Did you *find* any trip wires when you were examining Mrs. Yingling? Or any shoe-pads?"

"I didn't have the opportunity to fully investigate. But I did find," she raised her voice over my snort, "a length of black thread—precisely where Mrs. Yingling was sitting. Along with another dead cricket."

"Are you suggesting that tiny woman somehow moved a massive table with a piece of thread and a dead bug?"

"Of course not. But the thread was likely part of some other mechanism that caused the rapping. Either that or, as the Fox Sisters did, she may have simply been cracking her joints."

"Right."

"That's how they do it. For certain people, cracking a toe or ankle or knee joint can make a noise resembling rapping. If I had more opportunity to examine the chamber we were in, I'd be able to tell you precisely how it was done. All of it. It was all fakery and fraud."

"No mechanical device caused Mrs. Yingling to speak in that strange, dark voice, and—"

"On the contrary. It could easily have been some sort of voice-altering mechanism attached to her throat—did you notice how high her lace collar was? And how thick the column of her neck appeared? Of course you didn't." She *tsk*ed and I rolled my eyes as she launched into her familiar speech. "The art of observation is lost on the average individual—no, it is lost on every individual I have ever met—with the exception of my uncle and my father."

"What about Inspector Grayling? As I recall, he matched you fact for fact at the crime scene inside the British Museum."

As I hoped, my own diversion derailed her. Mina gave her little sniff, as she often did when she had no response to something. But the reprieve didn't last long, and she continued her lecture without even acknowledging my jibe about Grayling.

"I had been expecting some sort of occurrence in which the medium pretends to take on the spirit of a deceased person and speaks in an altered voice. The combination of a vibrating device that changes the pressure on the larynx with excellent playacting skills easily explains what you saw and heard today, Miss Stoker. And that is why I am certain Mrs. Yingling is taking advantage of our grieving friend Miss Ashton to extort great amounts of money from her. No wonder the princess is concerned."

I leaned across the carriage toward her. "Then explain, Miss Alvermina Holmes, if you are so accomplished at deduction and observation, how that elderly woman knew an old man's pet name for *me*. And how she even knew *of* the old man—Mr. O'Gallegh." I used Mina's full name purposely, and was rewarded as she winced. But to my surprise, she closed her mouth and blinked, as if my words had finally penetrated.

"Hm."

For a moment, I thought I had her. But no.

"A simple matter of research." She waved away my question with a flap of her hand. "Mrs. Yingling is obviously well versed in her performances, and she wouldn't have come ill-prepared. She would have spoken to people, learned all about you—"

"But, Mina." I spread my hands wide. It was better than trying to strangle her. "Not only did Miss Ashton not know I was to attend, but there is no one who could have told her—or anyone—that Mr. O'Gallegh called me Linny-Lou."

"What do you mean?"

"Mr. O'Gallegh . . . he was the cog-filer near our old street in Bloomsbury, before we moved to Grantworth House more than a year ago. Who knew I was friends with an old merchant man who died twelve months ago, and especially who called me a pet name no one else had ever heard? There is no one who would know or care."

"Someone must have told her. Or told someone who told her."

Her words were stout, but for the first time, she seemed uncertain. I pressed my advantage. I needed her to understand. *Something real had happened in that parlor.* "I know there are many mediums who've been proven to be frauds—but I don't think she's one. Mr. O'Gallegh was killed by a vampire. I was there the night he died. No one but he and I and my mentor knew what happened. Did you hear him—the voice,

I mean—tonight? He spoke of Judas's minions. He meant vampires. No one else could have known about that night."

Mina's mouth was slightly open, and she stared at me without blinking. In the shadowy carriage, her eyes were wide and white around the irises.

"I had finished my initial training as a vampire hunter—"

"Venator," she murmured.

Of course she had to correct me. Could she be any more annoying? I gritted my teeth and continued. "That night I was to hunt and slay a vampire on my own. I've told you . . . I can sense the presence of an UnDead. One was in the vicinity. I was with Siri, the woman who trained me—"

"A *female* mentor? Fascinating."

"—and I came upon Mr. O'Gallegh. The vampire was still feeding off him. It was a terrible sight. . . ." I squeezed my eyes closed for a moment to try and erase the memory of that horrible image. "I . . . froze. I—my mind blanked. . . ."

I opened my eyes. Mina watched me closely, and I could almost read her mind. She wanted to know how a person "chosen" to hunt vampires could be so shaken by the sight of blood. As if I hadn't berated myself for that enough over the last year.

For some reason, it was important she understand. "It wasn't the blood that affected me. It was—oh, there was so *much* of it, and his body was torn and open, his insides spilling out. Horrific. And then the vampire looked at me. I held my stake in my hand, I remember that. I hefted it in my grip. And

87

I remember lunging toward the creature, just as Siri taught me . . . but it felt as if I was running through deep water. I couldn't move fast enough. And then I. . . ."

My voice trailed off. I couldn't tell her what happened.

The truth was, I didn't *know*. I didn't remember. I didn't even recall if I'd actually *killed* the UnDead or not.

And if I hadn't . . . did that mean Siri had killed the creature for me? And was that why she'd disappeared the next day? I hadn't seen her since.

Had Siri given up on me? Had I made such a mess of things that she had to leave?

"And then . . . *what*?" Mina demanded.

The carriage stopped with a violent lurch that slammed me back into my seat and tumbled Mina to the floor. People outside were shouting. Whistles blew and bells rang. I had never been so grateful for a traffic delay as I was at that moment.

"Are you hurt?" I pulled her back into the seat, her skirts and petticoats a violent froth of lace and satin. It's no easy task for a woman to pick herself up when she can hardly bend at the waist, thanks to the steel or bone corset that encases her.

"Not really." But I noticed she was moving a little stiffly. "Except for my . . . er . . . posterior."

I looked out the window but couldn't see what had caused the ruckus or the blockage of traffic. The gas lamps weren't on yet because it was still midday, and the fog was relatively light for once. I made out a conglomeration of carriages, flower-sellers, wagons, and pedestrians. The sounds of barking dogs, continuous shouting, and more clanging bells filled the street.

All at once, the door to the carriage opened. Mina froze and I gaped at the shadowy man who appeared there.

"Who are you?" I reached for the small knife in the hidden pocket in my shirtwaist. And where was my coachman?

The man looked from me to Mina. In the uneven light, I had the impression of white-blond hair from beneath a low-riding bowler hat, a dark suit with a high-necked coat muffling the neck and chin, and a slender, crooked nose.

"I gots a li'l sumpin fer ya." He moved suddenly, pulling a hand from his pocket.

I bolted out of my seat, knife gripped, blocking him from entering any further or releasing whatever was in his gloved fingers. "Get out, or I'll give you a little something of my own." My blade, small as it was, caught a bit of light and glinted wickedly. I loomed over him, aided by the height of the vehicle. I could kick him in the torso hard enough to send him flying.

"As ye wish, then." He edged back, then his hand moved again, sharply. An object flew into the carriage. "'Ere ye are."

He was gone in a swirl of dark wool, slamming the door and disappearing into the loud night . . . but not before I caught a good glimpse of one familiar eye, laughing up at me.

# Miss Holmes

*Of Clumsy Umbrellas and Honey-Creme Mandarins*

Miss Stoker muttered an unladylike term which I will not repeat here. She glared at the carriage door, and I realized she wasn't upset or unsettled in the way I expected. She was furious.

"What on earth . . . ?" I willed my heart to stop pounding while also having the presence of mind to latch the carriage door. I didn't relish any more surprises. I had no idea what had happened to the lock in the first place, as well as our driver. Perhaps he had left his post to see what caused the traffic snarl.

The strange man in our carriage had disappeared as quickly as he'd come, and I was so taken off guard by his sudden presence, it took me a moment to reflect upon my natural observations.

His hair was false, attached to the hat he wore, and the one boot with which he'd stepped onto the carriage threshold was well made and polished . . . utterly at odds with the rest of his shabby, ill-fitting attire. He wore well-fitting gloves. One was patched over the left thumb.

As I reviewed these facts, along with my impression of the man's height and age, Evaline scrabbled about on the floor among our skirts, still muttering epithets. At last, she came up, holding a wad of cloth.

Wrapped in it was Dylan's telephone-device, sleek, silver, and fully intact. As Miss Stoker manhandled the object into her palm, she must have pushed a button, for the thing lit up, revealing all of its small, colorful images. At least it didn't launch into those loud, screeching noises it sometimes made.

By then, the pieces had clicked into place. "It was that individual . . . from the opium den, during the affair with the Ankh. The young man, the pickpocket who lives in the stews. Pix."

"Right. Apparently he found a way to put electricity back into this."

"He has a very odd and inefficient way of delivering it." I tried to forget that the last time I'd seen the shady (literally and figuratively) character, I'd been slung over his broad, half-clothed shoulder as he hauled me from a burning building.

"You're right about that. Pix prefers the dramatic, and he likes to take me—and everyone else—off guard. He has a need to be in control. I wouldn't put it past him to have even arranged the traffic problem. Caused a vendor to overturn in the street, or a sewage canal to overspill or something of that nature."

"So you brought it to him last evening."

"Yes. He didn't say he'd be able to fix it so quickly." Miss Stoker's face settled into a thoughtful expression. "Curious. Last night he tells me there are rumors the UnDead have returned. And today Mr. O'Gallegh speaks to me in a séance."

"*Supposedly* speaks to you," I reminded her. "I'm not yet convinced."

"Of course you aren't. Either way, it all seems very . . . coincidental. So perhaps it is true. The UnDead *are* back. As you've pointed out too many times to count, there are no coincidences."

"Indeed. Which is why I shall be visiting Mrs. Yingling first thing on the morrow."

"Why? And how do you know where she lives?"

"I obtained her calling card and address before we left. Miss Ashton might have sent everyone into a bit of a spin but I, at least, had my wits about me. I made certain to inquire about possible future séances from our esteemed medium, including information about her rates. As I suspected, her fees can be quite high. As for your second question—why: I intend to determine where and how she got the information about your Mr. O'Gallegh. She's either a fake, and someone provided her with that information, and she wants you to be her next victim, or . . ."

"Or, it really was the spirit of Mr. O'Gallegh speaking through her."

I rolled my eyes. The medium had played us false, just as she'd been doing to Miss Ashton. I was certain of it.

I had no doubt I would solve this case tomorrow.

Drat.

The next morning, I set out for the British Museum on my way to confront Mrs. Yingling. I had some books to return to Miss Adler's office and was hoping to speak to her . . . and perhaps see Dylan. I kept having this odd fluttery feeling whenever I remembered how he'd leapt into action and saved the Queen two days ago.

I relived the scene in my mind over and over again: his strong arms, propping up our esteemed monarch as if she were hardly more than a rag doll. He'd had a calm, yet intense and determined expression as he went about saving her life. And afterward, he'd been nothing but circumspect and modest.

A true gentleman.

I had just replaced the borrowed items on the bookshelf when the office door opened and he walked in.

"Good morning, Dylan." I resisted the urge to smooth the front of my skirt and adjust my lace-cuffed sleeves. I had chosen one of my favorite walking ensembles of apple-green and emerald trimmed with snowy white when I dressed this morning, and it looked well even on someone as tall and gangly as myself.

If only I could do something about my Holmesian nose!

"Hey, Mina. That's a really pretty dress." He wore a crisp white shirt with a dark brown waistcoat and trousers. Prince Albert's gear-ridden cufflink glinted from the knot of Dylan's necktie, and I approved of that embellishment.

His coat and hat were missing, which told me he'd not left the Museum this morning, and his clean shoes bore out that fact. The only element of his appearance that indicated he was a foreigner from the future was his dark blond hair. It was so long it hung to his brows and over his ears, flipping up gently near his square jaw. He'd gotten better at shaving (he claimed the devices used in his time were much different than the mechanized ones employed by gentlemen today). I saw only five tiny nicks in his skin and the small patch he'd missed at the corner of his jaw.

I should explain that Miss Adler had taken Dylan under her wing, so to speak. Because he was reluctant to leave the Museum lest he miss an opportunity to return to his time, she'd arranged a position for him as her assistant. He'd been living on the premises for the last month, and she provided him food and clothing as well.

He pulled out his telephone-device and waggled it at me. "I'm so happy Evaline got this recharged for me. She didn't tell me how she did it, but I'm not complaining. When she dropped it off yesterday, she mentioned you'd gone to Miss Ashton's already."

"Yes, we attended a séance at her house. And today I intend to visit the medium who conducted it in order to prove her a fraud."

"A séance? We tried to do one once, using a Ouija board, but nothing happened."

I had heard of the "spirit-talking" boards, for they were all the rage in America and to a lesser degree, here in London, but I'd never had the desire to examine one. "Our medium resorted to speaking in the spirit's voice, and using some rapping sounds to communicate instead of a planchette and a list of the alphabet. Would you like to come with me to interrogate her?"

As soon as the words came out of my mouth, I felt my face heat. How forward and improper I was!

But it was easy to be that way with Dylan. He didn't treat me or Evaline the way most men treated young women: as if we hadn't a valid thought in our heads, as if we were meant to be little more than pretty or wealthy dolls trussed up in fancy clothing and admired from our perch on a settee.

"Totally. I'm dying to get out of this building and into the sunshine."

We both glanced toward the window. Gloomy and drizzly— as usual. "At least it's fresh air," he said with a grin.

A clean, modern horseless taxi took us from the Museum to Glasner-Mews, where Mrs. Yingling kept rooms in a Mrs. Ellner's boardinghouse. Particularly self-conscious about being alone in the vehicle with a young man, I occupied myself by pointing out sights and landmarks. But I noticed that, unlike during our trip to Marlborough House, Dylan didn't seem as interested in the sights. In fact, he seemed introspective as he held the silver device in his hands, turning it over and over in a random fashion.

"Is something bothering you, Dylan?"

He looked up from the seat opposite me. Even though the light was sketchy in the taxi, I was easily able to read his expression. Uncertainty and sadness. My insides shriveled a little. What a silly question. Of course something was bothering him. His home, his place, his *world,* was a hundred and twenty years in the future. He didn't belong here.

Before I could say anything else, he spoke in a low, musing tone. "I can't stop thinking about it. . . . *I saved Queen Victoria's life.*"

"It was brilliant, Dylan. *You* were brilliant. How did you know what to do?"

"It's basic first aid training where I come from, especially if you're an Eagle Scout like I am. Plus my father's a doctor. He works in the emergency room—the part of the hospital where they bring people who need to be treated urgently. I've heard all sorts of stories from him over the years. Guess I've even learned a few things too."

I decided I could ask later about what an eagle scout was. Dylan didn't seem to be the type of person to be interested in ornithology. Instead, I focused on his other revelation. "Your father is a physician?"

"Yes." He grew quiet again, and I searched in vain for something to say.

Did he miss his father as much as I missed my mother?

Was it worse for Dylan, knowing that he'd left his parents, albeit not by his own volition—or was it worse for me, whose mother had left with no explanation and little communication in a year? At least *she* could come back if she wanted to.

My throat hurt and my eyes threatened to sting. I was relieved when Dylan spoke again.

"But the thing is . . . I saved the Queen's life. And I was the only one who could have done it. Yet I didn't change the course of history. The Queen doesn't die—I mean, she wasn't supposed to die yet. And she didn't."

"So you did something that only someone from the future could have done, but you didn't change the course of history."

It just occurred to me that Dylan knew when Queen Victoria would die. What else about the future did he know? A shiver rushed over my shoulders, ending in an unpleasant twist in my belly. That was dangerous. And fascinating.

"Yes. Isn't that weird? But there are a lot of strange things about this whole mess anyway," he muttered.

"I should think. Time travel is quite strange in and of itself." And yet there was a part of me fascinated by it, and its implications. Imagine if one could go back in time to the scene of a crime—just when the deed was being perpetrated?

"But it's not just that," Dylan mused. "It's . . . well, there are things in *this* London of 1889 that are very different from what I learned in history books. And so maybe . . . maybe I *did* change history—your history, this *alternate* history—by saving the Queen's life." Dylan's expression was miserable. "And if I'm in an alternate history, how in the hell am I *ever* going to get home?"

For once, I didn't have the answer. "You saved someone's life. That's the most important thing. It's always the most important thing."

Dylan seemed particularly moved by my words. "That's exactly what my dad always says. Saving a life is the best work a person can do."

Forestalling any further conversation, the taxi lurched to a stop. We'd arrived at our destination.

The driver engaged the vehicle's side-lift. I appreciated these mechanized platforms, for it kept the chances to a minimum that I would trip on my skirts or catch a heel on the edge of the vehicle. The small lift was smooth and silent as it lowered me to the tiled walkway and the driver handed over my umbrella as I stepped down.

Glasner-Mews was a clean, well-kept neighborhood filled with shops, residences, and boarding houses at all five street-levels. While it wasn't a particularly affluent area like

Hyde Park or St. James's, it certainly wasn't the dingy, dangerous Whitechapel where that character Pix resided.

"We have to go to the third level." Managing my umbrella, I led the way to the nearest street-lift while avoiding puddles of water, mud, and other waste. A demure young lady would have waited for the gentleman to offer an escorting arm, but as has been previously noted, not only did Dylan usually forget to do so, but I lacked the propriety Society requires of its young women.

After I nearly decapitated him while digging for a ha'penny in my bag, Dylan liberated the umbrella from my clumsy grip. He held it over my head as I placed the coin on the street-lift's small metal tongue. The tiny tray clicked back as the mechanism gulped down my fare, belching and coughing the whole time.

The ornate brass gate opened. Taking care to gather up my skirt, which was always in danger of being trapped by the closing doors, I stepped into the grillwork-sided platform with my companion. It was a tight fit, placing me in pleasant, close proximity to Dylan. He gave me the warm, crooked smile that always made my insides swish pleasantly. I was relieved that he seemed to have pulled out of his doldrums.

The gears groaned and chains rattled as we rose above the street-level with little jerks. Moments later, we alighted and began to walk along the narrow upper walkway toward 79-K.

In this part of London, the buildings rose so tall and wide above the throughways they seemed almost to connect over the street. The balloonlike air-anchors attached to the cornices of each roof bumped and shifted in the sky as their weightless pull helped keep the corners of the brick structures from crashing into each other.

Street vendors called out at all levels, hawking their wares. Because the raised walkways were so narrow, allowing hardly enough room for two people to stroll abreast, the sellers were relegated to parking their carts so half the vehicle hung out over the street below, anchored by brass manacles the size of wagon wheels—which was why the vendor-balloons were such a welcome invention. Carriages clattered along on the ground below. People shouted, dogs barked, shutters thudded, a church bell clanged . . . and feathered through it all was the familiar hiss of steam.

"Something smells really good." Dylan wielded my umbrella like a gentleman's walking stick as he took in the sights.

It was a rare event in which he wasn't hungry, eating, or at least thinking about food. But in this case, I couldn't disagree with the sentiment. The scents of flaming carrots, shredded-meat pies, puffed plums, and frothy vanilla teas filtered through the air.

"Honey-Creme Mandarins, miss," called a man from across the air-canal. "Fresh from the crystallizer, still warm!"

"Would you like one? My treat."

I accepted Dylan's offer with alacrity, for honeyed mandarins are one of my favorite sweets. He remembered to offer
me a gentlemanly arm as we walked over the fly-bridge, crossing the road three levels above the ground.

The lowest street-levels were the meanest in the sense
that they were the dirtiest, dingiest, and most unpleasantly
aromatic. Sewer chutes rushed alongside the roads, and the
primitive walkways were narrow and often flooded with rain-
water or sewage that splashed up as various forms of ground
transportation rumbled past. The higher the street-level, the
cleaner, lighter, and more expensive the area. The lifts were
the only way to travel between levels. Therefore, if one didn't
have a coin to feed the machine (or if the mechanism was dis-
abled), one was destined to remain at the lower level—either
permanently or temporarily. And the higher the level, the
greater the cost of the ride.

It was, my father had once said in a rare moment of
candidness, a way to keep the riffraff segregated from the
privileged.

Vaguely uncomfortable by this pronouncement, I nevertheless couldn't deny its truth. Every time I was forced to pay
to rise above the ground level, I couldn't help think of his
words. I wondered what it would be like to have no choice but
to have my skirts constantly dragging through the muck and
water—among other disadvantages.

"Here you are, Mina." Dylan offered me one of the
small, warm bundles.

The plum-sized orange looked delicious, its peelings folded back halfway like a lotus flower, revealing plump segments glistening with a glaze of honey-creme.

"How do you eat it?" he asked in a low voice as we left the vendor. I couldn't help but notice he had three more of the treats in his hand, and I hid a smile.

"The best way is to peel off one petal at a time and eat a segment. But some people just bite in. Once it starts to cool, the honey-creme flakes off more easily, so it's best to eat it right away."

We strolled back across the fly-bridge, enjoying the sweets, doing what Dylan charmingly called "people-watching." He offered me a second mandarin, and I declined, then pointed out that he had a tiny flake of glaze on his chin. He suggested I use a napkin to dab at the corner of my mouth, and I didn't even flush.

We noticed a young beagle hound with ears much too long for his puppy body bounding around on the streetwalk below and stopped to watch him for a moment. Although I don't particularly care for canine creatures, I found him to be quite adorable. He was brown-and-black-spotted over a white coat and he kept tripping over his ears.

Spending such a pleasant time with a handsome, attentive young man, I was almost able to forget that I was a Holmes—a young woman destined to remain unmarried and unattached. We Holmeses, as Uncle Sherlock had pontificated many times, were above the base emotions that affected (and, he claimed, weakened) other people, for our lives and minds were dedicated to cold, factual observation and clean, logical deduction. Emotions such as love or anger or fear simply clouded the brain and were a waste of energy.

And according to my uncle and father, as a female I was even more at risk of such weakness.

At last, the idyll ended as we reached 79-K. As Dylan went to throw the glaze-filled papers away, I pushed the call button on the door. A bell chimed, then there was a soft humming sound. A peephole door rolled open on invisible gears, revealing a brown eye set beneath a thick brow.

"Yes?"

"Mrs. Ellner?" I asked. "I'm here to visit Mrs. Yingling."

"Oh, well, then, one moment, please."

"Do you mind if I wait outside?" Dylan asked. "I want to watch that airship come through here. And that vendor with the meat-pies is calling my name."

I hadn't heard anyone shouting Dylan, but I shook my head. "Not at all." Watching one of the oblong airships make its way between the buildings to a mooring station was always a sight to behold.

I turned back to 79-K. The peephole had eased closed and I heard it latch into place, then the door swung open. Now I was able to see that the brown eye belonged to a homely woman who stood no taller than my shoulder.

Calluses on her fingers—*a hand-knitter.*

Well-mended, relatively new clothing, clean shoes, ivory comb in hair—*pride in her appearance, has an income that keeps food on the table and clothing in the trunks.*

No wedding ring, no other jewelry, no sign of male presence—*the Mrs. was widowed.*

And, from all appearances, comfortably prosperous on her own.

"You're here to visit Yrmintrude, then. I haven't seen her yet today, but come in, come in. She came back in after tea yesterday from visitin' 'er newest, most luc'ative client. Would be a good thing, I 'ave t'say, because Yrmy—well, now I should stop rambling. Her room's down this way." She beckoned for me to follow her slow progress down a narrow hallway. Mrs. Ellner had a pronounced limp, due to a misaligned ankle that needed to be adjusted, and her pace was maddeningly slow.

We passed three doors before my guide stopped, and she rapped on the door. "Yrmy, you have a visitor." Then she turned to me and explained, "If you was a man, I'd have you be waiting in the public parlor for her. But her female clients, well, what 'arm can it be to allow them to wait in the hall? I know why you're here, and it's of a personal matter, of course, so it's best not to be seen." She smiled knowingly.

When we heard no sounds beyond the door, Mrs. Ellner knocked again, more loudly this time. "Yrmintrude! You've got yourself a visitor!"

"Perhaps she's in a back room and can't hear you." I'd felt a prickling certainty that something was wrong.

"It's only one room. She cain't help but hear me." My concern was reflected in the landlady's eyes, and she produced a key.

A sharp clink, the clunk of a bolt being thrown open, and then the door swung wide.

"Yrmy!" Mrs. Ellner lumbered past me with newfound speed.

I followed more slowly, already sniffing the air and scanning the chamber.

There was no need to rush, for it was obvious Mrs. Yingling wasn't going to be awakening ever again.

# MISS HOLMES

## Miss Holmes Investigates

M rs. Yingling lay beneath a thin blanket, her head on a pillow. She could have been sleeping, except that the rousing cries emitting from her landlady's mouth hadn't caused even a twitch.

Mrs. Ellner had repeated her shrieks of "Oh my gad" countless times before she accepted the fact that her friend was deceased. Fortunately, I was able to intercept her before she disrupted the crime scene too much. There was no blood, no obvious sign of injury, but it was immediately clear to me Mrs. Yingling had not died a natural death.

"Perhaps you might want to notify the police," I suggested.

"The police?"

"Indeed. Your friend has been murdered and the Met generally like to investigate such events." I was proud of myself for leaving out the phrase "attempt to," for my uncle would not have been so circumspect.

"But how could she be murdered? She . . . there's no blood. No one was here—"

"Mrs. Yingling was left-handed, was she not?"

"Why, yes, I do recall she was, but what does that have to do with anything?"

"It means she was murdered. I'll remain here and make certain the scene isn't contaminated—"

"The what?"

I drew in an impatient breath. "I'll make certain no one disturbs any clues. Can you send someone to call for the authorities?"

"Yes, yes, I suppose I best." She hobbled toward the door. "There's that young fellow what lives just above Mr. and Mrs. Barnley . . . I'll call him."

I didn't hear the rest of her speech, for I was busy examining the chamber. Much as I was loathe to have the authorities bumbling about, they had to be notified. Therefore, I had to work quickly to finish my investigation before they arrived. I wished mightily I had brought my larger reticule, complete with my new, self-mounting Ocular-Magnifyer and other investigative tools . . . but I hadn't expected to come upon a murder. Since this wasn't the first time I'd been caught unprepared at a crime scene, I was doubly irritated with myself.

The space was fairly generous for being a boardinghouse room. Two windows offered a modicum of light, despite the neighboring building hardly two arms' lengths away. A new rug and expensive wool cloak indicated a recent change in Mrs. Yingling's financial situation.

I checked the haphazard stack of books on the floor next to the bed and wasn't surprised to find that the sensational novels of Wilkie Collins and Mrs. Radcliffe, with their ghostly characters and screaming women in white nightgowns, made up a good portion of the collection. A pile of papers rested neatly on the small table acting as a desk. A chair was ajar from the writing surface as if someone had just stood up and walked away, leaving a cup and pencil to the right of the papers.

Inside a trunk I found two false hands cuffed with lace and attached to strong, nearly visible threads along with a filmy white material resembling a shroud. There was also a small, curious device that produced a puff of cool, foul-scented air as well as a small slate with a pencil hidden in its frame—obviously for "spirit-writing." It appeared I had been correct in my opinion that Mrs. Yingling was a fraud.

And now she'd been murdered. But why? And by whom?

Could it be a coincidence that, merely the day after performing a fake séance for the niece of Sherlock Holmes, Mrs. Yingling had been found murdered? I highly doubted it.

It could have been no more than eight minutes since Mrs. Ellner left, but I heard the sounds of rapid footsteps approaching. The authorities.

Aware my time was running short, I bent over the unfortunate medium's body for further examination. My observations confirmed the lack of injury or any mark on the corpse, at least insofar as what was revealed by her long-sleeved night rail. She appeared just as I'm certain the perpetrator intended: a frail, elderly woman who'd died painlessly in her sleep.

Except . . . I peered more closely at the skin near her mouth. Drat that I didn't have my Magnifyer with me, but even with the naked eye, I could see a trace of red around her lips. My attention returned briefly to the cup on the table and I sniffed at the air once more. And smiled in satisfaction.

The footsteps, which had been rushing closer, came to an abrupt halt in the doorway. I heard an odd strangled sound and looked up at the newcomer.

"*Inspector Grayling.*" I straightened abruptly from my examination of the body.

"Miss Holmes. I hardly know what to say." His voice was filled with irony and something like distaste.

"That is quite unusual," I replied coolly, despite the heat rushing over my cheeks. "You, having nothing to say." I was trying to free my recalcitrant heel, which had somehow gotten caught in the lace of my petticoats, without exposing either of my ankles. Or the fact that I was struggling to do so. Pressing my advantage—if I actually had one—I continued, "Has the Scotland Yard uniform changed, or were you merely on a day off?"

My comment was prompted by his casual state of dress. He wore well-fitting brown Betrovian wool trousers perhaps two years out of fashion but nevertheless well maintained. His waistcoat was missing, and he wore only a white shirt and a hastily flung-on coat, as evidenced by the misaligned seams over his broad shoulders. One of the braces that held up his trousers peeked from the off-kilter neckline of his coat. He lacked both hat and gloves (although that wasn't unusual for the young inspector). He was due for a shave. However, his shoes were buffed and clean.

"My residence," he said, his voice as emotionless as mine, "happens to be three blocks from here. Mrs. Ellner is an acquaintance of my neighbors, and as such, I was summoned from what, yes, happened to be a morning spent at home. I had a late night last night." His curling, gingery hair did appear rumpled, and his face slightly ruddy due to his Scottish heritage as well as his obvious effort in arriving expediently at the scene.

"At the theater, perhaps?" I asked, trying and failing to imagine him escorting a young woman, dressed in frilly pink or sunny yellow, to a show. "Or Cremayne?" The old park, though not as popular as it once was, offered street-jugglers, pleasant walks, and other entertainments. I had never been there myself, but I understood it was a pleasant place for a group of young people to pass an evening's time. "Perhaps a music hall?"

"I'm afraid not."

Instead of elaborating, he walked into the chamber, examining it as I had upon my entrance. I closed my eyes, sending a hope off into the ether that he wouldn't mention anything about the Ocular-Magnifyer that I should have had with me. The one *he* had sent to me after the Affair of the Clockwork Scarab, to replace one that had broken in his presence.

"I was told this was a murder scene," he said after a moment of quiet perusal and air-sniffing. "Would you care to elaborate on that as well as on your presence here, Miss Holmes? Perhaps you know something about the victim that I do not."

"She was a medium, a spirit-speaker. I attended a séance at which she presided yesterday"—he gave me an astonished look at which I set my jaw—"and presented some information that was very obscure. I came here today to determine how she'd come by this sensitive information, and to prove that she was a fraud. With a bit of observation, I'm certain you'll agree with my deduction. Her landlady and I found her just like this. She was very frail yet seemed in good health, quite well-spoken, left-handed, and exceptionally adept at faking communication with the so-called spirit world."

He trained his attention on the body, then the table, and finally at me. "Definitely murder."

# Miss Holmes

*In Which Miss Ashton Makes a Startling Confession*

Inspector Grayling was still investigating the murder scene when I took my leave nearly an hour later. Even more of a cognoggin than I, he employed a complicated device to take measurements of a faint set of muddy footprints on the window-sill, for we had both agreed that was how the murderer entered and exited the chamber. I watched him manipulate the slick footed mechanism, not even attempting to hide my fascination while it crawled about, clicking as it ticked off the numbers he needed.

It was when Grayling went on to employ a simple Eastman camera to make pictures of the area that I decided to take my leave.

Of course I had done my own examination, as well as completed a very satisfactory interrogation of the landlady and several of the neighbors. In addition, I'd collected a sample of the dirt at the window and was taking it home for analysis.

As I walked out of 79-K and looked for Dylan, I heard a horrible barking wail. Remembering the entertaining beagle pup that had been playing one level below, I hurried over to the side of the street-railing and looked down. To my dismay, it was indeed the creature. His hind leg had been caught in one of the metal grateworks that acted as a vendor-balloon mooring. He wailed pitifully, tugging and twisting and dancing about. I seemed to be the only person to hear the distressed sound over the normal city noises.

Before I could determine the best way to help the poor fellow, a figure came from nowhere, vaulting over the walkway's edge and to the level below.

It took me only a moment to realize it was Grayling. He must have been working at Mrs. Yingling's window and heard the distressed pup—then vaulted out and down to rescue the poor thing. He landed flat-footed on the lower streetwalk and had the little pup liberated in a trice.

I turned away, ignoring the odd feeling in my chest. What a foolish, dangerous thing to do, leaping out of a window and over the railing! I shook my head. Grayling could have easily misjudged his landing and gone tumbling down to the street level.

*Tsk*ing to myself, yet unable to dismiss the memory of the lanky detective vaulting smoothly from one street-level down to another, I walked off. Surely Dylan was in the vicinity, patronizing another meat-pie vendor or indulging in a flaming carrot. I needed to find him, for I had many things to contemplate in regards to my investigation. And I certainly didn't want to be caught gawking at the Scotland Yard Inspector, either.

When I located my companion several blocks away, standing near the airship mooring dock, I launched into a description of my discovery of Mrs. Yingling's body.

"She's dead?" Dylan was, as I'd expected, eating again—this time a raisin-salad sandwich. The sweet rose-colored juice had stained the waferlike bread and wrappings, and a pink raisin plopped onto the ground as he took another bite.

"Not merely dead. Murdered." I took his arm, noticing again how solid and firm it was. I was certain he could launch himself out of a window and down a street level too.

"What are you going to do now? Do you think it's related to the Willa Ashton case?" He wiped the last bit of juice from his fingers as we strode along with me setting the pace at a brisk, efficient one.

"I hardly think Mrs. Yingling's death is a coincidence. I suspect there is more to this case than a fraudulent medium trying to make money."

Before I could expound further on my suspicions, we heard a loud mechanical squeal, then a violent crashing sound. Shouts and screams erupted from below.

People ran over to the edge of the streetwalks and looked down. A horseless carriage had crashed into another vehicle and overturned. A mangled bicycle was protruding from beneath the wreckage. Even from three heights up, I could see bodies on the street and splashes of bright red blood spilling over the cobblestones.

Bystanders were already helping to extricate the victims. A burly man and his companion heaved the carriage upright, and it landed on its two wheels with a loud thud. Others were arranging the injured persons on coats and blankets that had been laid on the filthy street.

Dylan's arm was tight beneath my fingers, and I felt him move a little, as if to pull away. "I should go down there. See if I can help."

"I'll come with you."

We hurried to the nearest street-lift and had to wait for it to return to our level. By the time we climbed on and it lumbered its way down to the ground, the police had arrived as well as some medical help.

I didn't see the auburn-haired Grayling and assumed he'd been too far away to hear the accident, or perhaps on his way back to the Met by the time the incident occurred.

"Alvermina, what on earth are you doing down at this level?"

I whirled to find my famous uncle standing at the edge of the crowd. A tall, gangly man cursed with the sharp, Holmesian nose and receding dark hair, he brandished a walking stick.

"Hello, Uncle Sherlock." I didn't bother to answer his question and instead responded with one of my own. "Are you investigating a case? The missing boy from Bloomsbury, perhaps? I see Dr. Watson is here with you." The shorter, bespectacled man crouched next to one of the accident victims.

"In fact I am on a case, but not the boy from Bloomsbury nor even the other from Drury-lane. The Met believe they have them well in hand, the fools, and have instead asked me to consult on a bloody fire on Bond-street. Might as well be sending me off to investigate the pickpocket gang. Waste of my brain cells."

As Uncle Sherlock pontificated on Scotland Yard's lapses in judgment and blundering attempts to investigate crimes, I noticed Dylan had approached Dr. Watson. They were speaking intently, gesturing to various accident victims in turn. My friend seemed very serious—even earnest. He stood slightly taller than my uncle's companion, and despite his too-long hair, he appeared every inch a Brit. A handsome, confident young man who had garnered the full attention of the esteemed Dr. Watson.

Dylan looked as if he belonged. And as I watched him, I became aware of an unfamiliar sensation spreading warmly through my limbs.

*I didn't want him to leave.*

"Do you not agree, Alvermina?"

My attention whipped back to my uncle. "Of course. And would you *please* refrain from calling me Alvermina?"

Uncle Sherlock blinked. "Whyever should I? It's a magnificent appellation. A traditional family name, bestowed upon my grandfather's mother. You are fortunate to have such an esteemed moniker."

For being so brilliant in some things, my uncle could be quite cloud-headed in others. I was saved from replying by the approach of Dr. Watson and Dylan, the latter now wearing a defeated expression. Nevertheless, he greeted my uncle politely, and we watched the victims being loaded into medical cabs. When they were finished, there was nothing left to do but find our own transportation and continue on our way. My uncle and his companion chose to take a street-lift and therefore had to walk several blocks, but I was able to find a taxi.

"They can't even give them blood," Dylan muttered as we climbed into a horseless hackney. "Watson claims there are some instances when a blood transfusion has been successful, but it's very rare. And forget about surgery. . . ."

"Blood transfusion? Transferring blood from one person to another?" I had the exceedingly improper urge to sit next to him and pat his (ungloved) hand. He had changed from calm and controlled to bereft and confused, and he obviously needed comfort.

"It's such a common practice in my time. It's so *frustrating* to see things that could be so easily treated . . . and knowing there's nothing that can be done with current medical practice." He worried Prince Albert's cufflink, still studding his tie. His expression was bereft. "It's just not fair. It's not *right*. I can see what needs to be done, but I can't do anything about it."

"I'm sorry, Dylan."

He shook his head, his mouth a thin, dark line in the drassy light. "I need to go *home*."

I nodded. He was right.

Despite my own desires, he didn't belong here.

The next morning when I came out of my chamber, I found our housekeeper, Mrs. Raskill, vigorously dusting the fireplace mantel with her Spizzy Spiral-Duster.

I glanced toward my father's bedchamber. The door was open a crack, a sure sign he wasn't here. "Has he been home?"

Mrs. Raskill shook her head, then went about her dusting, but not before I saw a flash of pity in her face. "Not as of late."

While everyone in London—perhaps England and even on the Continent—knew and lauded my uncle's deductive abilities, only those close to the Prime Minister and the Queen knew how valuable my father, Mycroft Holmes, was to our national security. He spent his days at the Home Office, doing whatever it was he did to protect and serve the British Empire. And more often than not, he carried out the rest of the evening and night at his gentleman's club in Mayfair.

In contrast, my uncle went out about on the streets and to the docks, dens, and rookeries as needed. He worked any case that appealed to him, whether it was for an individual of means, title, or not.

My father did all his investigating and strategizing from a desk and restricted himself to working for the government.

And yet . . . they both possessed the extraordinary Holmesian mind. My uncle acknowledged that, should Mycroft ever bestir himself and become physically active in his pursuits, he would outshine even Sherlock Holmes.

And I was his daughter—the child of a quietly brilliant, neglectful man . . . and a beautiful, vivacious woman.

Grief squeezed in my chest. I couldn't help but look at the mantel, at the picture of my stunning mother. It was the only photo of her remaining in the house. And she, at least, had been aptly named: Desirée. The only visible trait I'd inherited from her was my thick, chestnut hair. Why couldn't it have been her charming nose? Or her petite figure?

Mother left a year ago. I didn't know why. It probably had something to do with my father's style of life. But it could just as easily have had something to do with her awkward, bookish, socially inept daughter.

And it was one puzzle I no longer chose to contemplate.

She'd been in Paris at least for a time, for I received three short letters from her, each carefully devoid of anything pertinent. Even close examination netted me little information except that my mother had indeed written them, they *had* come from Paris, and she had to change ink bottles while penning one of them. The inconsistencies in her penmanship indicated many stops and starts during the composition, as if she'd had a difficult time determining what to write.

They gave no explanation for her sudden departure, other than vague platitudes like *It's for the best*, and *You'll understand the reason someday, Mina.*

The last letter came ten months ago.

"Mina?"

Mrs. Raskill had been speaking to me and I forced myself back to the present. "Yes, a pot of tea and some toast would be excellent."

"And a piece of ham," she insisted, pulling on the cord of her Spizzy for emphasis. The duster whirred softly as she lengthened the string, then when it was released, whizzed into an energetic spiral that she claimed did a much better job gathering up dust than a manual feather duster.

While Mrs. Raskill was preparing my breakfast, I sent a message to Miss Stoker wherein I invited her to join me in calling on Miss Ashton. It wasn't because I was particularly fond of Evaline's company or felt that she would be terribly helpful in my questioning of Miss Ashton, but more of a professional courtesy. After all, the princess had engaged both of us on the case.

I didn't expect my so-called partner to accept the invitation, for I assumed she'd been wandering the streets of London all night, searching for the elusive UnDead, and would still be asleep.

To my surprise, the messenger returned with an affirmative response, indicating Miss Stoker and her carriage would call for me at half-past ten. The convenience of having private transportation made up for having to wait for her arrival.

I had finished my tea and toast and nibbled on a slice of ham under the watchful eye of Mrs. Raskill when the Stoker carriage arrived. Bundling up a generous reticule, I bid our housekeeper good day and left the house.

"Good morning, Evaline." I commenced to settling in my seat. This was no simple process, for aside from my heavy skirt, ungainly bustles, and ever-present umbrella, I now had the cumbersome reticule to deal with.

"What in the blooming fish is in your bag? Are you going on a journey? Am I dropping you at the train station?"

"Tools and other accoutrements. After the surprise I encountered yesterday, I vowed I would never leave my house without my investigative equipment."

"You look like a new governess, arriving at the door of her latest employer." Evaline gave a merry chuckle. "Or a Gypsy woman traveling about."

"At least I won't be caught unprepared." My reply was haughty, but I became acutely aware of how frumpy I must appear, lugging my large bag. I was dressed neatly, but practically, in a simple cocoa-brown and cream-striped bodice with a dark green skirt. My fingerless gloves and small top hat were dark brown and with only minor embellishments. In a sly nod to my cognog tendencies, I'd pinned my favorite mechanical firefly brooch to the left side of my bodice.

On the other hand, Miss Stoker looked quite fetching in her fashionable but unexciting handmaker clothing. Her frock was of fine quality and excellent tailoring (from Madame Burnby's shop), and in a style that resisted the urge to be too lacy, flowery, or ruffly—and certainly not like the new Street-Fashion mode, which I found quite fascinating.

Although there were faint shadows under her eyes, Evaline's gaze wasn't dim or weary. Her daydress bodice was a lovely rose color, with a mauve underskirt and ruffles. The bonnet atop her head was little more than a fabric saucer, perched at her crown and slightly to the left. It had an elegant curve that allowed for the high bundle of her dark hair in the back, and was trimmed with tiny rosebuds and white daisies. I had coveted a similar one in a certain shop off Pall Mall, but it had more of a cognoggin element with a mechanized butterfly pin with wings that beat elegantly and some tasteful, gear-ridden flowers.

"Right, then. What surprise did you encounter yesterday, Mina?" There was a bit more levity in her voice than I appreciated.

"Mrs. Yingling's dead body."

Miss Stoker's reaction to my blunt announcement was quite satisfactory. She goggled as she made a shocked noise.

Thus mollified, I proceeded to tell her of the events in detail.

"And Grayling agreed with you that it was murder? How in the blooming fish did you know?"

"Inspector Grayling only agreed with me *after* I practically spelled out the clues for him," I informed her crisply.

"I see. Surely he was grateful for your assistance." Her eyes danced. "So how *did* you know she'd been murdered?"

"Elementary, my dear Miss Stoker. Mrs. Yingling was left-handed, which I observed during our séance. But on the table where she had presumably been sitting and writing, as well as drinking, her cup and writing instrument were on the right side of the papers. Clearly, someone else had been in the chamber and positioned the pen and cup to make it look as if she'd been working and then gone to bed afterward."

My companion looked at me skeptically. "Maybe she moved them herself—accidentally bumped them out of place."

"The angle of the pen and cup were both too precise and at the same time utterly wrong for having been randomly moved."

"Maybe someone else was sitting there and writing."

I shook my head. "The paper had smudges on it—the same sorts of smudges that a left-handed person makes because their palm brushes across the fresh ink as they write across the page. Someone else was obviously present besides Mrs. Yingling."

"And so you think she was murdered simply because someone else was in the room?"

"Considering the fact that no one was seen coming or going from Mrs. Yingling's chamber, the faint sweet smell I noticed immediately upon entering the closed room, and the raw redness around her mouth, it was quite obvious to me—as well as to Inspector Grayling, once I prompted him—that she had met with foul play."

"So how was she murdered?"

"Poisoned. Asphyxiated with chloroform—which has a sweet, chemical smell. As I'm sure even you noted, the woman was very frail and elderly. It would take little effort to hold a rag over her face whilst she slept, and chloroform is a rapid, if not unpredictable, killer—and it can burn the skin. Hence the faint red marks I noticed around Mrs. Yingling's mouth."

"And then the murderer moved her pens and papers around?"

"Likely he or she was curious about whatever work the old woman had been doing, and was perhaps checking to make certain there were no incriminating notes therein. That was the perpetrator's only mistake—well, besides not cleaning off his or her shoes—setting the scene on the table. If he or she had not taken the time to do that, I might not have identified the crime so readily. Either the culprit didn't know Mrs. Yingling was left-handed, or didn't realize the mistake when everything was arranged."

"And what about the dirty shoes?"

"Both Inspector Grayling and I found evidence that Mrs. Yingling's window had been recently opened. There was a bit of lime-soaked mud on the transom, presumably from the shoes of the intruder. I managed to obtain a specimen and have already used my laboratory to identify it as being from Miss Ashton's neighborhood, where you may have noticed there has been quite a bit of work being done on the roads. However, I believe the sample is specifically from Miss Ashton's front porch."

Miss Stoker's expression had changed from challenge to one of astonishment. "Blooming pete's, Mina, I do believe you're as smart as your Uncle Sherlock."

My cheeks warmed, but I took her heartfelt compliment as my due and nodded. "Thank you."

"So if Mrs. Yingling was murdered—"

"There is no doubt in my mind."

"—what does that have to do with Willa Ashton?"

"That's precisely why we are going to speak with her. It cannot be coincidental that the day after Holmes—and Stoker—begin an investigation by attending a séance, one of the main players is found murdered. But this turn of events has given me a completely different view of the case. At first, I suspected the plot was all Mrs. Yingling's: she was taking advantage of Miss Ashton's grief over losing her mother and younger brother in a relatively short time. She was clearly a fraud, obviously attempting to cull as much money from her victim as possible. But someone else is involved. Perhaps he or she hired Mrs. Yingling and fed her information that only a person close to Willa Ashton would know—"

"But what about Mrs. Yingling's message from Mr. O'Gallegh?" Miss Stoker simply would not give up that point. "That was *real*, Mina. You have to admit that."

"I admit no such thing. She faked everything else; she surely faked that. I merely got sidetracked from determining precisely how when I found her body."

"And what about that cloudy green stuff at the ceiling? That was real, too—"

"That sort of so-called ectoplasm can be easily manufactured with colored cotton gauze, gas, or even steam. Miss Stoker, I find spirit-talking and visits from beyond even less likely than the existence of the UnDead."

Evaline balked. Her lips pressed flat together as she fixed a cold gaze on me. "You don't believe vampires exist."

"I've never seen one."

"And therefore they must not exist. Because Alvermina Holmes has never set eyes on one." Her lips twisted into an unattractive sneer.

"Unlike certain people, I prefer to rely on scientific fact and objective observation rather than legend, fiction, and hearsay."

"Even after the whole affair with the scarabs and the Ankh? And Dylan traveling through time?"

I sniffed. "The affair with the Ankh was nothing more than a madwoman who believed she could reanimate an Egyptian goddess. But we saw no evidence she ever did, or that it was even possible. And as for Dylan's journey . . . were you not listening to what he said about string theory? There *is* scientific explanation for time travel. And he's here, is he not? One cannot refute *that*."

Our conversation was interrupted as the carriage stopped in front of the Ashton residence. I led the way up the walk, aware that my companion was grumbling about me under her breath. I ignored her in favor of examining the two terra-cotta pots of geraniums on the porch. I smiled to myself as I stooped to scoop a bit of the salty-muddy residue into a small envelope. I'd just shoved it into my reticule when the door opened and the butler greeted us. He showed us to the parlor, where we found our hostess sitting with her friend Amanda Norton.

Miss Ashton rose and greeted us with a warm smile. "Good morning, Miss Stoker. And Miss Holmes. What a pleasant surprise. And you've arrived in time to join us for elevenses."

As we took our seats, Evaline began to rattle on about the weather and the imminent re-opening of New Vauxhall Gardens. Obviously I couldn't launch into my interrogation while Miss Norton was present, so I took the opportunity to observe both of the young ladies while the elevenses repast was served.

Our hostess's skirts had cat-paw pricks on them again, although there was no hair clinging to the hem. There was a scratch on her wrist from the cat, less than a day old. The shadows under her eyes were darker than they had been two days ago, and her delicate features were pinched with exhaustion. Yet her face glowed with pleasure and she seemed genuinely happy to see us.

I turned my attention to Amanda Norton. Upon our first meeting, I'd been struck by her sharp, intelligent eyes and quiet demeanor. She was a plain young woman with brownish hair and unexceptional features, including a chin that was too small and pointy to be attractive. Yet one couldn't call her homely, and she certainly wasn't burdened with a massive nose.

Her attire was of good quality and recent fashion, and her pale yellow gloves were pristine—*pays close attention to detail.*

A man's fine-quality handkerchief peeked from the drawstring of her reticule—*she was attached to or being courted by a beau.* I could make out the initial *J* or perhaps *T* embroidered on it.

Every time a carriage clattered by or there was a movement in the hall outside the parlor, Miss Norton glanced at the door—*she's expecting someone or something.*

Was she anticipating Mrs. Yingling's arrival, perhaps? If that was the case, Amanda Norton was bound to be disappointed.

"Miss Ashton mentioned you had put her in contact with Mrs. Yingling. Were you particular friends with the medium?" I asked.

Miss Norton's teacup rattled into place on its saucer. "I'd attended her séances twice and was impressed by her skills at communing with the spirits. She put me in contact with my grandmother, who's been deceased for three years. I thought Willa would appreciate the chance to speak with her mother . . . especially in light of Robby's disappearance. She needed any comfort she could get."

"It's a shame, but Mrs. Yingling is dead," Evaline announced.

"Oh!" Miss Ashton gaped, wide-eyed. "Oh, *no. Poor* Mrs. Yingling!"

"The unfortunate, darling woman!" said Miss Norton. "But she was so very frail, one cannot be too surprised. Did she die at her home? How did you learn of this?" Her cool gray eyes fixed on me, and I felt the hair lifting along my arms at the challenge in her gaze.

"Mina called on her yesterday and found her—"

I had to interrupt before Miss Stoker could divulge too many details. My uncle taught me it's best to keep any information about an investigation close to the vest, so to speak. "I was hoping to consult with her about my own . . . erm . . . spirit-talking needs and I went to visit her. You've been to her flat, Miss Norton? The landlady and I found her in her bed. She appeared very peaceful."

"How terribly sad. To die all alone." Miss Ashton's eyes filled with tears.

"It *is* a tragedy." Despite my disdain for fakery and frauds, I meant my words. While death was an inevitability for all of us, being forced into that state by another individual was a case of Nature gone awry.

Before I could press on to other matters, a knock sounded at the parlor door. A pudgy woman with pure white hair poked her head in. "Miss Ashton, Rightingham has just answered the door to Mr. Treadwell. The young gentleman would like to know if you are at home."

The swift wash of pink that flooded Miss Ashton's cheeks and the sudden light in her expression indicated that she would, indeed, be home for Mr. Treadwell. "Would you mind terribly if he joins us? I'm certain he won't stay long. We can continue the conversation after."

"Not at all." Miss Stoker glanced at me, for she had clearly noticed the same reaction from Miss Ashton, but I had turned my focus to Miss Norton. She'd straightened in her seat and was patting her hair as she turned toward the door. *Aha.* The anticipated arrival had occurred.

Mr. James Treadwell appeared to be in his middle twenties. He was neatly dressed and well groomed, and his well-tailored clothing indicated simple yet tasteful means. His head of thick, dark hair shone when he removed his hat, and he had a pleasant countenance.

Frayed cuffs on right sleeve, cufflink askew, slightly smudged with dirt—*right-handed and writes a fair bit.*

Left shoe worn on inside and rear—*had a foot injury, likely a break, that was recently healed.*

Chalky ash on brim of hat—*rode the underground train from Gatfield station.*

The corner of a handkerchief protruding from his pocket—*the fabric and edging matched the one in Miss Norton's reticule.*

I made these observations as he was introduced to Miss Stoker and me. Then Mr. Treadwell took a seat on a settee near Miss Ashton, whose cheeks had remained faintly pink.

"I'm afraid I've interrupted your visit." He smiled around the table at us as our hostess poured his tea, then set his cup under the Sweet-Loader.

It clicked and whirred as she said, "Cousin Herrell isn't here today. I'm sorry you've missed him."

Mr. Treadwell didn't appear the least bit sorry he'd missed Cousin Herrell. In fact, he seemed quite the opposite, for his attention was fixed on Miss Ashton. "Ah, well, I wasn't certain he'd be here, and I knew it was a gamble when I set out to come. I've only returned to Town from Chewsbury and wanted to speak with him about an investment opportunity—ah, I'm sorry. I don't mean to bore you with talk of business." He picked up his teacup and sipped. "Slightly sweet, no milk. Just the way I like it . . . you remembered, Miss Ashton."

"Of course."

I decided to intervene before the blush on our hostess's face caused her honey-blond hair to go up in flames—and the daggers from Miss Norton's eyes actually pierced someone. "Moffett's Corner is one of my favorite places to get a ham and pickle sandwich. Did you enjoy yours, Mr. Treadwell?"

He blinked and set down his teacup. "Indeed I did, Miss Holmes. How did you know I was there . . . and what I had to eat?"

"I noticed the corner of a wrapper sticking from your pocket, and from the type of dust on your hat—which is from the chalk factory near Gatfield—I was easily able to deduce which train you rode this morning. Therefore I knew you'd passed by Moffett's—one of the only three shops in London that use that type of paper to wrap their food. There is a bit of mustard juice on the wrapper, which indicated the type of sandwich you chose."

"Why . . . that's extraordinary!"

Miss Stoker reached for a lemon biscuit. "Mina does that all the time. She even tells the Met how to investigate crimes."

My cheeks heated under the sudden regard from the others. "It's a simple matter of observation and deduction."

"Oh, Mr. Treadwell, I'd almost forgotten. I have the handkerchief you lent me. I was splattered with mud from a bicycle passing by." Miss Norton directed the latter part of her explanation to the rest of us as she extracted the fabric from her reticule. "It was very kind of you to see me home afterward."

"It was my pleasure, Miss Norton. I'm relieved you seem to have suffered no further damage than some mud spots on your gloves." He folded it neatly and tucked it into an inside pocket.

"Indeed, I have not." Her smile was warm and wide, but I could see the underlying tension.

I transferred my attention to Miss Ashton, curious as to whether she noticed the undercurrents that were glaringly obvious to me. She turned to the tea service, adjusting the cloth napkins and replacing the top of the Sweet-Loader. She still sported a faint flush on her cheeks, but now her lips were firm and drawn.

A moment later, after our hostess remained unusually quiet, Mr. Treadwell rose reluctantly. "I've taken your time long enough, Miss Ashton. Please give your cousin my best, and perhaps I will see him at the Parshalls' card party on Saturday."

"Oh." Miss Ashton's face lit up once more. "I believe he *is* planning to attend. I begged him to escort me, and he has agreed. So we—er, *he*—shall see you there."

"I shall be doubly anticipatory of that evening, then," he said with a little bow.

"My word! Look at the time!" Miss Norton fairly bolted to her feet. "I must be leaving too, Willa. Terrible news about Mrs. Yingling. We shall have to find another medium for our séances straightaway. But in the meanwhile, I am late for a fitting at Madame Burnby's. Would it be too much to ask for me to share your carriage, Mr. Treadwell? I fear if I wait for a hack, I'll be even more tardy and will lose my appointment."

"Oh . . . why, of course I will see you to the shop. It would be my pleasure."

It would clearly be hers as well. *Well played, Miss Norton.*

They took their leave, but before I could resume my questioning in regards to Mrs. Yingling, Miss Stoker said, "He seems quite taken with you, Miss Ashton."

"Who? Oh, oh . . . you mean Mr. Treadwell." Our hostess dropped her gaze. "I'm certain that's an exaggeration. He's so kind to everyone. He's a friend of Herrell's."

"Your cousin lives here with you, then?" I was determined to take control of the conversation.

"No, but since returning from his European tour, he spends a lot of time here. His townhouse had a fire and he hasn't found permanent new rooms. Or he stays at his club, if he's in Town. Robby and I have been living with Aunt Geraldine since Mother passed on—Father died ten years ago, and I hardly remember him—and thus my cousin has taken it upon himself to act as an older brother would." Her expression was so sad, even I felt a twinge.

Evaline patted Miss Ashton's hand. "It must be very difficult for you. But we want to help."

"Do you think you could find Robby? Is that why Princess Alix sent you? I didn't have an opportunity to ask when you visited before."

I shook my head. "She sent us because she's concerned about your . . . attachment . . . to spirit-talking. That perhaps you're being . . . taken advantage of. Or—"

"I'm not *mad*." She drew herself up, sudden fire in her eyes. "And I'm not delusional. I don't believe Robby is dead.

And there is no doubt my mother has been speaking to me through these séances."

Silence hung over the parlor, broken only by the soft plopping of the Sweet-Loader dropping an excessive number of sugar lumps into Evaline's tea.

"We mean no offense, Willa—may I call you Willa?" asked my companion at last.

"Of course." She rubbed her forehead, covering her face with a trembling hand. "I apologize for my outburst. It's just that Aunt Geraldine keeps harping on me about this. She is furious that I am spending my money and time on séances. Even after she attended yesterday's session, she's become even more insistent I cease working with mediums. But I cannot seem to let it go. My visits from Mother are *real*. And she's telling me what I already know: that Robby is still alive . . . and in danger. But . . ." She bit her full lip. Her breathing sounded harsh in the tense, silent chamber. "I must be truthful, mustn't I, Miss Holmes? If you are to help me?"

"Of course. You must tell me everything."

Willa nodded. "Very well, then. You see . . . Mother visits me at night too, in that greenish cloud. She is begging me to save Robby. And . . . there are times, great spots in my day, that are blank. And empty. As if . . . they've been erased." Now she raised her face, her cerulean eyes wide and guileless. "I am afraid, Miss Holmes. I'm *afraid*."

# Miss Holmes

## Coincidences and Conveniences

At Willa Ashton's announcement, I glanced at Evaline, then back at our hostess. "Considering the fact that Mrs. Yingling was murdered, in my opinion you *should* be apprehensive." My words were purposely blunt, for I wanted her full attention.

"*Murdered?*"

"I'm afraid there is no doubt. And I'm just as certain her untimely death is related to your situation."

"But . . . why? And how? Oh, the poor, *poor* woman." Miss Ashton's eyes filled with tears, making them appear even more luminous. "How terrible for an innocent woman to be caught in the midst of something so . . . terrible."

I refrained from pointing out that the medium was by no stretch an innocent. "I intend to answer those questions during the course of my investigation. I suspect someone wanted Mrs. Yingling dead before she could divulge some pertinent information—specifically, who was paying her to fake your séances."

"Pay her? For faking the séances?" This question from Miss Stoker had me holding back a sigh. We had already discussed this in the carriage. Could she not follow even the simplest train of deduction and put the facts together? I was beginning to understand my uncle's frustration with Dr. Watson.

"At first I believed Mrs. Yingling was merely taking advantage of Willa's need to find out what happened to her brother." I turned back to our hostess. "She would continue to string you along with vague messages—giving you hope that your brother could be found—for as long as she could. But when I examined her rooms, I noticed several things that pointed to a sudden large influx of funds—surely more than you'd paid her in the last fortnight, even if you were being generous. Two pairs of spun wool and brass gloves from Betrovia, each set worth more than a governess's monthly wage. An antique rug from Persia, recently placed on the floor. And, most telling of all, the deed to a small house in Sussex. The date of transfer was only one week ago."

"You might have mentioned these facts earlier. Maybe she had saved enough money from her other clients."

I gave Miss Stoker a quelling look. "My careful interrogation of her landlady indicated Mrs. Yingling had very few clients over the last six months, and none were as regular as Miss Ashton. Even Miss Norton, who introduced Willa to the medium, had seen her a mere three times over three months.

The woman had been behind on her rent for half a year and only recently caught up. It was only because the two ladies were close friends that she hadn't been evicted."

"Right."

"To confirm . . . Miss Ashton, I presume you haven't paid Mrs. Yingling upward of five thousand pounds since you began to consult with her."

"No." She gaped. "Not even close to that amount."

"Therefore my theory must be correct. Someone had very recently paid her a large amount of money, and as you were her only regular client, I deduce it's related to your situation. Add in the fact that immediately after I participated in her séance, Mrs. Yingling was killed. Obviously, the culprit doesn't want me to be closely involved, for he or she must know there is nothing that gets past a Holmes. I wouldn't be surprised if that was the impetus for removing the unfortunate woman from the scene—for fear she would divulge information about the scheme. Either willingly or accidentally."

"That's *terrible*." Willa had gone pale.

"Murder is, indeed, terrible. And so is bilking a young woman of her funds through illegal means."

"But who would do something like that?"

"Never fear. I shall soon determine the perpetrator's identity. I've already deduced he or she was someone who frequents your street here in Mayfair, and, quite likely, came through your front door some time in the last day or so."

"My front door?"

I nodded regally, thinking of the sample I'd just taken from the porch. "I shall be able to positively confirm that theory when I next return to my laboratory. Therefore I deduce Mrs. Yingling was murdered because she possessed information someone didn't want me to discover. I spoke quite openly about my intent to visit her—and if the murderer learned of this, therein lies even more evidence for the evil deed. He or she wanted to silence the medium before I spoke to her. When a Holmes is on the case, the evildoers know their time is limited."

Both Evaline and Willa were gawking at me. "Right, then. What now?" asked my partner.

"We must determine who would benefit from Willa's relationship with Mrs. Yingling—or any spiritualist."

"But why would anyone care if I consulted a medium?" Miss Ashton appeared utterly bewildered.

"That is the question, indeed. I have several theories."

"Of course you do," muttered Miss Stoker.

I ignored her. "First, the instigator might wish for your time to be occupied or your mind distracted. Or, he or she—and I lean slightly toward the villain being a female person—"

"Why?"

"Because poison is known as a woman's weapon. Sneaky, requiring no great strength or speed, and it generally doesn't leave a violent, bloody mess."

Miss Stoker thought about this, then nodded as if I needed her approval. I continued, "Or, he or she wished for certain messages to be given Willa during the séances."

"Messages? What do you mean?"

"Perhaps the villain wants you to believe Robby is alive so that you spend time searching for him? So you are distracted?"

"But that's just it," Willa said fretfully. "I seem to be receiving conflicting messages."

My eyebrows rose. "Please explain."

"Sometimes Mother is very adamant that I should stop worrying about Robby. She says he is happy and well and with her. And other times, her messages indicate that I must find him. That he's in danger."

It was all I could do to keep hidden my disdain for these blithe statements. "Messages from a dead woman? Is it any wonder they are conflicting?" This time, I was quick enough to move my ankle before Evaline's toe slammed into it. Between her pinching, poking, and kicking, I was becoming sore and bruised.

"You have only two theories?" Miss Stoker asked, clearly challenging me.

"Of course not. There is a third—and most likely—theory. Someone is attempting to make Miss Ashton go mad . . . or at least *appear* to be crazy. Willa, who would benefit should something happen to you?"

"Do you mean, who would inherit my money? Why . . . Aunt Geraldine, I believe. She's my mother's sister, and mine and Robby's inheritance comes from our mother's side. Aunt Geraldine is my guardian and my closest living relative; she came back from France to take care of Robby and me when Mother died."

"Not your cousin Herrell? Or any other relative?"

She shook her head. "He's from my father's side of the family. And I have no other family. Except . . . Robby."

"And until you reach your majority, who manages your money? Surely you don't have control of your inheritance yet."

"Oh, well, it's Cousin Herrell, of course. He's been doing so since Father died. And I won't gain control of any of my inheritance until I turn twenty-five, unless I marry first."

Quite enlightening. My range of suspects was growing by leaps and bounds.

Willa's voice choked with emotion. "Dear gad, this cannot be happening! All of these theories and suspicions simply cannot be true. I don't believe any of them!" Her cheeks flushed, but this time from indignation and vehemence. "And I know my mother's visits . . . well, I know she's really here! I can feel her."

Before I could respond, someone knocked on the door. At Miss Ashton's invitation, the good housekeeper poked her white head around. "The post has arrived. There is a letter for you, Miss Willa. It's from an Yrmintrude Yingling."

Our hostess fairly bolted from her seat. "From Mrs. Yingling? Why . . . how could that be?"

"Perhaps she mailed it before she died," Miss Stoker suggested.

"Or someone mailed it for her. After she died." I was very eager to get my hands on that letter. "Or, more likely, she wasn't even the authoress."

"It's rather eerie to get a letter from a dead woman." Miss Ashton looked down at the missive as if it were possessed itself. Then she broke the seal.

She scanned the note, then went back and reread it. When finished, she looked up at us, her eyes bright with enthusiasm. "Mrs. Yingling sends me the name of a woman— let me read it to you. 'Miss Louisa Fenley and her assistant, Espasia, have a great familiarity with orb devices such as the one you possess. Miss Fenley is also a spirit-talker of renown. I will contact her to ascertain whether she would be willing to experiment with us and your glass.' So you see, now I have someone to take Mrs. Yingling's place. How fortunate!"

Indeed. How *conveniently* fortunate. How *coincidental* that Mrs. Yingling should have somehow managed to post a letter with such important information to Miss Ashton . . . and then find herself murdered only hours later. Especially since she had announced her intention of helping Willa use the spirit-glass herself.

I railed on about these so-called conveniences and educated Miss Stoker about the absence of true coincidences in nature as we drove away from Miss Ashton's home a short while later. Thunderous clouds and an accompanying heavy rain made the afternoon dark as dusk. The drumming downpour nearly drowned out my lecture.

"Something is afoot here, Evaline!"

"You've said that. Thrice already, Mina."

"And the letter purporting to be from Mrs. Yingling. I examined it closely—"

"I saw you. I was there."

"—and I am certain she was not the writer, although it is a fair copy of her hand and on her stationery. But there are none of the ink smudges from a left-handed writer. They are always there, however subtle or faint."

"I know. You've mentioned that. Multiple times."

"Which gives an excellent explanation for why the writing implements and papers were rearranged improperly on Mrs. Yingling's desk. The murderer killed her, and then wrote the letter, copying her penmanship as well as possible."

"Now that makes much better sense."

"And aside from all that, Miss Ashton truly believes her deceased mother is visiting her. I suspect after one night spent in her chamber I'd be able to explain to her exactly what is happening. Either she's imagining it, or someone is playing a vile trick on her."

"Or perhaps her brother really is alive, and she can save him, and her mother is trying to help."

"The thought has occurred to me as well. *Not* that Miss Ashton is truly receiving messages from beyond," I was quick to say, "but that Robby might still be alive. He's not the only boy to have recently gone missing." When Evaline looked at me blankly, I sighed. "Do you not read the papers? There's a boy from Bloomsbury and one from Drury-lane both gone missing in the last two weeks. Disappeared without a trace. It wasn't until Uncle Sherlock mentioned the cases that I realized they could be connected to Robby's disappearance."

"But you still won't allow the possibility that Willa—*and I*—have received messages from beyond."

My entire life was built around scientific fact and tangible, visible elements. To even consider things that could not be explained by physics or chemistry or any other natural law would disrupt my entire belief system. It wouldn't make sense, and the very thought was unsettling.

"Mrs. Yingling was a fraud. There is no possibility of messages from the spirit world."

"Maybe," Miss Stoker said stubbornly, "only *part* of her was a fraud."

The vehicle rolled to a stop and I peeked out. The tall, black turreted building loomed above us, sleek and glistening with raindrops. "Ah, we've arrived."

My companion stepped onto the platform and was lowered to the street after me. A generous awning stretched over the walkway, keeping us out of the rain.

"What is it we're going to see again? I can't believe I let you talk me into this," she grumbled.

"It was on the way home. Even a handmaker like you might find it enlightening. We are going to see an exhibition about a device called the Analytical Engine, which could potentially compute mathematical problems. Charles Babbage made several designs for this machine before he died, but it was never built. Mr. Oligary is showing a display of Mr. Babbage's drawings and prototypes, as well as some of his other inventions. There is talk that Oligary might attempt to have a version of the Analytical Engine built."

"Great. Just what I wanted: An afternoon with a bunch of cognoggins, talking about gears and gadgets and things that move." Miss Stoker followed me into the building. "Why can't we be visiting a collection of ancient weaponry? That would be much more interesting."

"I suppose you haven't any money with you." I was already digging in my oversized reticule. "As usual."

"Blooming fish, we have to *pay* to see it?"

I supposed it was only fair that I cover her expenses, since I'd had to drag her anyway. I handed two shillings to the gatesman, who ushered both of us into the exhibition area.

The inside of the Oligary Building was as sleek and colorless as its exterior. At each corner, there was a lift that rose to the highest, fifteenth story, stopping at any other necessary floors on the way. In the center of the structure, the grand hall boasted a vaulted ceiling three stories high and painted white with black cogwork designs. The walls were gray, white, and black-tiled, and the white tiles had imprints on them of different Oligary products (cogs, gears, levers, and the like). Six tall palm trees sat in alternating black and white pots at the perimeter of the room, each with its own gas lamp shining on it. The floor was also black and white tile, like a massive chessboard.

Once we entered the exhibition area, I lost track of Evaline. She barreled ahead of me, hardly glancing at any of the displays. I took my time, examining the drawings and various parts of the mechanism.

"Right this way, Miss Babbage. Mr. Oligary is expecting you."

I turned to see a well-dressed man gesturing to an attractive young woman as he navigated through the display. Presumably the Miss Babbage to whom he'd been speaking, she appeared to be concentrating fiercely on something. Her brows were furrowed and her lips moving. The young woman wore a fashionable blue daydress and a smart bonnet that covered a coiffure of white-blond hair.

"Miss Babbage." The man hardly disguised his impatience. "Mr. Oligary is waiting."

"Come now, Olympia." An older couple appeared from behind another display cabinet. The woman was speaking, and there was a layer of affection in her voice that had been missing from the previous speaker. "This won't take long, and then we can return home."

"What? Oh, yes, Merry, of course," said Miss Babbage, blinking and looking around as if she'd just been awakened. She began to walk more quickly now.

I returned to my examination of the cogs, pins, and pistons of one section of a device called the Difference Engine, which had been a predecessor of the Analytical Engine.

"*Mina.*" Evaline curled her fingers around my arm. Her voice was urgent and her eyes bulged wide.

"What on earth—?"

"There's a vampire. *Here.*"

# MISS STOKER

## Evaline Engages

Mina rolled her eyes at me. "A *vampire*? Don't be ridiculous."

"Not so loud!" I grabbed her reticule, fumbling inside the massive bag. "I don't have a stake. You must have something in here I could use—"

"A vampire, *here*? But . . . it's the Oligary Building. It's . . . daytime. It's . . . there *aren't* any vampires in Lon—"

"Mina, stop babbling and help me find something to use for a stake before he gets away!"

Blast. What if he already had? I stilled for a moment. No, he—or she—was still here. Somewhere nearby. I could tell by the eerie, unpleasant chill that wafted over the nape of my neck, even though there was no draft.

I hadn't realized right away what it was. I felt the prickling chill, but it had been so long since I'd encountered an

UnDead, and only once at that. But who could forget the uncomfortable sensation of the presence of evil?

"Ah." I pulled an object from the depths of Mina's bag. "This could work."

She was a picture of skepticism and indignation. "You can't use my—"

But I'd already snapped the wooden dowel from whatever the device was (some sort of measuring implement) and shoved the reticule back at Mina. "I'm going to find him and kill him. You . . . er . . . you'd better get everyone else out of the building. It could get messy. Or dangerous."

"I can't just tell everyone to leave because you think there's a vampire in the building." The babbling Mina seemed to have gone, and my opinionated, controlling companion was back. And her voice was too blasted loud, for bleeding Pete's sake.

"*Hush*. How am I going to take him by surprise if he knows *I* know he's here? They walk around looking just like everyone else until they're ready to attack."

"Well, where is he? Is it that man over there?" She didn't actually point at the slender, pale gentleman standing off to the side, but she might as well have done so.

"I'm not sure who it is. It could be anyone." I tried not to feel foolish, but the skepticism in my partner's face made it difficult. "I'm going to have to walk around. When I get near enough, I'll know who it is." The sensation would grow stronger the closer I got to the UnDead, so I'd be able to identify him that way.

"I'm coming with you. I want to see this so-called vampire with my own eyes."

"Right." Who was I to argue? We were wasting time.

The display cases of half-built mechanisms and sheaves of notes and diagrams were even less interesting now that I had an UnDead to track. The uncomfortable sensation over my shoulders became more pronounced as I walked through the gallery. My palms were shamefully damp. Yet energy rushed through me.

I was ready. I was going to do this.

I paused regularly to *feel,* trying to get a sense of which direction to go. At the same time, I chafed with impatience. The longer it took me to find the UnDead, the more likely I'd find a victim, too.

Something bumped into me from behind. I spun, the slender wooden stake raised. "Mina! What are you doing?"

"My apologies. I didn't mean to—"

"Forget it. And don't follow me so closely." Blooming blasted fish, why on earth was I saddled with a clumsy know-it-all for a partner? She should stick to murder investigations and leave the vampire hunting to me.

"Where is he?"

I had to pause to check my innate sensor. "Through this door, I think."

"Miss Babbage went this way. There was a man leading her off to meet with Mr. Oligary. And an older couple, presumably her parents or guardians, were with her." She pointed. "There they are, over there by that entrance to the tower. But I don't see Miss Babbage."

I hardly heard what she was saying as I approached the door. There was no sound when I undid the latch and pulled the door open. My makeshift stake felt terribly flimsy as I peered into the dark vestibule. Adjusting the weapon in my damp hand, I felt the telltale prickle. Sharp and cold.

I was going in the right direction. The vampire was nearby.

My breath was unsteady. What if my weapon wasn't strong enough to do the job?

Mina swished in behind me as I slipped into the chamber. A spiral staircase gleamed metallically in the low light, leading up into one of the towers. But there was also another door ahead of me that would likely lead to the exterior. The area was dusty and filled with cobwebs, lit only by rainy, gray light coming through two small window slits.

Mina started to speak and my hand flashed up to stop her. I strained to listen, aware that the seconds were ticking by. Nothing but the distant sounds of people strolling through the display.

Then—a muffled cry, choked off . . .

I gathered up my heavy skirts and started up the spiral steps, still clutching the stake. My slippered feet made soft ringing sounds on the metal stairs. Mina clumped up behind me, the distance between us growing.

Something thumped above me, and I pounded faster up the dark steps. My skirts were heavy and my corset was tight, but I pressed on. The only part of me not perspiring was the nape of my neck.

The chill there was so cold it burned.

All at once, a dark figure loomed over me in the narrow stairwell. A flash of glowing eyes told me I'd found my quarry.

I barely had time to duck before a powerful hand swooped down, narrowly missing me. I slammed into the stone wall, dropping my handful of skirts as I grabbed at something—anything—to keep from falling. The wall was rough and cool, and there was nothing to hold onto. . . .

My foot stepped into air and I tipped backward. My free hand flailed and I grasped fabric . . . *yes*. The vampire's coat!

I gave a sharp yank. He shifted off-balance but held steady, and neither of us went tumbling. By now, I found my feet and looked up. Big mistake.

Two red eyes burned down at me. White fangs gleamed in the drassy light. I was aware of the stake in my hand . . . so flimsy in the face of this threat. The enthralling gaze captured me. I couldn't even blink.

My world slowed . . . became sluggish. My heart pounded, and I felt as if I'd been shoved underwater. My breathing turned shallow. Everything faded away but those eyes . . . red . . . glowing . . . hypnotic.

I was hardly aware when he grabbed my arm. Pulling me off my feet, he bored into me with his stare. He smelled . . . it was the scent of age and evil. I forced myself to remember the stake in my hand, digging deeply into my mind . . . *use the stake* . . . trying to remember Siri's lessons.

But the vampire's pull was strong. The world wavered around me as I struggled to pull myself out of it. My arms were like stone, heavy and cumbersome. A strong band crushed my torso.

The cold, rough stone wall was against my spine, trapping me. A hand grasped the back of my skull. Sharp fingernails dug into my scalp, yanking my head back. Baring my throat.

I smelled stale blood on his breath as he drew closer, still holding me with his gaze. His fangs gleamed, lethal and long. My veins leapt and pounded as if waiting for release, thudding madly in my throat and in my chest, swelling in anticipation.

He was going to bite me. I knew this . . . I fought it . . . deep inside I struggled to break free from his gaze.

*The stake.*

The world pressed down on me. I dredged for strength, calling on my training, my desire to succeed . . . my need to prove myself. My calling.

*Use the stake.*

He plunged his fangs into my shoulder.

# MISS STOKER

## *Miss Holmes Is Gravely Disappointed*

A s the vampire swooped forward, his gaze released mine. The thrall shattered just as his fangs penetrated my skin, sliding in with hardly a prick of pain. My veins erupted, the blood coursed out. . . .

But I was free.

The stake was still in my hand. His chill mouth fastened on my skin as blood drained from my body, pumping forth. Warmth bled from me but I focused on my weapon. Still imprisoned against the wall, I shifted my arm loose.

I drew in a deep breath, fighting against the soft lull of having the life sucked from my body. My arm reared down and back, my elbow slamming painfully against the wall. I tightened my grip on the stake.

Then I rammed it up and into the vampire's torso. Precisely where Siri had taught me.

Time stopped.

The vampire froze. And then he exploded in a poof of foul-smelling ash. He was *gone*.

I dropped the stake and it made a hollow sound as it rolled across the metal step. My knees were shaking and I sagged against the wall.

*I did it.*

Covered with vampire dust, I gasped for breath. The wall became a support rather than a blockade as I leaned against it.

I had proven myself. Inside I danced and trembled, and a great rush of light roared through me. Even so, my knees were too weak to support my body.

Just then Mina appeared, panting and bedraggled. Her hair fell in strands from her temples and she carried an object that beamed a slender light. "Can't . . . run. . . . Corset . . . too . . . dratted . . . tight," she gasped. "What . . . happened? Did you lose . . . the vampire?"

"Dead. I killed it." I couldn't contain a boastful grin.

"Dead? Already? Where?" She actually sounded disappointed. Then her nose wrinkled. "Is that what I . . . smell? That awful . . . stench? Like a corpse. Is that . . . dust?"

"Yes. It's UnDead ash. What do you expect?" I brushed some of the residue off my skirt.

"I didn't even . . . hear. . . . How did you do that so . . . easily?"

The warm trickle pooling in the hollow of my collarbone was blood. "I'm a vampire hunter. It's supposed to be easy for me. It's what I'm meant to do. So I guess you believe in vampires now, hm?"

But even as I said that, I remembered the imprisonment of his thrall, the sluggish feeling . . . the sleek penetration of his fangs.

I should have known better than to look in his eyes. That was a beginner's mistake. It could have been my death.

Never again.

"Oh, gad! You're bleeding." Mina, having caught her breath, began to dig in that obnoxious reticule. Apparently unaware that I'd been bitten by my victim. Which was amazing, given her considerable "observation" skills. "I think I have a handkerchief in here somewhere."

"And some paper?"

A new voice had both Mina and me spinning to look up. A figure stood on the steps above us, her bonnet askew and her gloves missing. She appeared to be trying to repair her sagging hair in the back.

"Miss Babbage!" Mina said.

*Miss Babbage?* Blooming Pete, how could I have forgotten about her? Mortification swept over me. She might have been the vampire's next victim if I hadn't shaken off the thrall.

"Paper," she said again, this time with a tone of impatience as she withdrew her hand from the back of her head. She held a pencil instead of a hairpin. "I'm in need of paper. Even a scrap. Otherwise I'll ruin my sleeve again, and Merry will be annoyed. I think this is a new bodice."

She didn't appear to be worse for wear, although she did seem a bit distracted. I saw no sign of vampire bites, and the chill at the back of my neck had evaporated along with the UnDead. Clearly, she wasn't a vampire herself.

"Are you all right, Miss Babbage?" I asked as Mina produced a small journal from the depths of her bag. "Were you injured?"

"Much obliged." Ignoring my question, she took the notebook. Using the wall as a desk, she began to scrawl quickly on a page of the book. Thanks to Mina's small light, I was able to make out numbers, arrows, and other shapes. "I've been trying to figure this out for *weeks*," she muttered.

She filled the paper, writing down into the corner until her notations were very small and squashed at the edge of the page. Then she tore the paper out, flipped it over, and continued to write.

At last, she made a satisfied sound and handed the notebook back to Mina. She folded the paper and tucked it inside her sleeve, then jabbed the pencil into the back of her hair. Her bonnet was still askew. "Now then. Who are you? And what happened to that awful man? His eyes turned *red*. Most curious."

"I'm Mina Holmes. This is Evaline Stoker. We . . . er . . ." She glanced at me as if to ask what exactly she could say— a miracle in its own right.

"Are you hurt?" I asked, aware I was still bleeding. I needed to attend to my bite as soon as possible, but I wouldn't shirk my duty again. At the same time, I couldn't stop smiling.

I'd killed a vampire. Now I'd proven myself. I was still dancing inside, still in shock at how quickly and easily it had happened.

And neither of my companions had any idea the importance of what I'd accomplished!

"Injured? Me? Not that I've noticed." Miss Babbage checked her hands and arms, then over her shoulder as if to confirm her posterior was still in place. "No. I seem to be intact. Did something happen?"

She was a very odd young woman.

"You weren't attacked by the man with the red eyes? We were under the impression you were being taken off somewhere where he might . . . erm . . . ravish or otherwise injure you."

"He did get a bit rough," Miss Babbage replied. "He pushed me against the wall. And his teeth—*wait* a moment." Her face became lax and her gaze blank, as if she were trying to remember something. "May I have that book again?"

She pulled the pencil from her hair. When Mina didn't immediately give her the journal, she withdrew the paper from her sleeve and began to write on it once more.

Mina glanced at me then back at the red-headed young woman. "Miss Babbage. Were you not afraid? Did that man attack you?"

"Yes, I believe he did." She was still writing. When she finished, she shoved the pencil back into her hair. "But then he must have heard someone coming, because he wrapped me tightly in a heavy cloak and threw me to the floor. I bumped my head."

A bump on the head would explain a lot. "Well, you're safe now. He's gone and will never bother anyone again," I announced, brushing the last bit of vampire ash off my arm.

"Who?" Her eyes were owlish.

At that, I gave up.

"Why would a vampire be at the Oligary Building? I was under the impression they didn't come out in the daylight—although it *was* raining today. That must be enough of a barrier from the harmful rays of the sun. Unless the vampire was in the Oligary Building all along. . . ."

"I don't know," I said for the hundredth time.

Mina had begun her interrogation the moment we climbed into my carriage. Apparently, she had already forgotten her disbelief in the UnDead. Now she wanted to study them as closely as she'd studied women's face powders.

I thought about calling her out on it, but why bother? She'd just argue me into exhaustion—just like she was doing now, with her incessant lecturing. Or she'd sniff and change the subject.

"And what was that vampire trying to do, taking Miss Babbage off into that tower? Did he choose her on purpose or was it just convenience? Aren't you curious? Didn't you want to know? Why didn't you at least engage the creature in conversation before doing away with him? Once I got the Ankh talking, I learned a great many things from her before she tried to kill us."

"It was *obvious* what he was doing: trying to feed on Miss Babbage. Or, at the very least, abduct her. I didn't have the time to ask him. Blooming daggers, Mina, I'm a vampire hunter, not a vampire inquisitor!"

"But why Miss Babbage? And why at the Oligary Building? And why in the middle of the—"

"*Alvermina.*" My teeth gritted so hard my jaw hurt. "If my great-great-aunt Victoria Gardella stopped to interrogate every vampire she came across as a Venator, she wouldn't have killed half the ones she did. She probably would have been killed herself. He was doing *what vampires do:* feeding on young, helpless women. Or whoever they can find in a pinch. It was probably convenience. He was hungry and she was there."

Mina gave me an unpleasant look, probably because I called her by her despised name. Possibly because I made a very good point. She adjusted her seat in the carriage and thumped her reticule. "It was quite fortuitous for you I was in possession of my equipment. Or you would have been caught without a weapon with which to *hunt* your vampire. And, incidentally, you ruined my new Allister-MacLeader Depth Perceptor. I hadn't even had a chance to use it."

"I'll get you a new one." I realized a good portion of my sudden weariness had to do with the still-oozing vampire bite on my shoulder.

Mina must have noticed at the same time. "Gad, I'd for-gotten about your injury. Did he cut you?"

"No, he *bit* me. Siri told me the best thing to do is put salted holy water on it, so we'd best find a church. Unless you have some in that blooming elephant bag of yours."

"I'm not a vampire hunter, therefore I don't carry those sorts of accoutrements. Although perhaps now I should con-sider. . . . Nevertheless, on the next block. Saint Ursula-on-the Sea. We can stop there and get water from the font. I even have a cup." She thumped the reticule again.

"Splendid."

I had no idea how much it stung to have salted holy water poured on a vampire bite . . . but unfortunately, I found out.

I gritted my teeth to keep from shouting at Mina when she dumped a whole cup of it on my bite all at once. The siz-zling pain was worse than the actual injury.

"My gad! Look at how it bubbles up." She peered at my wound as I struggled to keep from groaning. "It's amazingly frothy and pink. It's absolutely fascinating how it dissolves like that. And the bleeding's stopped."

"Brilliant." The front of my bodice was now soaked with salted holy water, as well as stained with blood. I hoped I was going to be able to get into the house without Florence seeing me . . . let alone noticing the wound on my neck. Blast.

"Mr. Starcasset didn't describe that sort of detail in his book." Mina was still examining my injury. "Would you be averse to allowing me to collect some of this residue? I'd relish the opportunity to study it in my laboratory. And perhaps a sample of your blood as well, so I can discover the difference between—"

"No," I said flatly. "Not necessary. I have no intention of getting bit again by a vampire anyway. For all I know, that was the only vampire in London. So no blood, no sample, no residue."

Mina sniffed, crossing her arms over her middle. "Very well. But it could be helpful in the future."

Not at all, I thought. I wasn't going to get bit again.

It was *easy* for a trained vampire hunter to slam a stake into the heart of an UnDead. All I had to remember was not to look him in the eye.

If I remembered that, I'd be invincible.

# MISS HOLMES

## Deductions, Theories, and Suspects

Two days after Evaline killed the vampire at the Oligary Building (the implications of which I was still mulling), Miss Stoker and I arrived at Miss Adler's office just before noon.

The four puncture wounds on my companion's shoulder had almost completely disappeared. It was quite miraculous, and I would insist she allow me to do a more thorough examination if it should occur again.

I was still quite stunned and even a little disbelieving about the appearance of the UnDead. After all, I hadn't actually *seen* the creature. But I certainly had *smelled* something, and there were the marks on Evaline's neck.

"Do you have any further information on the death of Mrs. Yingling, or the Ashton case?" Miss Adler asked as we gathered in her office.

To my disappointment, Dylan wasn't present, but I resisted the urge to question his whereabouts. "I was considering a visit to Scotland Yard today to determine whether Inspector Grayling has made any progress on our investigation. I'm surprised I haven't had any communication from him regarding the crime. Particularly since I am the one who pointed out that it was, in fact, a murder."

"An excellent point, to be sure, Mina."

Although she was perfectly groomed in a fresh lemon-colored daydress and a particularly fetching bonnet with yellow roses that matched her ever-present gloves, Miss Adler appeared even more weary than she had on the day we visited Princess Alexandra. I wondered if she'd been ill, or if something had been keeping her up at night.

Whether by accident or design, there was very little one could deduce about Irene Adler from her appearance, other than her excellent taste in fashion. This was part of the reason she'd been such a formidable opponent for my uncle during the Bohemian affair.

I smoothed my skirt. "I have confirmed one new and important fact, however. Evaline, do you recall the terra-cotta pots by Miss Ashton's front door? A lime and salt residue had seeped through the bottoms of the pots, mixing with dirt and fragments of dried geranium petals and cricket legs. I had some on my own shoes from our first visit, and I am certain you do as well. I took a fresh sample of it yesterday, and it matches the same residue on Mrs. Yingling's window sill. Therefore, as I suspected, the murderer—and whoever is trying to upset Miss Ashton's life—has been through her front door recently. Specifically, since those pots were put there."

"Which eliminates the servants or any delivery people, as they always enter through the rear," Miss Adler said. "Whom do you suspect, Mina?"

I straightened, preparing for a detailed monologue. Miss Stoker appeared ready to bolt. I ignored her and launched into my discourse. "In order for a murder to occur, there must be motive, means, and opportunity. As far as opportunity and means—we already know the villain has used the front door at Miss Ashton's. Thus our list of suspects who have come into the house via the front entrance include the obvious: her Aunt Geraldine, her Cousin Herrell, Willa herself, Miss Norton, Mr. Treadwell, *and* anyone else who has visited since Thursday last. Which is when the geranium pots were placed on the porch. I *asked*," I added pointedly, looking at Miss Stoker. She closed her mouth. "That would include Evaline and myself, of course, but I feel confident we can both be eliminated."

My partner gave an unladylike snort and rolled her eyes. "I should hope."

I continued. "First, one must consider motive. Why would anyone want to upset Miss Ashton's life—to make her appear mad, or cause distraction by making her believe her brother is alive? I'm going to focus on the former first: Someone is trying to get her out of the way. It's the most likely motive. There is, of course, money involved—and even more if Robby is ever pronounced dead, for Willa or her heir will inherit his portion."

"True."

"Thus, Willa's spinster aunt inherits upon the death of either child. Therefore, I am looking very closely at Aunt Geraldine. Although the woman has wealth of her own, for some, there is never enough money. She lives in the house and would have easy access to all of the chambers in order to arrange any of these shenanigans. However, there are at least two other prime suspects as well. Would you care to give it a go, Miss Stoker?"

Evaline gave me an unpleasant look, but nevertheless sat up from her slouched position in the chair. "Right then. Well . . . hmmm . . . if we're talking of women, Miss Norton strikes me as intelligent enough to do something of this sort. You saw how easily she manipulated Mr. Treadwell into driving with her. And she obviously is attracted to him, while he can't seem to decide between Miss Norton and Willa. As for motive . . . well, if she wants Mr. Treadwell badly enough, she might do anything she can to get her rival out of the way. We saw how much the young women in the Society of Sekhmet were willing to risk for a man they desired."

"Precisely along my train of thought. Love can be the strongest of all motives. But there is one other factor that you didn't mention, which makes Miss Norton an excellent suspect: She is the one who introduced Willa to Mrs. Yingling. An excellent deduction, Evaline."

"You needn't look so shocked," she grumbled. But I noticed she smothered a pleased smile.

"There is one more major suspect. Mr. Herrell Ashton would retain control of his cousin's not insignificant income if she were placed in a lunatic home or was otherwise out of the picture. And if she married, he'd lose control of her income at that time."

"So would Aunt Geraldine," Evaline pointed out.

I nodded in agreement. "Of course. You are getting quite good at this, Miss Stoker."

"I'm more than just a vampire hunter. And now I'm a *successful* vampire hunter." She glanced meaningfully at Miss Adler.

Our mentor's eyes widened and she appeared utterly shocked. "Do you mean to say you've encountered and killed a vampire?"

Although I hadn't finished my monologue, I allowed the distraction so we could bring Miss Adler up to date on Evaline's recent accomplishment.

When we were finished, Miss Adler said, "And this all occurred at the Oligary Building? In broad daylight?"

"It wasn't exactly broad daylight," my partner said. "It was pouring down rain all day and very dark. As long as the sun doesn't hit their skin, it doesn't bother them. He probably shielded himself with a cloak or umbrella from the carriage to the door. But it doesn't surprise me, for I've heard rumors that there has been a revival of *La société*—here in London."

"*La société*?"

There was an odd note in Miss Adler's voice. She seemed surprised, and yet not surprised. Nevertheless, I launched into an explanation. "*La société de la perdition* is a sort of club that, for lack of a better term, socializes with vampires. The types of people who frequent the purlieu are of the sort who enjoy—"

"I'm familiar with *La société*," Miss Adler said, interrupting me more sharply than necessary. Then she smiled briefly at me, as if in apology. "Of course I am aware of the history. But the group has been defunct for decades, and to my knowledge, was never here in London."

"Yes, of course. It proliferated on the Continent, in Paris in particular, but also Vienna and Amsterdam. The group identifies itself with an image of a seven-legged, spindly spider for obvious reasons. Spiders draw blood from their prey just as the UnDead do," I added for Miss Stoker's benefit.

"*Really?*"

"So it's possible *La société* has come to London, along with at least one vampire. One would assume there are more than the single UnDead, however." Miss Adler's fingers, which had been lax on the desk, had curled up tightly during this conversation. "That would be most unfortunate."

The office door opened, and Dylan strode in. His coat fluttered and his honey-blond hair shifted silkily in the light. He smelled of the outdoors, of the Underground, and of something medicinal and antiseptic.

I'm ashamed to admit that the mere sight of him caused my heart to do a little arrhythmic bump, and suddenly my corset felt more restrictive than it had only a moment earlier. He was so handsome, and his presence seemed to shrink the size of the chamber.

"Oh good—you're all here," he said without preamble. He gave me a warm smile that lingered a bit longer than it did on the others. "Hi, Mina."

"What have you been up to?" Miss Adler asked as he took a seat. "I've hardly seen you in the last few days. Have you been spending your time on that project you mentioned to me?"

I couldn't help a small flare of disquiet. Why did Miss Adler know about Dylan's "project" and I didn't? I believed I was becoming his confidante and friend, that he was sharing things with me he wasn't sharing with anyone else. Perhaps he was like that with everyone—whoever he was with, he spoke to as he did with me. Some of my pleasure at his presence dimmed.

"What project?" Evaline asked—thankfully, just as ignorant as I.

"Mina sort of knows about it," he said. My heart bumped again and I felt better—even though I wasn't precisely sure what he was talking about. "But let me start from the beginning.

"So there's a kind of joke about time travel, like, from my time. It's kind of a rule—the first thing someone should do if they ever find themselves having traveled back in time."

"Try to find a way back?" Evaline asked.

He gave a short laugh, which made his blue eyes light up. "Well, that too. But there's something that could be done to prevent terrible happenings in my time. And if you travel back in time, you're supposed to try."

"What are you supposed to do?" I asked, looking at him closely. My body had gone cold. "Kill someone?"

"Well . . . no. Not necessarily."

But I was upset. Surely Dylan wasn't talking about hurting someone? "It's rather obvious, isn't it? To prevent something 'awful from happening' in the future, the easiest and most expedient way is to remove the individual who caused it. What awful thing are you talking about? A war?"

"Yes. But the point is, if someone travels back in time, the desire is there to *do* something to change horrible things that happened. If possible. But not by hurting anyone. Of course I wouldn't do that!"

"But if you did something that altered history . . . wouldn't that affect a lot of other things? Science, government, inventions—possibly your own life? It could affect whether you were even born."

"Yes, you're right. I mean, it's all spelled out in a movie—er, a story—called *Back to the Future*. If you mess with the past, it can totally screw up the future and *erase* you. So, of course, I can't follow the Number One Rule of Finding Yourself Back in Time." Dylan grinned as his fingers gestured, like he was putting those words in quotation marks. "But that did get me to thinking, and that's the point of what I'm trying to say—I can't change the future, as much as I might want to try. But I'm here, stuck here, for who knows how long. There doesn't seem to be anything I can do about it for now—I know you're trying to figure it out, Mina, and I am, too . . . but like I said, if the scientists from my time can't figure out how to travel through time, how can we?"

"We can. We *will*," I vowed. Even though I ached at the thought of him leaving, I knew it was the right thing.

He gave me a look that made my lungs stop working and my heart bump off-rhythm again. "I know. And if anyone could figure it out, I'm sure it would be you."

"So . . . your project?" Evaline's tones were ironic and impatient.

"Yeah, right. So, anyway, I got to thinking . . . I am here. And if I'm here, I should be doing something—something worthwhile. I mean, I've been put here for a reason, right? I can make a difference."

"Like saving the Queen's life," I said softly. I was beginning to understand.

"Exactly. I can . . . I know things from the future that can help people—people who are injured or hurt. I might be able to save lives here and now. Like, I was telling Mina the other day, for example, we do blood transfusions routinely in my world. And so, I've been spending a lot of time with Dr. Watson."

"But you have to be careful," I interjected, suddenly nervous. "What if you do something that *does* change history?

You can't introduce inventions and knowledge now that haven't been discovered yet. It could create a disaster."

His expression was sober. "Exactly. But I have to do *something*. I saw all those people hurt and dying after the accident the other day—Mina, you were there, you saw how awful it was. And I knew I probably had knowledge—lots of bits and pieces—that could save some of their lives. And so I have to do what I can. It's my calling. My . . . destiny. It's why I'm *here*."

There was a heartbeat of silence after his earnest speech. He and Evaline and I looked at each other. It was an odd moment, one of solidarity.

Each of us in our own fashion felt that way about something—Evaline about keeping the mortal world safe from vampires, me about finding the truth and solving problems my father and uncle would never find important enough, but that were, nevertheless dangerous and life-threatening . . . and Dylan, with this difficult task of helping people without affecting history.

"Brilliant," applauded Evaline. "That's brilliant, Dylan." She was smiling.

I wanted to agree, but I also comprehended the delicacy of his plan. Our eyes met and I knew he did too.

But he was smart and brave and thoughtful. If anyone could walk the tightrope of past and future, I had faith it would be Dylan.

"What do you say, Mina?"

I blinked and realized Miss Stoker was talking to me. I got the sense she'd been waiting for more than a few moments. "About what?"

"Willa Ashton sent word around this morning—she'd like us to attend a séance with her new medium. Shall we go?"

"Most definitely," was my firm reply. "I look forward to exposing Miss Louisa Fenley as a charlatan as well. I just hope she's still alive when we get there."

Once in Miss Stoker's carriage, I learned the séance was not to be held at the Fruntmire-Ashton household again, but at the medium's parlor.

"Miss Fenley can afford a private parlor for her séances? The better to arrange for all matter of fakery, then."

"Apparently, it's rather good business being a medium," Evaline replied dryly.

"Only until one is exposed."

Miss Louisa Fenley turned out to be a much younger and agile prospect than the unfortunate Mrs. Yingling. I estimated her to be twenty-five or thereabouts. Of rather plain appearance with unremarkable brown hair, she seemed calm and pleasant. Yet her eyes were constantly moving about as if to drink in every detail from her guests. As she examined us, I observed a variety of things about her as well as her parlor.

Garbed in flowing skirts with unusually stiff petticoats—*the better to hide movements or devices beneath them.*

Delicate, clean hands with long slender fingers devoid of ink markings, yet faint scrapings at the wrist—*nimble fingers that can make quick work of ties or manacles, and the evidence of such in the marks.*

Parlor walls covered with silk wallpaper hangings—*the better to obstruct imperfections or hidden openings in them.*

The floor: new, smooth and level wooden planks, covered by a rug in the center—*likely overbuilt on top of some other space, with the rug to draw attention away.*

Windows draped with heavy curtains—*allowed exit and entry as needed.*

Before introductions were finished, I had already identified several ways in which Miss Fenley was a cheat.

"Is this your spirit-cabinet?" I gestured to the small wooden structure built into one side of the parlor. I had heard about such things, but never seen one used.

"It is. Would you like to examine the interior?" She seemed aware of my skepticism.

I eagerly accepted and spent five minutes doing so. The cabinet was hardly larger than a bed, were it to be positioned vertically. Three sides were wooden and the fourth was curtained, isolating the medium so she wouldn't be disturbed while the spirits were manifesting. Of course, that was just an excuse to allow the medium privacy to do whatever she needed in order to produce the so-called Para-Natural effects.

"When I use the cabinet, I'm bound with ropes to this chair," Miss Fenley told me as I checked to see whether the cabinet had a false rear entrance (it didn't). "In order to prove that I'm not doing any manipulations myself, and that anything that manifests itself is due to spirit activity. The ties can be sealed with wax so one can determine that they haven't been undone."

I sniffed, but continued my examination. No false rear. No false sides. The chair, which appeared decidedly uncomfortable, had spindly legs and nowhere for tools to be hidden. I had to admit, against my better judgment, I was becoming more curious about how the medium conducted her so-called séances and produced spirit phenomena.

I had seen a magic show once wherein the performer extricated himself from seemingly impossible bonds in mere seconds. I suspected that ability—rather than a connection to the spirit world—was the most important skill a medium such as Miss Fenley could employ.

Her assistant appeared at that moment, emerging from a small door in the side of the parlor. She was older than the medium, a woman with dark, graying hair and a personality to match.

"Espasia is simply here to ensure that nothing unexpected occurs during the séance."

"It could be very dangerous to Miss Louisa if she is interrupted or otherwise disturbed while communing with the spirits," Espasia intoned darkly.

More likely, it was very dangerous to their charlatan business if Miss Louisa was exposed while doing whatever it was she did inside the spirit-cabinet. Thus Espasia was there to ensure we didn't see anything we weren't supposed to.

"Shall we begin?" Miss Louisa looked at her assistant and then said unexpectedly, "We won't be using the spirit-cabinet today. I feel that Miss Holmes in particular would prefer to keep me in sight at all times."

"Of course. But we must dim the lights." Espasia looked at me in challenge. "The spirits won't manifest unless it is in near darkness."

"I suppose the light is harmful to them," I managed to say without sounding terribly sarcastic.

"I'll sit next to you, Miss Fenley," Miss Ashton said eagerly. Despite an increasingly thin face drawn with weariness and strain, she looked lovely but fragile today. Her hair was arranged in a soft knot that allowed gentle curls to spring free near her temples, and her pale blue eyes sparkled with enthusiasm and hope.

We arranged ourselves around a small table thus: Miss Fenley, Miss Ashton, Miss Stoker, Espasia, and then myself on Miss Fenley's other side. I surreptitiously attempted to move and shift the piece of furniture to determine how easily this could be accomplished. To my surprise, it seemed to be fixed to the floor.

"Please take the forearm of the person to your left, thus creating a powerful circle that will allow the spirits a safe place to gather," Miss Fenley told us.

I offered my right arm to Miss Fenley and took hold of Espasia's left one, at the same time asking, "But where is the spiritglass, Miss Ashton?" For wasn't that the reason she had contacted Miss Fenley in the first place? I had anticipated it being in the center of the table, the highlight of this séance.

"Excuse me, I must dim the lights a little more." Espasia stood as Miss Ashton replied to my question.

"I neglected to tell you that after my initial consultation with Miss Fenley, we decided to attempt to contact Mother without the oracle—er, spiritglass this first time. But I've left it safely in my chamber for now in case we decide we would need it."

I was not surprised at this explanation. The spiritglass was merely an excuse for our villain to redirect Miss Ashton to another medium of her—or his—choosing. I was certain the cornerstone of the plot against her was that Willa Ashton continue her experimentation with spirit-talking.

"Now then," Espasia said from my right side as she settled back into her seat, "we must settle into a quiet and respectful mood so the spirits can manifest."

In the near darkness, she offered me her forearm. I grasped it once more . . . and realized it was not the same limb she had previously extended. No person is completely symmetrical, and there are slight differences in our bodies, such as one limb being slightly more muscular than the other.

Aside from that, the sleeve on this arm had an uneven seam on it and a loose bit of lace, and the other one hadn't.

A prickle of anticipation sizzled through me as I realized what she'd done: twisting in her seat so that her left hand, which she reached over to hold Miss Stoker's arm, was of the same limb extended to me to grasp. No one would notice her odd position and the angle of her arm. This trick left Espasia with a free right hand, hidden in the dark, able to do whatever must be done in order to conduct the séance.

I grinned. I would let the performance unfold for the time being, for I am always appreciative of good showmanship. However, I would be speaking with Miss Fenley in short order.

"Now, let us become quiet," said the medium in an atmospheric voice. "And ask the spirits to join us."

Silence descended over the parlor.

In our dimly lit chamber, everything was still but for the soft sounds of breathing. I identified Miss Ashton's as the shallow, desperate one. In the far distance, I could hear the sounds of the city: rumbling cart wheels, horses clip-clopping, the hum of machinery and self-propelled vehicles, voices shouting, calling, shrieking.

Miss Fenley stiffened next to me, and then I heard a sharp rap. "They are here," our medium said. "They've accepted our invitation."

"Is Mama here?" Miss Ashton asked.

*Rap, rap.*

"Yes, she is present."

Suddenly, the table moved, lifting and tilting sharply. I nearly sprang from my seat.

Miss Ashton gave a little shriek as Espasia exclaimed, "Do not release your grasp! Hold tight!"

"Look!" cried Miss Ashton. "Above!"

As if guided by an unseen hand, a square object floated through the air. At the same time, I heard a sharp, discordant note from a violin. I spun to look in that direction, but saw nothing. Another jarring shriek emitted from an out-of-tune violin.

Something clattered onto the table next to me and I looked over to see a slender object rolling from where it had landed on the table. A writing implement. And, *blast it*, I'd been staring in the other direction when the pencil appeared. I'd fallen for the common technique of distraction.

The floating white object came nearer, hovering over our heads. The table jolted once more, causing Miss Ashton to gasp.

"Why is she so angry? What's wrong with my mother?"

"Remain calm." Espasia's voice lashed out. "The spirits will speak . . . but only to Louisa. And only if you remain silent."

A rush of cold air blasted through the room, and I turned quickly to see one of the filmy wallpaper coverings fluttering. The eerie chill that had settled over my skeptical self eased when I realized how that effect had been accomplished. A gust of wind from behind the silk or through a hole. Louisa and Espasia must have a partner, or some sort of automated mechanism.

When I turned back, I saw the floating white object had settled itself in the center of the table. It appeared to be a piece of paper.

"The spirits wish for me to write their messages," said Miss Fenley. "They have given me the tools. Espasia, please raise the lights slightly."

When Espasia stood to do this, Miss Stoker and I released her arm (which was, of course, the same arm due to the woman's manipulations in the dark). As I expected, when she returned, she offered each of us different arms—me her right one, and Miss Stoker her left one, now that we could see in the light.

"You may release Louisa," the assistant said. "She's going into her trance. Please do not make any sudden movements or sounds or the connection may be broken . . . and she could be injured."

The young medium closed her eyes, holding her hands straight out in front of her, resting them on the table. The pencil rolled toward her right hand. She reached out and caught it before it careened off the table.

I knew how she'd done it, and I watched to see what would happen with the paper. Louisa's body went rigid. Her eyelids fluttered and her arms began to vibrate as her breathing became rushed and audible.

Suddenly, Espasia's arm tightened, then her whole body jolted. I had to turn from Louisa to Espasia, for she'd begun to shake violently. I knew better than to be distracted, but the poor woman seemed to be having a seizure.

The logical part of my brain knew such a thing could be faked, yet when an individual seems to be losing control beside one, it's difficult to ignore. The older woman stilled as quickly as she'd begun to shake, and I was turning back to watch Louisa again when Espasia spoke, startling me.

"Linny-Lou . . . I have a message for Linny-Lou . . ." The voice was deeper and smoother than her normal one, and an unaccountable shiver streaked over my shoulders. I realized the arm which I'd been holding had become unnaturally chilled.

"What on—" Miss Stoker began, then choked off when Espasia continued.

"Well . . . done . . . Linny. . . . You have proven yourself . . . worthy. You will . . . receive . . . confirmation . . . soon."

With an awful, gurgling sound, Espasia jolted in her seat and then sagged in place.

Beyond the older woman, I could see the faint outline of Miss Stoker's figure, frozen in shock.

"Espasia?"

Her arm was returning to a normal temperature, and I could feel its pulse beating rapidly. It was an excellent act, I told myself. She must have put something on her arm when she rose to change the lights and it made the skin turn cool for a moment. And anyone with training could fake a seizure.

"Yes. Yes, I am here," Espasia said in her normal voice. "Please do not speak. You will disrupt Miss Louisa."

Of course. With a mental sigh, I turned back to Louisa, realizing in disgust that Espasia's performance had been merely another distraction.

"The spirits are speaking to her." Espasia's voice was steady and calm, as if nothing had happened moments ago.

Sure enough, I could hear the sound of a pencil scratching over paper. Louisa held the writing implement with one hand, and her other fingers settled on the paper to hold it in place.

However, she wasn't looking down at the writing. Instead, she stared into nothingness above all of our heads, her face lax. In the dim light, her eyes seemed darker and deep-set, eerie in their blankness. At last, the pencil fell from Louisa's hand and she bowed her head. Her chin sank into her chest and she breathed steadily.

After a moment, Espasia broke the silence. "Louisa, come back to us." She pulled her arm from my grip and rose, walking over to turn up the lamps.

Immediately, I snatched up the paper. The writing, as one would expect, was irregular, messy, and heavy. I could barely make out the words, written over and over again:

*Willa . . . Help me. Help me help me help me.*

# Miss Stoker

*Wherein Our Heroines Crash a Party*

"What a nonsensical thing for a spirit to say," Mina remarked dryly as we drove away. "'Help me?' Truly? What precisely is an earthbound mortal supposed to do to assist a spirit? If one believes in Spiritualism, then the spirits are the ones with great capabilities. That's only one of the numerous reasons I'm convinced someone is attempting to turn Willa Ashton lunatic, or worse. Leaving her a vague message such as that is only fodder for greater worry and more strain on her mental being—and a greater addiction to the séances."

For once, I found myself in agreement—at least regarding Willa. "So you believe it was all fakery."

"All of it. The pencil was magnetized, and that's how it moved across the table to her. She likely wore a magnetic bracelet, slipping it off and on when we were distracted. The gust of cold air was emitted through a small hole in the wallpaper via some sort of bellows mechanism. The floating paper was obviously transported by thin wires or threads, and when we were distracted, the strings were cut. The table . . ." Here her words became less strident. "I haven't figured that one out yet, for I'm certain it was bolted to the floor. We shall have to pay Miss Louisa another visit tomorrow. At that time, you can divert her attention while I investigate further. As well, I will be interrogating her to find out whether one of our suspects has been in contact with her."

"Right. And what about Espasia's performance?" I'd waited for the opportunity to bring up that portion of the séance. I didn't think even Mina Holmes could come up with an explanation for it.

"Performance is the correct term. She's a consummate actress—as most of these charlatans are."

"Her arm turned ice-cold. And there is no way in which she—or anyone—could have known I killed a vampire last week. Let alone my nickname."

"Pish." Mina flapped her hand. "Willa Ashton could easily have told her about your nickname, and the previous séance. Gad, for all we know, Mrs. Yingling might have done so before she died. As for the vampire slaying . . . well, Miss Babbage knows you killed a vampire. As do Miss Adler, Dylan, and myself."

"Yes, Dylan must've rushed off to tell Louisa Fenley I killed a vampire last week. No, wait, it was probably me, and I simply forgot. Providence knows it couldn't have been that cloud-headed Babbage girl. I don't think she can hold a single thought for more than thirty seconds."

"I'm not suggesting any of those things actually happened. I'm merely pointing out that you and I aren't the only people who knew a vampire was killed at the Oligary Building. Any one of the individuals I mentioned could have carried the story, by accident or design, and therefore the information could have been given to Miss Fenley. After all, she did meet with Willa Ashton. She knew we'd be invited—*of course she did*," she said, drowning out my arguments. "Willa would have told her all about us—and so she did her own research in order to be prepared."

I folded my arms across my middle and glared at her. Drat and blast! There were times when I would have been happy to be *without* a partner. Mina Holmes could be so exasperating with her know-it-all attitude.

"Fine. Right. It couldn't have been real," I said loudly and untruthfully. "You are so bleeding stubborn. So what now, pray tell? I'm certain you have a *plan*."

"As I've already mentioned, we are going to pay another visit to Louisa Fenley tomorrow—er, no. On Wednesday. For tonight, we're going to attend the opening of New Vauxhall Gardens."

*That* was the best idea I'd heard in a long time. It would make up for having to attend a card party with Florence tonight when I'd rather be out searching for more UnDead. I was fairly dancing with impatience to get back on the streets with a stake in hand. But even though I didn't protest, Mina took it upon herself to inform me why we must go to Vauxhall.

"Surely you heard Miss Ashton comment that she, her aunt, and her cousin had been invited to attend the grand opening with Miss Norton and her brother, along with Mr. Treadwell. It's the perfect opportunity to better observe three of our suspects, particularly in Willa's presence."

"Three of our suspects? How many do we have?"

"At least four. Perhaps five. But tonight we will be able to observe Miss Norton—whose brother happens to be a doctor, although I suspect the significance of that fact might be lost on you—as well as Cousin Herrell. Mr. Treadwell might as well be counted a suspect as well, since, if he were to marry Willa, he would take control of her money. But there's no point in driving her lunatic to do so. Yet he has been in the house through the front door and thus he cannot be eliminated from consideration. I managed to determine what time the group was meeting, and where. We can accidentally encounter them, and I'm certain we'll be invited to join their group."

"Mina, I'm surprised at you. I didn't think you enjoyed social gatherings."

"I don't. But in this case, it will be a necessity."

A necessity to wander through the brand-new, most modern pleasure garden ever designed? I couldn't think of anything more exciting . . . and I was certain if there were any vampires in the vicinity, they'd agree, too.

The original Vauxhall Gardens had been a popular place for casual afternoon and evening entertainment through the early part of the century. But the park closed in 1854 and pieces of the land had been sold off to different buyers.

Five years ago, Mr. Oligary bought up some of the parcels again. He claimed he wanted to recreate the pleasure gardens in a more modern setting, as a way to thank the City of London for supporting his industry. My brother Bram snidely remarked that it was no more than a way for Oligary to compete with the popular Crystal Palace area in the south of London.

Honestly, I didn't care why or how they were reopening. Despite the fact that I'm more of a handmaker than a cognog like Mina, I can enjoy the pleasures of modern technology when it comes to entertainment.

The original gardens were known for pleasant walkways, dimly lit and convenient for young men and women to dally . . . as well as pickpockets. And surely vampires, too. There had been mimes and street jugglers, organ grinders and acrobats, as well as food vendors and even circus acts. I could only imagine what Mr. Oligary might have designed for what he called the Most Modern Pleasure Park of Our Time.

Mina and Dylan, who'd been happy to act as our escort, met me a street away from the Gardens. Even from a distance, the lights and sounds of celebration filled the air.

When I noticed Mina's dress, I stared in surprised envy. Who helped her put that together? The tall, gawky girl usually wore neat, understated, but otherwise unremarkable clothing. But tonight she had somehow put together an ensemble worthy of a second look.

An external black corset, laced tightly in the front and back, covered a sheer, fitted black bodice that buttoned up the front into a high collar. It resembled a close-fitting man's shirt; I'd never seen anything so striking. Neither lace nor ruffles trimmed the sleeves, collar, or bodice hem of the shirt. Instead, small copper cogs and grommets had been sewn into holes in the sheer fabric along the edges, giving the hems a glinting appearance. Her black skirt fell in a straight, graceful line from her hips to the tops of her shoes. A dark green lace overskirt billowed out over the narrow lines of the underskirt, giving it an ethereal look and changing the entire shape of the gown. The bustle at the base of her spine was an interesting combination of forest-green lace, black satin, and shimmering copper chains.

Mina's hair was pinned up in place, and covered by a small top hat decorated with slender black feathers and a green and white polka-dotted ribbon. A scrap of black netting from the hat brim hung rakishly over one side of her face. She wore short green fingerless gloves with laces threaded through metal grommets and cogs from forefinger to wrist. I craned my head to see if I could tell what sort of shoes she was wearing with such an amazing outfit. Boots—or daisies, as Pix had called them—would be wondrous.

I was definitely going to have to let Florence force me to go shopping. Soon.

"What on earth are you staring at, Evaline?" Mina asked after we'd strolled along a number of steps.

"I was admiring your ensemble." I smoothed my own frock. Mine happened to be a split skirt, but even so, it was still much fuller than hers. To help me blend with the shadows, it was midnight blue trimmed with unexciting black rickrack. I had feathers, as well as a bit of lace and ruffles, but nothing as unique as my partner's. "I didn't realize you were such an admirer of Street-Fashion."

"On occasion, I find it worth the time and effort to patronize the shop in a particular alley off Pall Mall." I heard the satisfaction in her voice.

"What, don't you like my clothes too?" Dylan teased. He was walking between the two of us, one on each arm, and seemed to be enjoying himself. "I picked them out all by myself."

"They're very nice," Mina told him. "Now, Willa indicated she and her cousin were to meet Miss Norton and her brother at half-past eight near the entrance. We must hurry if we're to accidentally encounter them. Ah, there she is. Oh! And her aunt is with her—number four in our list of suspects. How fortuitous."

My companion quickened her pace just enough that we crossed in front of Willa, Aunt Geraldine Kluger, and the young man helping them down from a carriage.

"Why, Miss Ashton! How pleasant to meet up with you."

"Evaline! And Mina!" Willa seemed just as delighted to see us as my companion was pretending to be. "Herrell, darling, these are my two friends. Aunt Gerry, you've already met them, I believe." She introduced us and Mina did the same with Dylan.

Mr. Herrell Ashton was about the same height as Mina, and had neat sandy-brown hair. He wore long sideburns and a trim mustache. The man beamed and bowed during the introductions. "How wonderful to meet you. Willa has been chattering on about her new friends quite often over the last days, and her auntie and I are pleased she's at last having some social engagements. It's been a difficult month. And here are the Nortons. And Treadwell is with them!"

"We'll make a party of it. Do say you'll come with us!" Willa looked hopefully at Mina and me.

"Of course. Mr. Treadwell, Miss Norton, it's a pleasure to see you again as well." Mina gave a brief curtsy and I followed suit.

"Likewise." The handsome young man extricated himself from Miss Norton's grip. He bowed to all of us, but his attention was on Willa the moment he lifted his head.

I was wrong. Mr. Treadwell wasn't at all torn between the two young women. He obviously preferred Willa Ashton. A quick look at the other young woman's dark, furious expression was all I needed.

Amanda Norton had shot to the top of my list of suspects, regardless of what Mina Holmes thought.

We joined the group and paid our fare. I'd even remembered to bring money. The entrance to New Vauxhall was through an ornate iron gate. It was flanked by tall shrubs and a stone wall, so that you could see very little of what was beyond until you stepped through. The gate led us into a tunnel-like entrance made of ivy and climbing roses so thick it would have been dark inside without the small lights.

As we walked through, Mina nudged me. "Talk to the cousin. See what you can find out about Willa, and anything else in that house."

"*Me?*" The last thing I wanted to do was stay with this staid, boring group. I'd thought to slip off into the shadows the moment the opportunity arose. Dylan would be alone with Mina, which—from the way he'd been gazing at her, I thought he'd appreciate—and I could be on my way. "You're the detective. You're the one—"

She shook her head impatiently. "I intend to speak with Mr. Treadwell." She took my arm and came closer so she could speak without being heard. "And observe Miss Norton and Aunt Geraldine in the meanwhile. You can—erm . . . charm Cousin Herrell. I have no doubt you can inspire him to talk. You're beautiful and vivacious, and you understand how to flirt and converse with a young man."

I nearly tripped. Had she just complimented me—or was that a veiled dig? "Very well. But no complaining if I don't find out what you want to know."

The timing was perfect, for we were exiting the tunnel of greenery and found ourselves inside New Vauxhall.

"My word." Miss Ashton turned in a slow circle. "I've never seen anything like this."

Our entire party had stopped to look around in amazement. I would have done so myself if Mina hadn't given me a shove toward Willa's cousin.

Even so, I noticed three moving walkways spiking out from the entrance like spokes on a half-wheel. Lights danced everywhere. They were attached to hundreds of hand-sized hot-air balloons, anchored to trees, posts, buildings, and even the ground. Stone walls, trees, and shrubbery loomed in every direction so you couldn't see very far down any particular path. Large gateways made of cogs and gears opened and closed to allow groups of people to enter in waves.

The moving walkways were wide enough for three people to stand abreast, and footpaths led into what seemed to be a clockwork fairytale land. Flowers bloomed everywhere, filling the air with a sweet, floral scent and covering up the unpleasant stench of London. Small mechanized butterflies and birds darted about, along with gear-ridden fireflies as big as my thumb. They cast small, colorful glows as they danced in the air.

Signs offered several options for entertainment. One pointed left to ANIMAL CURIOSITIES. Another to MEDALLION MAZE & CLOCKWORK LABYRINTH. RIVER STROLL & BOAT PARK.

JUNGLE FAIRE. CAROUSEL OF THE GODS. And OLIGARY'S OBSERVA-
TION COGWHEEL appeared to be straight ahead.

A faint mist lingered down one of the paths, and down
another, tiny winking lights of pink, green, blue, and orange
beckoned like little fairies. Mechanical fireflies. I could hear
music in the distance . . . and in a different direction, applause
and laughter.

"Evaline." Mina jabbed me in the arm. She was strong
for being a mere mortal female.

I refused to give her the satisfaction of rubbing the spot
and pasted on my sweetest, most innocent smile.

"I'm so pleased to finally meet you, Mr. Ashton," I said,
boldly offering Willa's cousin my arm.

"The pleasure is mine, Miss Stoker," he said, obliging by
taking my hand and settling it loosely inside his elbow. "I'm
delighted Willa has found some new friends. She became
quite a hermit after Robby disappeared."

Someone in the group, probably Mina, had chosen the
path leading to RIVER STROLL & BOAT PARK. Blast. I'd wanted
to see the OLIGARY'S OBSERVATION COGWHEEL.

"It's a terrible thing. She doesn't want to give up hope
that he can be found, but at the same time she must accept
whatever it is and go on with life. But I'm certain you're doing
everything you can to help find him." Blooming fish . . . was
that *my* voice? Syrupy and sweet?

"Indeed I am. I've spent nearly an hour every day walking about in Smithfield, asking if anyone has seen the young

man. I feel as if it's my fault." Mr. Ashton shook his head sadly. "I shouldn't have—"

"What do you mean?" A spark of interest caught me. If there was a chance Robby *was* still alive, perhaps his cousin had information that could help.

Mr. Ashton looked down at me as if suddenly remembering he didn't know me very well.

"My goodness . . . I didn't realize how tall you are, Mr. Ashton. You must have excellent horsemanship." I bumped gently into his side as we walked, coming closer to his person than was strictly proper. I smiled beguilingly up at him . . . and the tactic seemed to work, for his smile grew warmer.

"You're upset about Robby," I prompted. "What happened?" The sooner I got the information Mina wanted—or at least *some* information—the sooner I could slip off and have some real fun. If there were any more vampires in London, surely at least some were here tonight.

I had three stakes on my person, along with a knife and a curious old weapon called a mace. It was only the size of a peach pit, studded with small spikes and hanging from a chain the length of my arm, but it could inflict some damage. With the number of people here and the dark walkways, I could only imagine how many pickpockets, thieves, and hopefully UnDead would be taking advantage.

Encountering that sort would be *my* preferred entertainment here in the gardens.

Mr. Ashton focused on the path ahead of us. "The truth is, I can't help but feel partially responsible for his disappearance. I used to take him with me to the boxing club. He liked to watch the fights. One night, he wanted to come with me, but I . . . well, that particular night, I had other plans that weren't appropriate for a boy of eleven. But he was stubborn and insisted on following me nevertheless. He hitched a ride on the back of my carriage! When I discovered he'd done so, I became angry and hailed a cab to take him home. I should have taken him back myself, but I . . . well, I didn't."

"He never returned? What did the cab driver say?"

He made a sad sound. "We never saw him again. The cab driver said he jumped out of the vehicle after only a block and ran off."

"Why does Scotland Yard think he fell into a canal? There could be hundreds of other explanations for his disappearance."

"The boxing club is near Pristin Canal. I don't know if you're familiar with it, but the railings are nonexistent there, and the sides are steep and deep. There were two men who saw someone fall in, but they were too drunk to save the person. And likely too drunk to have known what they saw anyhow. But if someone did drown, it could have been Robby."

"How terrible." I lapsed into silence, trying to determine what other questions Mina would ask. I could think of nothing more . . . but perhaps that was because I spent more time peering in the shadows, hoping to see a pair of glowing red eyes.

Our conversation turned to lighter topics, and my companion made a few jests about the mechanized fireflies and their incessant buzzing. He had me laughing unexpectedly as we passed small trash compactors that chugged along, sweeping up refuse. Smoke belched from their rear pipes. Side gates opened temptingly as we approached, then closed when we walked past. Beyond the cogs and gears of the ornate side-gates, I saw shadowy figures and winking lights. The entire pleasure garden seemed to be a large maze with a variety of entertainment centers. A body of water was close by; I could smell it on the air.

Miss Norton and her brother trailed behind us, conversing with Aunt Geraldine. Mina, Dylan, Willa, and Mr. Treadwell were directly in front of us. A fountain suddenly appeared to my right. Water spurted up in a slender, elegant stream, arcing over us, then sparkled down into a small pool on the other side of the path, spraying us gently. Miss Norton gave a little shriek. I did not.

"It's a pleasure to walk with a young woman who doesn't mind a few droplets. It can be quite strenuous on the ear, those unexpected shrieks." My companion grinned down at me, and I gave a little chuckle.

"Then I shall attempt to keep any such shrieks firmly tamped down, Mr. Ashton. I should hate to injure your ears."

A trio of jugglers dressed like harlequins appeared from the shadows. Their faces were painted white with black diamonds. Each had four red balls and they began to walk along with us as they juggled, passing the balls back and forth over our heads, weaving in between and around us.

A man in a cape and tall black hat stood near a park bench, playing a mournful song on the violin. It was eerie and sad, yet oddly beautiful. A young couple stopped to listen, then I heard the clink of coins being dropped into his violin case.

"So, Herrell . . . how is Miss Willa?" asked Dr. Norton as he joined us. His sister had walked ahead to accompany Mr. Treadwell and the others. "You mentioned earlier there was an incident. Can I be of assistance?"

My escort sighed and I felt his arm tighten. "I'm very concerned about her." He patted my hand. "You'll hear about it soon enough, I trust. Best that you hear it from me."

"What is it?" I was only half listening, for I suddenly felt a chill over the back of my neck. Blast it all, I wasn't certain if it was a real breeze or a vampire.

I looked around. The jugglers had left us. The violinist was still playing, his eye-patched face nestled into his instrument. A group of five young men came jaunting along the footpath, loud and boisterous, pushing and shoving. A man riding a bicycle, its front wheel nearly as tall as me, came spinning down the path. Lights glittered on his spokes, and a little puff of steam came from the back. A trail of golden glitter followed in his wake.

"Willa did something terribly frightening yesterday. She climbed on top of the roof of the south tower and appeared to be attempting to fish," Mr. Ashton said grimly. "She brought up a pole with her, and was casting the line off into the air. Fortunately, this was right in the middle of the day and one of our footmen saw her."

This grabbed my full attention. "She wasn't hurt?"

"My *word*," said Dr. Norton. "Did she come down safely?"

"Only with some difficulty. It was quite an unsettling experience."

"What explanation did she give for doing such a foolhardy thing?"

We'd stopped at the edge of the footpath and I remained silent as they continued.

"She claimed . . . pah, I can hardly speak it. She claimed her mother told her to do it, that it was the only way to save Robby! That if she could catch his soul on a hook, where it floats over the tower, she could bring him back to earth."

"Has the poor girl gone *mad*?" Dr. Norton's eyes were wide.

"That is precisely my concern." Mr. Ashton sounded weary. "I very much fear. . . ." He stopped and seemed to notice me again for the first time. "You're a dear friend of Willa's. Have you seen any evidence of this?"

I didn't correct his assumption, although I felt guilty about allowing him to believe we were close. "No. Did she say how or when she received those instructions?"

"No, and I didn't want to upset her further by pressing." Mr. Ashton ran a hand over his face, rubbing his brow roughly. "Her aunt has threatened to cut her off from doing any more séances, and I'm inclined to agree. We both felt she should have remained home tonight and rested. But she insisted on coming."

All of a sudden, a figure appeared at the edge of the pathway. A discordant note startled me, and I was reminded of the ghostly music during Miss Fenley's séance. But when I looked over, it was only to see the eye-patched violinist. Still playing screechy, unpleasant notes, he gestured to his open violin case with a booted foot. The gentle music he'd been playing moments ago had gone, replaced by this loud, unpleasant noise.

"Devil take it—pardon me, Miss Stoker." Mr. Ashton gestured at the musician. "Only cease your playing and I'll line your bloody pockets with coin." He dug in the deep insides of his coat and tossed a handful of coins into the case.

One of them flipped out and landed on the ground next to my foot. Without thinking, I bent to pick it up just as the musician stooped as well.

We both reached for it at the same time, and I looked at him full in the face.

Bloody, blooming, blasted fish.

*Pix.*

But this time, there was no humor in his expression, no flash of levity in his exposed eye. Only cold darkness. He took the coin and gave a short, jerky bow. Then he collected his case, tucking the violin under his arm. "Good even'n, guvnors. . . . Miss."

I caught a glimpse of his flat, hard mouth just before he turned away. A gate behind him opened, and he walked through, melting into the shadows.

# Miss Holmes

*Wherein Our Heroine Encounters Creatures of
the Four-Legged and Finned Varieties*

A s we strolled along the crowded path in New Vauxhall,
my hand curved around Dylan's arm. As requested,
Evaline inserted herself into a conversation with Mr. Ashton.
I hoped she didn't forget she was actually supposed to obtain
information. She seemed more interested in smiling up at him
and making flutter-eyes. Anyone watching would think the
two of them to be engaged, or at the very least sparking.

After we extricated ourselves from the midst of some
energetic harlequin-garbed jugglers, I saw that Evaline, Mr.
Ashton, and Dr. Norton had stopped to listen to a violinist.
The musician wasn't particularly good—frankly, the screeching notes were torture to my ears, and I couldn't understand
the attraction—but at least my partner was still with her
quarry.

"I need to speak with Mr. Treadwell," I murmured.

Dylan bent closer to me than was strictly necessary, and I found myself surrounded by a pleasant male scent as he replied, "Shall I distract Miss Norton for a few minutes? Get her to walk on ahead with me?"

"If you can dislodge her from Mr. Treadwell's side, yes. And Miss Ashton and her aunt as well."

"And then afterward, maybe we can take a boat ride. Just you and me, you know, if it's proper. I'd like to talk to you."

"I'd like that." My tongue seemed to have stuck to the roof of my mouth. A boat ride. Alone? Under the moonlight?

It wasn't proper at all . . . but I didn't care. Hardly anything I'd done in the last month or so had been strictly proper.

"Cool. I'll approach Willa and Amanda, and—"

"And I'll pretend to have a problem with my shoe," I said. "Mr. Treadwell seems gentlemanly enough to stop and assist while you move the others on ahead."

Things worked precisely as planned—no surprise, given my foresight in waiting until Miss Ashton and Miss Norton were safely in Dylan's presence before I pretended to trip.

"Thank you so much, Mr. Treadwell," I said when I had "fixed" my heel. "The Gardens are lovely, but I'm afraid I wouldn't have been comfortable walking along this path alone. I see the others have left us behind. Although there are several other people about, I prefer to be with ones I know."

"I don't know where Mr. Ashton and Dr. Norton have gone off to." He glanced back. "Or your friend, Miss Stoker. She seems to have disappeared."

I was about to reply when a small creature bounded out of the shadows in front of me. Startled but not frightened, I halted, still clinging to Mr. Treadwell's arm.

It was a spotted dog with floppy ears that nearly dragged on the ground. He was running about, barking as if released from some sort of confinement. His long ears went every which way as he dashed about, making awkward figure-eights on the path around us and the others in the vicinity. One of his rear legs was a mechanical one. It gleamed in the moonlight, making a soft metallic click as the limb leapt and bounded. He stepped on one of his ears and tripped, tumbling onto his face in a somersault, then twisted back onto his feet and dashed about some more. I could hardly contain a giggle.

"Angus!" called a voice from the shadows. "Angus, where are you off to?" Thrashing sounds and vibrations amid the shrubbery commenced.

As a rule, I don't care for animals, but this particular creature was utterly endearing with its too-big ears and stubby legs. I empathized with his ungainliness, having tripped over my own two feet (or skirts) more than once. I released Mr. Treadwell's arm and crouched on the path, calling for the beagle to come to me.

"Come here, doggie." I felt the unfamiliar strain in my legs and ankles from such an unusual position. My corset felt uncomfortably tight at the same time; I'd have to adjust my Easy Un-Lacer in the future. The green lace of my overskirt poofed out in a circle around me. "Oh, there you are. Nice doggie."

He settled on the ground, right on the edge of my lacy skirt, writhing in some expectant manner. His ears lolled about like a child's arms when making snow angels, flopping back and forth. His round white tummy was exposed and his mechanical leg fell wide from his torso, still moving reflexively. I got the distinct impression he expected me to rub his belly.

"Angus!"

Recognizing the voice, I looked up as the beagle's apparent owner emerged from the bushes. "Inspector Grayling!"

He looked from me to the beagle, then over at Mr. Treadwell, and then back down to me. "Miss Holmes. I do believe this is the first time I've found you crouched over something other than a dead body."

"Dead body?" Mr. Treadwell said with a horrified expression. (Of course the demure Miss Ashton would *never* be caught crouching over a dead body.)

I gave Grayling a quelling look, then replied to my companion. "Don't mind him, it's only a jest."

"Would you like some assistance?" Grayling offered me his hand as I began to struggle upright.

"No, thank you." I patted the canine creature on the head once more. Despite the weight and awkwardness of the layers of petticoat beneath my skirts, I was able to pull to my feet gracefully, without—for once—embarrassing myself. "Is this your dog, then?"

By the way Angus was jumping up on Grayling's legs and panting enthusiastically, the answer was obvious.

"Yes. The little menace slipped his lead and took himself off when we were walking through the park." But now there was affection in his voice as he bent to scratch the dog, who'd flopped on his back once more and fairly wriggled in ecstasy. "It's no wonder ye lost a leg, you little blunderbunt. Always getting into trouble, aren't you, boyo?"

"This is the beagle from last week in Glasner-Mews— who caught his leg in the metal hasp on the streetwalk. You got him free and had his leg fixed."

"How did you know about that?"

"I saw him trapped and crying, and then you . . . erm . . . you came out of Mrs. Yingling's window and jumped down a whole level to save him. Foolishly, I might add. What if you'd missed and fallen all the way to ground level?" The memory of his neat vault over the streetwalk railing was still embedded in my brain.

Grayling's expression changed into something unfathomable. If I didn't know better, I would have thought he seemed embarrassed. He cleared his throat. "You . . . er . . . saw that?"

"Yes." Goodness, my voice sounded rusty. I was forced to clear my throat as well. "Despite its foolhardiness, it was very . . . athletic."

"Aye. Right." His Scottish brogue was evident now. "Well, then. Thank you for capturing Angus for me. I'll tighten his collar to make certain he doesn't slip off again. Won't I, boy?" He attached a leash to the collar in question.

When Grayling stood, I realized for the first time he was wearing a coat with a badge pinned to it. (How had I not noticed earlier? Drat!) "You must not be here for pleasure, then, Inspector." I gestured to the metal shield.

"Ah, well. As it happens, Mr. Oligary suggested the Met might provide a bit of extra manpower for security tonight." He shrugged, once again seeming sheepish. "He was paying well, and Angus and I thought it would be an opportunity to see the inside of the New Gardens and get paid at the nonce."

Before I could respond to that enlightening comment, Grayling's attention wandered to Mr. Treadwell, then returned to me. "But Angus and I have interrupted your party, Miss Holmes. We should get on with our business. Come along, you scoundrel." He tugged firmly at the leash.

Angus didn't seem to like that idea, but after a moment, he succumbed to the inevitable and began to bound off happily once more—this time, attempting to pull Grayling along with him. It was a losing battle, for of course the pup was hardly a match for the tall, broad-shouldered detective. Nevertheless, he allowed his canine friend to lead him off.

It wasn't until they'd gone back into the bushes and, presumably, back to wherever the inspector was stationed, that I realized I'd forgotten to obtain an update from Grayling regarding Mrs. Yingling's murder. Where on earth had my brains gone?

"We should attempt to find the rest of our party." Mr. Treadwell offered his arm.

As we strolled along, I brought my mind back to the matter at hand and contemplated a possible motive for Mr. Treadwell. He had the means and opportunity to be behind the nefarious scheme, but I could conceive no reason he would want to ruin Miss Ashton. Love was as good a motivation as anything—as I'd recently learned during the Affair with the Clockwork Scarab. But as she seemed to reciprocate his affections, I could fathom no reason he'd want to turn her mad. Every indication was that he truly cared for her.

Where on earth had Miss Stoker gone off to? I needed to find out if she'd learned anything from Mr. Ashton.

The scent of water was in the air, and I knew we were approaching the eponymously titled River Walk. Voices carried on the breeze, and I even discerned the distant calls of some wild creatures likely from the Animal Curiosities exhibit. An interesting duo of peacocks—one living, and one mechanized—strutted across the path. The gear-ridden bird's tail was a magnificent display of glittering jewels: sapphires, emeralds, jet beads, and aquamarines set in a bronzed fan. Fortunately, the discordant violin had ceased to play and now I could hear the tinny sound of an organ grinder and, beyond, the rumble of some mechanized vehicles or machinery.

To the northeast, I noticed the top of a massive cogwheel turning above the trees. It was lit with small lights and

THE SPIRITGLASS CHARADE

appeared to have gondolas hanging from it, large enough to hold two or four persons. Oligary's Observation Cogwheel, I presumed. What a view one would have, sitting in a gondola at the top. Sitting beside a handsome young man . . .

Suddenly, there was a loud *pop-pop-popping*. A spray of red, blue, and yellow lights burst into the dark sky, coloring everything below. Mr. Treadwell and I, along with every other person on the pathway, stopped to observe the fireworks exploding above.

I watched in delight as a new round of dancing lights blazed above. Although everyone in the crowd was gazing up as well, I doubted they were calculating the trajectory of the discharged explosives, counting the seconds between launch and the resounding flare, and measuring how the different colors of illumination lasted for different lengths of time before they faded.

Uncle Sherlock had given Dr. Watson and me a lecture on his experimentation with explosives of this nature. I was attempting to confirm his theories regarding the angle of trajectory versus the span of the explosion, as well as using the smell that lingered in the air to identify the particular accelerant employed. If I had the opportunity to return in the daytime, I'd also examine the area for the detritus that would be left behind from the explosives.

Then someone screamed.

Perhaps everyone else thought it was part of the reaction of the crowd, or perhaps the sound was drowned out by the *pop-pop-popping* . . . but I heard it and immediately determined from whither it was coming.

No one else seemed to notice, but I didn't care.

I started toward the sound, and then heard another scream, followed by more urgent voices. Gathering up my long overskirt, I ran as fast as I could down a side path toward the noise. I might not be an inhumanly strong vampire hunter, but I wasn't about to stand around and do nothing if someone was in distress.

"Thief! Stop, thief!" someone shouted.

I tripped over a rock but caught my balance and kept going despite the strain of my lungs fighting against the tight lacing of my corset. My petticoats and skirts whipped around my legs, and I could feel the unfamiliar sensation of my bustle jouncing over my posterior.

A figure burst out of the darkness, nearly bowling me over. He had something in his hand like a reticule or pocketbook. I stuck out my foot in his path.

The boy tripped, but kept going, and I started after him. "Stop! Thief!"

Unfortunately, I doubt anyone could have heard me. I was using what little breath I could drag in to propel me after the pickpocket. The stones were uneven beneath my speedy feet and the items I'd secreted beneath my bustle and in the hidden pockets of my skirt—a Steam-Stream gun, an Ocular-Magnifyer, and even a wooden stake in case Evaline forgot hers—bounced alarmingly.

I don't know how I managed to stay with the thief, but I kept him in sight as he followed the narrow footpath along the River Walk. Providence offered me a hand by providing a stick or stone along the way, and the lanky, fleet-footed pickpocket tripped, nearly tumbling into the river. But he careened upright after, giving me a few precious moments to catch up to him.

I threw myself at his person as he stumbled back to his feet. Grappling with his coat, I held on, trying to wrestle him to the ground. This was a losing proposition, for though he was probably only fourteen or fifteen, he was tall and strong, nor was he hampered by corsets and skirts. He flung me aside and I staggered, almost taking a header into the bushes . . . but still I held on to his lapels.

"Help!" I shouted. My cry came out as more of a croaking gasp. Where on earth were all of the other hundreds of people I'd seen earlier in the Gardens? The fireworks continued to explode above, the green and blue lights flickering over the sharp-faced pickpocket. "Help!" My lungs heaved weakly inside my corset. Blasted thing.

We struggled, doing an awkward dance along the path, wrestling our way up a small footbridge. My assailant twisted suddenly, brandishing something long and silver.

"Let go, ye blasted bitch!" The knife flashed, then surged down toward me.

I choked out a scream as pain blazed along my arm. But somehow I continued to hold on, spinning us about and ducking at the same time. Then all at once, we were falling, tumbling over the side of the low bridge.

The water was a cold, hard shock and necessitated that I release the culprit. The river enveloped me, dark and heavy.

I was out of breath, restricted by the lacings around my torso, hampered by layers of skirt and petticoats. My gown became heavy and sodden, and I floundered in the depths, trying to reach the surface. Then my face broke into the fresh night air. I gasped, trying to gulp in more air before I sank again.

My arms moved frantically, my legs slogging amid tangled skirts. I knew how to swim, but I was weighted down . . . sinking into the cold darkness.

Suddenly, something grabbed me. I kicked out, struggling, grasping . . . but was too weak and tangled to have much effect. My lungs burned from holding my breath. When fresh air once again spilled over my face, I coughed and dragged oxygen into my restricted lungs. Strong hands pulled me out of the water. My vision was blurred, and I gasped, desperate to breathe, but my torso was banded too tightly.

I sagged weakly to the ground, the energy drained from my limbs. Blackness closed over me. Everything was tight, growing tighter, stiffer, closer. . . .

I felt a yank, a violent jolting at the front of my bodice. *Jolt, jolt, jolt.* My body jerked with each movement.

"Bloody . . . damned . . . corsets . . . ," growled my rescuer.

And then . . . *ahh!* Everything loosened. I dragged in my first deep breath in what seemed like hours—clean and cool and sweet.

The face of my savior was partly illuminated by a gaslight, making him appear golden and shadowy all at once. Water dripped from his curling coppery hair as he glared down at me, panting for breath of his own.

"What . . . the *devil* . . . did you think . . . you were . . . doing . . . Miss Holmes?" Grayling demanded.

"I. . . ." I was still gasping for air. He was looking down at me as if he wanted to throw me back into the river. And yet his expression made me feel warm and fluttery. Or maybe it was just the new breaths of oxygen.

"Chasing after a bloody . . . thief," he continued. "Blasted foolish . . . thing to do."

"He was getting . . . away. I had to . . . stop him."

"He had a knife!"

I could feel the blood seeping from my arm. "I didn't know that. Someone had to—"

"You almost *drowned*. Bat-headed female."

Grayling glared down at me, his breathing slower and deeper now. His mouth was tight and I could see his jaw shifting. Water plopped onto my cheeks and chest from his hair and clothing, yet it didn't seem to matter. He was close to me, propped on the grass, leaning over. Warmth seeped through layers of wet clothing into my hip and arm. His white shirt clung to his torso and I could see the outline of his shoulders and arms. They were surprisingly muscular for such a tall, lanky person.

He was looking at me strangely, and when my gaze was caught by his, I suddenly couldn't breathe again. I thought for a minute he was going to . . . move closer. My mouth went dry and I almost stopped breathing again. Then I looked away, my heart pounding sharply in my chest.

"I've been expecting a report from you," I managed to say, frantically collecting my thoughts. My throat felt as if it needed to be cleared. "About the Yingling case."

"A report?" His voice was strangled and he sat upright. "From me? For you? Miss Holmes, you are the most—"

His exclamation was aborted when a ball of fur blasted into the area, barking and yapping wildly. Long ears flopped on my face and claws scraped my arm as Angus leapt and bounded around us. His puppy weight settled on my belly, his tail slapping furiously against my jaw.

"Angus," Grayling said, in a much nicer tone than he employed with me but nevertheless filled with irritation. "Get off. Get *off.*"

He dragged the excited canine away and I took the opportunity to sit up. As I did so, gravity pulled my corset away. I reacted with an embarrassing squeak and clapped a hand back to my chest, pulling the two halves of the ruined garment into proper position. Fortunately, Grayling seemed too occupied with Angus to notice. Thank fortune I was wearing a dark undergarment beneath my sheer bodice, or—*gad.*

I stopped the rest of that thought. I couldn't even consider what might have happened otherwise, what Grayling might have seen beneath my suddenly loosened corset and the transparent fabric of my shirt. It was bad enough that he'd practically undressed me.

"You ruined my new corset." I staggered to my feet, still holding the sagging undergarment in place. Droplets of water flung everywhere. Angus leapt up at me, eager for attention, and I patted him on the head. It wasn't his fault his master was an expert at annoying me.

"My apologies," Grayling said stiffly, also rising as excited voices approached. "Next time, I'll let you gasp for air like a beached fish and hope you don't drown in the meanwhile."

Before I could make some sort of smart retort, he flung something dark and heavy—and dry—over my shoulders. I took his coat while holding my corset in place and managed to pull it over my sodden clothing, wincing only slightly at the pain in my arm.

"Mina! What happened?"

Huddling under Grayling's coat I turned to see Dylan rushing down the path. He was accompanied by the rest of our party . . . and a small crowd of others. But Evaline was missing, drat it.

"I was chasing a thief. We struggled, and I fell into the river."

"And got a bit of a slice in the process." Grayling was still dripping and Angus was still bounding around—although now he had a variety of newcomers upon which to employ his paws.

"Chasing a thief? Do you mean you were running after him?" a male voice said in shock.

"You should have called for help," agreed another. "There were plenty of people around."

"I've never heard of anything so . . . *improper*," a female whispered loudly enough to be certain I heard. "Chasing a thief. Running alone down a dark path. Young ladies have lost all sense of decorum in this day!"

"Proper young women don't *run*. They wait for assistance. Call for help."

"And they certainly don't fight. What was she thinking?"

Murmurs of agreement rose and I felt my temper rising as well. I didn't even look at Grayling, for hadn't he said the same dratted thing? Calling me a *bat-headed female*?

In my entire life, *no one* had dared insult my intelligence. My long nose, my graceless limbs, even my tone of voice and pedantic lectures . . . but never my intelligence.

"Come on, Mina," Dylan said, putting an arm around me. "Let's get you home."

I spared a brief thought for Miss Stoker's whereabouts and a farewell pat on the head for Angus—but not even a backward glance for the man whose coat I was wearing.

Inspector Grayling could drip all the way home in his sodden clothing for all I cared.

# MISS HOLMES

## *A Milestone for Miss Holmes*

Dylan helped me into the cab and I settled onto its seat. Fortunately, it was a midsummer's night and I wasn't cold as much as bedraggled and out of sorts. Yet I shuddered at the unattractive picture I must have made, even in the shadows.

I wasn't attractive on a good day, with my long, slender Holmesian nose and my too-long limbs and angular figure. But now I knew I must have looked hideous. My fetching little hat was gone and my corset was ruined. My injured arm was bound up, but there were bloodstains on my glove. I didn't even want to imagine the state of my hair.

"Are you all right? Are you cold?"

"No," I said, wishing I was. Perhaps then I could move closer to him, and . . . no, of course not. What on *earth* was I thinking? Here I was, half-clothed—thanks to that annoying Grayling. . . .

"You could have drowned. *Seriously*. You could have *drowned*."

"I know how to swim." Even to my own ears my defense sounded weak.

He shook his head, his eyes fastened on me from across the carriage. "You chased that thief without even thinking about the danger to yourself. And you must have really held on to him. . . . Like a barnacle or something." He gave an admiring laugh. "You're an awesome piece of work, Mina."

"Is that good?" I thanked Providence it was night and he couldn't see the color of my burning cheeks.

"Definitely. It means you're so cool and so different and unique and awesome . . . and yet challenging at the same time. It's a good thing."

"Right," was all I could manage. "Thank you."

"I know I've told you this before, but in my time, women aren't treated the same way they are now—told to sit and do nothing. Just get married and have kids. It's not like that." His eyes gleamed in the low light. "Don't listen to what those jerks were saying back there. They don't know what they're talking about. Some men wouldn't even have chased after that thief. You were really brave."

I was aware of an unfamiliar emotion bubbling up inside me. Warm and fluttery, it stole my breath. "Thank you."

I had no experience with this sort of dialogue—with anyone, and certainly not with a young man. My father hardly said two words to me. My uncle, on the other hand, constantly lectured and demanded I do more and better. My mother— There *had* been times of soft words, a gentle touch. Even encouragement.

Fighting off the weakness of grief—I would never allow myself to become like Willa Ashton, desperately holding on to someone I'd lost—I drew in a long, shaky breath and tried to think of a way to change the subject. I needed to ask if he had seen Evaline—for I had not before being bustled off to the carriage under the disapproving eyes of the crowd.

Before I could speak, Dylan moved to sit on my side of the carriage. I wasn't crowded when he settled next to me, likely sitting on my sodden skirts, his arm brushing warm against mine. Before I could react and explain how improper this was, he took my hand.

"I suppose this is totally improper," he said, reading my mind. "Me sitting so close to you. Us alone in the carriage."

I swallowed. I was no longer the least bit chilled. "It is."

He squeezed my hand tighter, and I became aware of how large his fingers were. How warm and sturdy. His thumb began to move over the top of my gloved one, and I could feel the gentle caress through the bloodstained, damp leather.

"You know . . ." Dylan's voice sounded odd, and his fingers twitched a little. "If we were in my time, I'd want to date you."

"Date me? Do you mean, determine how old I am? I don't mind telling you that; you don't have to guess. I'm seventeen, and—"

I stopped because he was chuckling, his eyes narrowed with humor, his fingers loosening. "Ah, Mina. Thank you. I needed something to break the ice."

I was grateful for the change of mood as well, and I smiled at him. The next thing I knew, he moved closer to me. His hand slid around the back of my head, his fingers into my soggy, sagging hair.

And he kissed me.

# MISS STOKER

*Evaline Investigates*

I slipped away from Mr. Ashton at the earliest opportunity, determined to track down the disreputable Pix, who kept turning up like a bad coin. But though I searched for over an hour, I couldn't find him.

As I wandered down the path from the Oligary's Observation Cogwheel, a fireworks display exploded above. Moments later amid the popping sounds, I heard shouts of "Stop, thief!"

Ah. I'd found Pix.

I smiled grimly and started over toward the cries, aware that the night had cooled a little. As I came around the corner of a deserted pathway, I saw two people struggling on a small bridge over the river.

Blooming fish! Was that Mina Holmes?

She looked ridiculous, clutching the hem of the thief's coat, her tall, slender body jerking and swaying as he attempted to shake her free while running away. Then a glinting blade slashed down toward her arm.

*Oh no,* Mina!

I was too far away to help. *Pix, you fool!* What was he thinking?

I ran faster.

Then the two battling figures fell off the bridge.

By the time they hit the water, I was at the shore. Two heads emerged and I identified Mina's. With a wave of relief, I realized her assailant wasn't Pix after all. I was just about to jump in to drag her out when another man ran from the shadows, stripping off his coat.

He dove into the water, a yapping puppy with long ears on his heels. I recognized Inspector Grayling by his height and curling gingery hair. Good. He could be the one to pull Mina out of the water.

That way *he'd* get her lecture, telling him everything he'd done wrong.

I watched as the thief paddled toward the opposite shore, where I waited in the shadows. When he slogged onto the grass some distance from the bridge, I was waiting for him.

He didn't have a chance. In a trice, I relieved him of the knife he still gripped, as well as the three drawstring purses and two wallets tucked into his pockets. Then I tossed him back into the river.

Valuables recovered. Thief submerged. And I hadn't even broken a sweat.

Mina and Grayling had been joined by others on the opposite shore and I hurried across the bridge. Skirting the back of the crowd, I placed the stolen items where they'd be found. I didn't want to rejoin our group, but I needed to make certain Mina wasn't injured. Since she was lecturing Grayling, I decided it was safe for me to leave.

I turned to go and glimpsed a familiar figure in the crowd. Miss Adler?

Craning my neck, standing as tall as I could, I peered through the throng. But the person I'd noticed was gone, or else I'd been mistaken. If it had been our mentor, wouldn't she have been assisting Mina?

Then I slid into the shadows to search for Pix and, hopefully, vampires. But by the time dawn broke, I'd found neither Pix nor an UnDead. I had, however, become very familiar with New Vauxhall Gardens. Frustrated, I returned home—for once entering through the front door.

Florence called sleepily from her room near the top of the stairs. "Evaline?"

"Yes, it's me. I'm exhausted, but it was very fun. I'll tell you all about it in the morning."

My sister-in-law had been thrilled about my social engagement with several young people tonight, so she had no complaints about the lateness of my return. As far as she knew, I'd been chaperoned with a large number of friends.

Then I heard her rustling in bed, and the soft, deep murmur of my brother. An unexpected wave of comfort washed over me, taking me by surprise. This was home. Where I lived with two people who loved me and who loved each other. They couldn't understand my life, but they still loved me.

Which was more than I could say for Mina Holmes.

The unusually strong, comfortable feeling of being loved and cherished remained with me as I climbed the stairs to my room. But as I drifted off to sleep, a different thought lodged in my mind: the memory of the dark, angry eyes of an irritated violinist.

When I woke the next morning, it was well before noon—somewhat unusual for me. But I had plans today, for I was going to Smithfield and Pristin Canal to poke around a bit and check out Herrell Ashton's story about his boxing club.

Mina Holmes wasn't the only one who could investigate.

I didn't send word to my so-called partner about my conversation with Cousin Herrell and Dr. Norton. Surely Mina was recovering from her dunking in the river. She'd probably stay in bed all day. And if I found out anything more about Robby Ashton's disappearance in Smithfield, I could tell her everything at once.

Pristin Canal was just as Mr. Ashton described it: deep, with its railings in disrepair, and smooth, sheer sides that wouldn't allow anyone to climb out once in the water. It was sludgy and smelled of rotting fish and gad knew what else. If you fell—or were pushed—you'd best be an excellent swimmer who didn't have a weak stomach.

I grimaced. I wasn't certain whether to hope Robby had drowned and was now at peace, or whether he had been somewhere else unpleasant or dangerous for the last month.

In Smithfield, where the meat markets and cattle trading took place, the second street-level buildings hung so far over the roads it was like walking through a tunnel. Little sunlight made it to the ground, and even someone as ungainly as Mina Holmes could jump from one side of the second level street-walk to the other.

Not far from the canal, a small, weatherbeaten sign on the brick wall of a narrow mews caught my attention. NICKEL'S FIGHTING-CLUB.

Could this be the boxing house Mr. Ashton frequented?

Intrigued, I turned down the passage. Just as I came to the small, black door that said NICKEL'S, I glanced toward the other end of the alley. A pub faced me and even from where I was, I could read the sign.

THE PICKLED NURSE.

That was the place Pix said two drunks had seen a vampire. Robby Ashton had disappeared in this vicinity. And during Willa's séances, I'd received messages about the UnDead.

*There are no coincidences.* Mina Holmes's strident voice rose in my mind.

Intrigued, I pushed open the door to Nickel's. Of course I didn't have a *plan.* I was going to wander in and see what happened. Did I think someone was going to come right out and tell me what I wanted to know? Of course not. But I'd done a good job getting information from Mr. Ashton last night.

Like most proper women, I'd never been in a fighting-club and I wasn't certain what to expect. The establishment smelled of sweat, blood, and cigar smoke. The place was a large room with low ceilings, two measly windows, and a planked floor covered with dirt. An older model of Mr. Jackson's Mechanized-Mentor leaned against one wall, tarnished and with one arm dangling. I had one of the newer devices at home. Florence thought it was to help me learn the waltz, but I used it for training to fight vampires.

My entrance didn't seem to draw any notice. Other than one sleek, muscular man in the corner, pummeling a bag hanging from the ceiling, the other half-dozen occupants were arranged around a boxing ring, watching a sparring match. The sound of fists thudding against flesh, laced with grunts and groans, was raw and primitive.

I edged closer, my attention drawn to the two fighters. Both had fabric wrapped around their hands and wore only trousers. Even their feet were bare. I found the sight of a man's unclothed torso both fascinating and unsettling.

At the Ankh's opium den, I'd seen bare arms and shoulders and a hint of chest—but this was even more risqué. The boxers were riddled with bruises, cuts, and blood mingling with sweat. Men, I discovered, had muscles that rippled—even in their backs. And the sight of broad, uncovered shoulders, gleaming with perspiration, made my face unusually warm.

Blood and spittle flew as the duo circled and sparred, thrusting with strong jabs and ramming shoulders, hips, and even heads into their opponents. I could probably learn something from them—

"Who the blazes are *ye*?"

I turned to face a bewhiskered man, who was decently clothed in a shirt and vest. But he looked as if he were staring at some sort of odd, foreign creature—that odd, foreign creature being me, a female.

"I'm . . . er . . ." Blast! This was what happened when one didn't have a plan. "I . . . uhm . . . Mr. Herrell Ashton—"

"*Ashton*? That bleedin' rat! Do you say you know him?"

Unexpected, to say the least. I gathered my thoughts quickly. "I don't know him well. Does he come here often, then?"

"Too oft for my taste. The man's up to 'is knickers— sorry, miss—in debt. He owes half the house for his wagers. Oy! Bernie! This gel here knows Ashton!"

His call had some of the spectators turning from the match. None of them looked pleased.

"You tell Ashton he best not show his face round here until he's got cash," one of them ordered me, then turned back to the fight.

"Did you hear about a boy disappearing from this area? Three weeks ago? It was Mr. Ashton's cousin, Robby," I asked the bewhiskered man, who seemed a little calmer now.

"Aye. There's talk he fell into the canal, but no one knows for cert. He used to come in sometimes with Ashton. The Yard come around asking questions 'bout him."

"Did you see him that night? Mr. Ashton said the boy followed him without him knowing. And then he sent Robby home, but he never arrived."

Mr. Whiskers shook his head. "Ashton was 'ere for a while. Then 'is little cousin showed up, an' 'e left. I ain't seen 'im since—an' that's what I tole the coppers. Cove knows better 'an to come in here without the glint he owes. But mark m'words, he best come up with it soon."

"Do you know where he went after he left? Or if there was another place he tended to frequent while he was in this neighborhood?"

"'Oo knows. All I know's I ain't seen 'im since that night."

"Thank you, sir." I mulled this over as I turned to go. Surely if Mina Holmes were here, she'd have a slew of deductions and theories. I wondered what Cousin Herrell's other, more adult pursuits were—the ones he didn't want Robby to experience.

I took two more steps toward the door, then turned back. "Have you heard any rumors about anyone seeing red-eyed men with long teeth around here?"

Mr. Whiskers stopped. "Red eyes? Glowing-like, in the dark?"

My heart beat faster. "Yes. Have you seen anyone like that?"

"I ain't seen nothing like that, but there's been some 'as talked about it at the Nurse over yonder. But I can't believe half of what them drunks say, all knockered up as they are. Though there could be sump'n to it, I spose, since more'n one of 'em claims it."

That was enough for me. I thanked Mr. Whiskers and left, heading to the Pickled Nurse.

Though it was just past noon, the alley was drassy as if it were twilight because of the overhangs above. And the pleasant London weather didn't help: once again, it was cloudy. Fog seeped down the streets and walkways, giving the neighborhood a frosty, eerie atmosphere.

It would be the perfect location for a vampire to lurk, even during the day . . . waiting for his or her prey, out of the sun and in the shadows.

As if to emphasize these thoughts, a chill passed over the back of my neck and settled there. I turned quickly, scouring the people walking by, focusing on the ones who stayed near the buildings beneath the overhangs. Could one of them be a vampire?

Or was it just a cool breeze?

But the chill persisted as I continued to the Pickled Nurse. I scrutinized the passersby, wondering if any of them were vampires—but not quite knowing how to figure it out. I was still new at this.

When I reached the pub, I pushed the doors open and strode up to the counter. It was early in the day, and this was a workingman's neighborhood, so the saloon wasn't crowded. A handful of men and one woman sat at various tables with tankards in front of them. The place was much quieter and cleaner than Fenmen's End. There were even windows studding the front wall, which allowed in what little daylight there was.

Behind the bar was a row of huge glass jars held in place by a cagelike mechanism. A small rail-like contraption ran along the front of the line. Each jar was filled with pickles and had a small chalkboard label on it with names like HONEY-GINGER SPICED, ZOOK SPEARS, SPICY ANISE, CURRIED CLOVE, and SOUR DILL.

Settling on a stool at the counter, I watched as the bartender took a coin from one of the patrons and slid it into a tray. Then he turned a dial and pushed a button. With a soft clicking sound, a spindly device ticked along the cagework in front of the jars, stopping at the one labeled FANCY HOT.

Two delicate mechanical hands popped open the top of the jar, and a third reached inside, withdrawing a long, dripping pickle. A small tray piled with butcher paper hummed along the row of jars, stopping so the pickle could be placed on the top sheet. Then the bartender wrapped it up in the paper and gave it to the patron.

Then he turned to me. "What's yer fancy, miss?"

I didn't suppose they had lemonade or tea, so I bravely ordered an ale. "Don't fill it up too high," I said, knowing I wouldn't drink it.

"Still the same price either way," he said, putting the drink on the counter. "What flavor?"

"Flavor?"

"The pickle. It goes in the drink, stir it up, give it some flavor," he explained with exaggerated patience.

"Oh . . . uhm . . . I'll have the plain Sweet."

While the mechanism retrieved my pickle, I plunged into my questions, keeping my voice low. "I've heard rumors some of your patrons have seen men with glowing red eyes."

The bartender paused from wiping pickle juice off the counter. "There's been rumors. I ain't seen nothing. But . . ." He shrugged. "Nothing would surprise me in this day and age. Glowing red eyes. Long white teeth. Spider pets. I've heard it all."

"Spider pets?"

"Yep'm. That one I seen myself. Man and a woman come in here with a small cage, this big"—he indicated the size of a loaf of bread—"covered up with a cloth. She liked the Honey-Butters; had about three of 'em in her ale at one time. That's extra, ye know," he warned. "More'n one pickle's extra."

"What about the cage?"

"Yeah. Guy 'ad an accent, too. He took off the cloth and showed me a peek. Inside was the biggest, hairiest spider I ever seen. Big as my hand." He shuddered. "Guy really liked spiders, too; both of 'em did. And then they come back some more times since. I don' like to wait on 'em, so I lets Luke do it. Coupla lunatics if ye ask me, takin' up w' caged spiders. Bloodsucking, crawly creatures. Ugh."

The hair on the back of my neck stood on end. "What makes you think they both liked spiders so much?"

"They had—both 'em did—a mark on the wrist. Right here." He showed me the inside of his wrist. "Had a long-legged spider on it. Creepy and ugly. Wouldnt'a seen it if she hadn't taken off her gloves 'cause of the pickle juice. You want another pickle?"

I hardly heard him. Surely the man and woman were members of *La société*. "Did you see where they went?"

The bartender shrugged again and gestured to the front windows. "I can't see much. But they went out and to the left, as I recall. Hard to forget them. He had a mark on his wrist, too. Looked like two small red punctures. Maybe he let that spider pet suck on himself."

*Or maybe something else had been drinking his blood. Something UnDead.*

"Ain't seen 'em for a while, and I'm glad to say it." He shuddered again, then turned to serve another patron.

Filled with excitement, I slid off the stool and, leaving a generous payment, hurried out of the pub. I knew it was unlikely I'd figure out where the spider couple had gone, but at least I could look around.

I could hardly wait to talk to Mina.

# MISS HOLMES

*Wherein a Legality Is Reviewed*

"Excellent investigative work, Miss Stoker." My approval was sincere, for she had uncovered quite a bit of interesting information. "Most excellent. You may become my Watson after all."

"Not bloody likely."

But I could tell she was pleased.

It was the morning two days after the events at Vauxhall. At my request, Evaline had picked me up in her carriage after breakfast. The game was in full swing.

"So what have we learned . . . That one of our suspects has large gambling debts, which strengthens his motive of wanting to maintain control of Willa's finances—particularly if he was beginning to see the writing on the wall of the resolution of Mr. Treadwell's courtship of his cousin. This information requires a closer look at Mr. Ashton, who, I confess, I hadn't given as much thought to until now. I shall endeavor to do so today when we visit Miss Ashton."

"So that's where we're going. Nice of you to tell me."

"Do you not think we ought to hear *her* side of the story—about what happened when she climbed out onto the roof and attempted to catch her brother's soul with a fishing pole? This latest development is quite concerning. She actually climbed onto the roof with a fishing pole. . . . Perhaps I was wrong. Perhaps the villain isn't trying to drive her mad, but to go so far as to cause her *death*. We must tread carefully from here on out, Evaline. We must watch over Miss Ashton very closely."

"I agree."

"As for your experience at the Pickled Nurse . . . It does seem to indicate, at the very least, the return of *La société*."

"And the vampires."

"Mm. Yes. I suppose one must accept that as well." Since Evaline's encounter with the vampire at the Oligary Building, I had reluctantly acknowledged the existence of the UnDead. But I wasn't at all ready to believe in spirit-talking and messages from beyond. That was simply ludicrous.

"Did you see Miss Adler?"

"Miss Adler? Where?"

"At New Vauxhall. I thought I saw her in the crowd of people after you were pulled out of the river. But if she didn't speak to you, I must have been mistaken."

"I would have noticed her. And surely she would have made herself known to me."

Or perhaps she wouldn't have. The lead ball that had settled in my belly since Vauxhall grew heavier. Perhaps Miss Adler had witnessed my debacle with the thief and agreed with the spectators. And Inspector Grayling, who'd called me bat-headed.

After all, when Miss Adler pressed me and Miss Stoker into service for the Crown, our mentor never indicated she expected us to engage in fighting and running and drawing attention to ourselves. At least, in public. And perhaps the princess had heard of my lack of decorum and was displeased. I pushed the worry away.

"I did, however, have the misfortune of encountering Lord and Lady Cosgrove-Pitt." That had been a moment of sheer mortification as I stood there with my hair dripping wet over my shoulders, required to be polite and deferential to the Parliamentary leader and his wife . . . the latter whom I had very nearly accused of being the murderous Ankh.

Not to mention that I was wearing the overlarge coat, complete with Metropolitan Police badge, that belonged to their distant relation. Fortunately, Lady Isabella hadn't seemed to notice.

"I'm not surprised. It seemed as if everyone in the upper crust of Society—and below—was at New Vauxhall Gardens last night."

The carriage stopped in front of Miss Ashton's home. As Evaline and I walked to the front door, it opened. This action was not due to our arrival, but the departure of a familiar gentleman—Dr. Norton.

"Sad business, Miss Geraldine, Herrell." The physician donned his hat. "Sorry to do it, but she needs protection."

Mr. Ashton appeared weary and resigned, and the spinster aunt leaned heavily against him as they bid Dr. Norton farewell. "I know. That's why I asked you to come. I knew I could trust you. Why, Miss Stoker! And Miss—er—Holmes."

Evaline exchanged glances with me. "Good morning, Mr. Ashton. We've come to visit Willa. Is everything all right?"

I had felt a prickle of unease when I saw Dr. Norton, and now it metamorphosed into apprehension. "Is she all right?"

Aunt Geraldine glanced from us to the physician, who tipped his hat and took his leave. "I'm afraid we've had another incident. Dr. Norton is quite concerned about my niece."

"Do lie down, Geraldine," Mr. Ashton said kindly. "This has been nearly as upsetting for you as it has been for Willa. I'll . . . see to our visitors."

"Thank you, Herrell, darling. I do think I shall go put a cold cloth on my forehead."

Aunt Geraldine went off and Mr. Ashton turned to us. "Willa is . . . a bit weary. I'm not certain she's in a condition to receive visitors."

I opened my mouth to argue, for I wasn't going to be dissuaded from seeing Miss Ashton. And apparently, Evaline was of the same mind. The change that came over her was amazing in its speed and effectiveness. Her face altered into one almost unrecognizable in its vacuousness: Her eyes widened and her lips parted slightly, and she gazed up at him as if he were the most fascinating individual on the earth.

"Oh, dear, Mr. Ashton." She placed herself directly in front of him, slipping a hand around his arm. Somehow she managed to manipulate him so we were facing the open door. "That's simply terrible news. I can't imagine how you all are holding up. But I'm certain you're being a solid rock for them both, aren't you?" She was very nearly batting her eyes at him, gazing up with large, thick-lashed hazel eyes. "Willa and Miss Kluger must truly rely on you and your strength to get them through this difficult time. But it all rests on your strong, broad shoulders."

I must admit, Evaline Stoker was quite brilliant in those moments.

I followed the two of them into the house as my partner murmured, "I'm certain you could use a moment of ease as well, Mr. Ashton. Perhaps a cup of tea, and you'll feel right as rain."

To my surprise, he agreed to this nonsensical suggestion and rang for a pot and some biscuits. Moments later, we were settled in the parlor and Evaline had made herself comfortable on the settee nearest Mr. Ashton's chair. He didn't seem to be at all put off by this development, for his knee was very close to my companion's skirt and he'd hardly looked in my direction. So much for concern about his cousin.

I could have asked about the incident, but I decided to leave that to Evaline. She seemed quite adept at extracting information from the man. I, on the other hand, wanted to speak to Willa uninterrupted.

Mr. Ashton didn't seem to notice when I excused myself, ostensibly to wash my hands. But Evaline gave me a wink as I stood, and I took it to mean she'd keep him occupied as long as possible.

Well taught by my uncle, I had committed the structure's floor plan to memory during my previous visits. I climbed the stairs, and once I arrived at the second floor, it wasn't difficult to determine which was Willa's chamber.

I ducked inside and closed the door, turning to face its occupant. "Don't make a sound. Your cousin and aunt don't know I'm here."

Willa's blue eyes were round with shock, but to my relief, they were clear and lucid. As I'd expected, she was propped in bed, golden hair falling about her shoulders and onto the pillow like a Rapunzel. The cat was settled on her lap, watching me with large, green eyes. Except for the dark gray circles under her own eyes, Willa Ashton appeared fragile and lovely. If Mr. Treadwell were the one to encounter her in this state, surely he would be even more charmed than he already was.

"Miss Holmes, thank goodness you're here." She was intelligent enough to keep her voice to a whisper, but I could hear the terror there. "I don't know what's happening to me."

"Please be calm. Evaline and I are on the case, and we aren't about to let anyone harm you."

"But what about me harming myself?" Her voice went a little high with hysteria, but she lowered it and swallowed. "I'm so glad you're here."

"Take a deep breath and tell me what's happened."

Her agitation eased. "There's a chair for you. Please sit." She gathered her cat closer, and I heard the rumble of its purr.

I observed the chamber. I wasn't surprised to see the ornate spiritglass sitting on a table in the corner. It was open, and its coppery-brass sides were folded back like a cogworked lotus blossom. The blue and green sphere sat in the middle, its colorful ribbonlike swirls moving as if alive inside.

Overall, the room was neat and clean, decorated with fine and expensive furnishings. Papered with pink and white flowers on green stripes, with frilly white curtains and a surprisingly soft cream-colored rug, her chamber was comfortable and inviting.

The dressing table was cluttered with earbobs, feathered hair combs, brooches, and small perfume vials. Lacy handkerchiefs, gloves, and silk stockings spilled from a drawer. Her large wardrobe was closed, but I suspected it held at least two dozen dresses.

Before I sat, I examined the papers next to the spirit-glass. I recognized one of them as the message Louisa Fenley had scrawled during the séance, purportedly from Willa's mother. The second paper had a similar message, presumably from a more recent séance. It read: *I cannot rest. Help me, Willa. I need you.*

The handwriting was identical to that from Miss Louisa's first séance, and was surely markedly different from the medium's normal penmanship. Nevertheless, I was certain she'd faked the "spirit writing." But again . . . what was the purpose? The only one I could deduce was to confuse, distract, and disorient Willa in an effort to have her eventually committed to a madhouse.

Someone who climbed onto a roof trying to catch her dead brother's soul with a fishing rod would appear well on her way to madness.

"Why did you go on the roof, Willa? Do you remember doing that?"

Her face turned pale as the sheets. "No. I didn't realize what was happening until I woke up . . . there. With the fishing pole. Way up there. I'm not even certain how I could have climbed up there." Her fingers trembled against the blanket and I felt a wave of sympathy for her. "And last night . . ."

"What happened last night?"

"I went to bed as usual . . . and the next thing I knew, I was. . . ." Her voice wobbled. "I was outside, standing in the street. In my *shift*. And . . . bare feet. I had a butterfly net with

me . . . apparently, I was trying to catch my mother's spirit."
Her voice broke. "This was just after dawn. A cog-cart nearly
ran me over. People were shouting and looking at me."

I schooled my expression, barely managing to keep from
displaying my shock. No wonder the doctor had been called.
"I see. And you don't know why or how you were prompted
to do such a thing?"

"No. I don't remember anything. And Dr. Norton was
here today for luncheon. He said he was stopping by to return
the gloves I loaned Amanda, but I know why he was really
here. Herrell and Aunt Geraldine . . . they're afraid I'm going
mad." Her breathing was rapid and shallow and her words
tumbled out. I feared she might hyperventilate or raise her
voice enough that we'd be heard. "And I begin to wonder if
it's true after all."

I understood her fears, and I certainly realized Willa's
precarious position. Thanks to the so-called Lunacy Law, it was
frighteningly simple to have an individual committed to a lunatic asylum. The opinions of a mere three persons were required
to send one to a madhouse: two physicians and one clergyman
or a magistrate. Any of whom could be bought or otherwise
manipulated as long as they signed the certificate—just as a
greedy, spirit-talking medium could be paid off to create an
environment where someone appeared to be going mad.

I'd never visited a sanatorium before, but I had heard
stories and read articles about the most famous one of course:
Bethlem Royal Hospital, better known as Bedlam.

It was not a place anyone wanted to be . . . especially the fragile, kind, *sane* young woman with whom I sat. I would *not* allow it to happen.

"I shan't lie to you, Miss Ashton. This is a grave situation. But Holmes and Stoker are on the job, and we have already made progress. I cannot imagine how frightening this must be for you. But I am quite certain you aren't going mad. In fact, I have the suspicion that you might have been mesmerized, and that is what is causing you to do these strange things like climbing on the roof."

"Mesmerized?"

"The more common term is hypnotized. Somehow, someone has learned to control your mind to have you do certain things—such as climb onto the roof with a fishing pole."

"Or wander into the street in the night in my shift?"

"Precisely. Usually, there is a signal that causes the mesmerized individual to go into a trance and conduct him or herself in the manner the hypnotist wishes. I must find out how and what that signal is. Once I determine how this hypnosis was done, I shall be that much closer to finding out who has done so." I peered at her closely. "Now, I must ask you another question. Should something happen to you, it's your understanding that your aunt receives your money. But what happens if she dies as well? Who would inherit her money?"

I could read the horror and disbelief in Willa's face as the implication of my questions sunk in. "First of all, Mina, Aunt Geraldine—she doesn't need my money. She has her own income, and it's quite comfortable. She doesn't need it, and she'd never do anything to hurt me. Never. And neither would Cousin Herrell."

"Who inherits if something happens to both you and your aunt?" I was already certain I knew the answer. "Is it your cousin?"

Willa nodded sadly. "Yes. Herrell would inherit. But *neither* of them—"

"The cold, unpleasant fact is, *someone* is trying to get rid of you. And they've either gotten rid of Robby as well, or they are taking advantage of his disappearance. He cannot be pronounced dead for at least two years after his disappearance, but I suspect the perpetrator isn't going to wait that long to get you out of the way. If you cannot think of anyone else who might want you . . . distracted, I must go with the facts."

I chose specifically not to mention Miss Norton. Not because I no longer suspected her—in fact, my suspicions were even more highly aroused now that I knew her brother was involved in Willa's potential incarceration—but because I thought it best to keep the idea of her marrying Mr. Treadwell out of the equation for the time being.

I had no patience for soothing lovelorn young women.

"Now, tell me more about these nighttime visitations from your mother. I've determined how the daytime séances have been faked, but I must turn my attention to the ones at night. When did they start? Before or after you began attending séances?"

"It was only a few days after Robby disappeared. I woke in the middle of the night and there was this greenish cloud in the corner of my chamber—there," she said, pointing toward the window. "I felt my mother's presence . . . I knew it was her. I wasn't nervous or frightened . . . and I *heard* her in my head. She told me 'Help Robby.' Over and over. It was after that happened, and after the strange dream I had about Robby, that I decided to conduct a séance."

"What strange dream about Robby? I don't believe you've mentioned it to me. Was this before or after he disappeared?" I tried to hide my frustration. How could I conduct an efficient investigation when I didn't have all the facts?

"After he disappeared. I dreamt I was walking through the streets at night, and I found him in a dark room with some of his friends. It was red and warm, and tiny fires, like fireflies, flitted around, burning everywhere. I felt . . . smothered. Everything was heavy and . . . I was sleepy . . . but it was so vivid. I can even remember the street . . . the buildings. It was nighttime. And there was a key hanging over me. Sort of floating. A big brass key, as big as my arm. Robby was so happy to see me. He wanted me to stay. But someone took me away. And then I woke up, in my bed. And . . . the strange thing is . . . my feet. They were dirty."

This had me straightening up sharply. "Your feet were dirty. Are you a somnambulist, Willa?"

"A what?"

"A somnambulist. A sleepwalker."

"No. At least, not until recently, when I climbed on a roof and walked out into the street."

This was not good news. Perhaps she had been mesmerized much earlier than I believed. The more information I obtained, the further I seemed to be from a solution.

"Very well, then," I said. "With your permission, I shall spend the night in your bedchamber to see if your mother will pay us a visit . . . or to keep you from leaving your bed in some new and dangerous fashion. Only then will I be able to determine how the trick is happening."

Willa's eyes glistened and she reached for my hand, grasping it tightly. The cat, disrupted by this activity, glared at me and then leapt off the bed. "Thank you, Mina. I know I shall feel safe with you here."

"You cannot tell a soul that I intend to be here. *Not one person.*" I aimed a forefinger at her. "For if there is a mortal presence behind these Para-Natural happenings, we cannot take the risk they might be forewarned. Promise me you'll tell absolutely no one. Including your maid."

"You have my word. On my mother's soul, I swear it." That presence of mind was back in her expression, and I was satisfied. "But how will you get in here with no one the wiser?"

"I have a plan." I rose from my chair and patted her cold hand. "Miss Ashton, you may expect me tonight at approximately half-past eight. Here, in this very chamber."

# MISS HOLMES

## A Sandwich Purloined

Upon returning to my home after the morning's interview with Miss Ashton, I settled into my chair in the library to think . . . and to knit. The rhythmic clicking and rote, familiar movements of wrapping yarn and sliding needles was my favorite way to relax and allow my thoughts to wander.

Uncle Sherlock played the violin when he was contemplating the intricacies of a case. My father whittled chess pieces. Thanks to my mother's influence, I knitted.

However, I'd hardly managed an arm's length of hand-knitting when Mrs. Raskill interrupted me. She was holding a dark wool coat with a badge on it. "Land o' stars, where'd you come upon this, Miss Mina? It looks like a real police badge."

Drat. I'd forgotten about Grayling's coat. "I have to return that today." I wasn't looking forward to seeing the blasted Scot again, but at least it would give me the opportunity to find out if he'd made any progress on the Yingling case—which could help in my contemplation.

Still, I couldn't dismiss the memories of him tearing my corset away and calling me a bat-headed woman—which infuriated and mortified me in turn.

"Well, I've brushed it all out and shined up the badge anyway." Mrs. Raskill ducked back out. "There was a loose button I sewed, and fixed the bit of a droop to the hem too. Coat's several years old, but it's some wear left in it."

"That was very kind," I called toward the closing door. "Thank you."

The clock on the mantel cranked to life, its cogs and gears spinning with alacrity as it announced the noon hour. If I was going to finish the preparations for tonight's excursion to Miss Ashton's bedchamber as well as make a visit to the Met, I must be on my way.

A short time later, I walked into the station of the Metropolitan Police, also known as Scotland Yard. A new building was currently being constructed, but as I well knew, the Criminal Investigation Department was still housed here. It was a matter of moments before I found myself approaching the office assigned to Inspector Grayling and his partner, Inspector Luckworth.

I'm certain one could understand my slight hesitation before announcing myself at the open door. I might even have changed my mind and left the coat with one of the clerks at the front of the office if not for the sudden familiar yip.

Drat. *Angus.*

The canine creature burst out of the office, leash trailing, ears flopping, mechanized leg clattering. He barked up at me, dancing around excitedly, trouncing my hems and shoes and pawing at my skirt. As it was one of my favorites (a cobalt-blue overskirt with a complementary black, blue, and maroon bodice, trimmed with jet beads and tiny pearls), I pushed him away in dismay. Yet I found it difficult to resist the big brown eyes and sloppy, happy tongue of the energetic pup. Despite my misgivings, I bent to pet him.

"Nice boy." I neatly avoided his enthusiastic licking and frantic paws. "Good boy." Now that I was looking at him in the full light, I could see his leg had been amputated at the middle joint. The mechanized limb replaced the lower part of his leg, but a cogged contraption enclosed and protected the upper part where it fit onto his haunch. I could hardly believe the pup had healed so quickly in a week's time.

"Miss Holmes."

Angus's master stood in the doorway. The expression on his face was a cross between chagrin and surprise.

"Good afternoon, Inspector Grayling," I said crisply, straightening up. "I've come to return your coat." I thrust the article of clothing at him, feeling awkward and uncertain.

He cleared his throat and accepted the garment. "Thank you." His cheeks appeared slightly ruddy as his attention swept over me.

I did the same to him, noting that he'd recently changed shaving lotion scents, ridden his steamcycle this morning in lieu of the Underground, and had purchased new shoes within the last day or two. He'd also had his thick auburn hair trimmed.

"It's brushed and the badge polished. And the button fixed as well. That's very thoughtful of you, Miss Holmes." He hung the coat on a hook inside the door.

"I'll pass on your gratitude to Mrs. Raskill. It was her doing," I confessed. "I see Angus has been availing himself of your hospitality by gnawing on your footwear."

"Oh, aye. The little menace seems to prefer the taste of my leather boots to the beef bones I give him to chew. I've had to buy two new pairs since the little boyo took over my house." Despite his words, Grayling seemed unaware when the menace in question flopped on the ground and began to sharpen his puppy teeth on the edge of his new boots.

"Erm . . . Inspector." I gestured to the little devil.

"Angus, nay there." He reached down to snatch up the dog. Ears flopped and a tongue swiped out, catching Grayling along his firm, square chin. "Little beastie."

"I've also come to see if you've made any progress in the investigation of Mrs. Yingling's murder." I pulled my attention from the dog and his enthusiastic affection for his master. Poor creature had no idea how misguided he was.

"Ah, the ulterior motive is revealed." Grayling set Angus back down. "Well, you might as well come in."

I stepped over the threshold into the office. It was immediately clear which workspace was Grayling's and which belonged to Inspector Luckworth. The latter was absent at the moment, but his desk was obvious, for it showcased cluttered stacks of papers, broken pencils and their shavings, a handheld magnifying glass, notepads, two cups, and, most telling of all, the childish drawing of a stick figure wearing a too-large badge and a too-small hat.

Grayling's work area was just as strewn with paper piles, but on his desk was an automated Ink-Stipper for refilling writing implements, the newest model of Mr. Kodak's camera, a stack of books (one of which I recognized as the excellent *Gray's Anatomy*), and a small wooden case that likely contained some sort of gadget. I also noticed an efficient-looking Ocular-Magnifyer, as well as a slick mechanized measuring device I immediately coveted. Next to the desk were a number of photographs tacked onto a wallboard.

Intrigued, I walked over to look at the board and was pleasantly surprised to find a collection of images from none other than Mrs. Yingling's rooms. Aside from the photographs, Grayling had included sketches of the room layout, as well as a draft of the position in which the body had been found. There was also a picture of what appeared to be a fingerprint.

"What is this?"

Grayling's cheeks became slightly more ruddy. "It's my case-wall. I find it easier to study and make observations when the information is spread out in front of me."

What a fascinating way to display the elements of an investigation. I was entranced.

"He stares at it for hours on end, he does," came a voice behind us. "Waste of time, I say, all those photographs and measurements. Good afternoon, Miss Holmes."

I turned to see Inspector Luckworth. He carried two paper-wrapped sandwiches (which immediately caught Angus's attention) and a new cup of something steaming. Coffee, from the smell. His gait was even, which indicated he'd finally taken my previous advice and had his mechanical hip adjusted— although he clearly hadn't changed his habit of trying to shave in the dim light of morning rather than lighting a lamp.

"Hello, Inspector Luckworth," I said. "Wife's been away to the Brighton shore for a few weeks, I see. Taken the children with her too, I presume."

"What? Hm? How did you know that?" He looked around as if to see the ghost of his wife or some other specter standing behind him, giving me the information.

I gestured to his desk. "The postmarked envelope from Hove and its accompanying letter signed 'All my love, Bettina' was the clue. Along with the small finger smudges on the paper itself. It appears your children are very fond of toffees."

Luckworth mumbled something about cheeky young ladies and unceremoniously dropped Grayling's sandwich on his desk. "Don't know why you're wasting your time with that Bertillon bloke's ideas." He settled into his chair with an ominous creak. "And now you're all worked up about that Doctor Frauds and *his* harebrained schemes. Detective work's not about photographs and measurements. It's 'bout long hours, lots of talking to people and tracking blokes down, and paperwork. Lots of blooming paperwork."

Clearly, that was Luckworth's biggest complaint.

I slid a glance at Grayling, whose mouth had tightened at his partner's diatribe. "Dr. *Faulds* has a sensible theory that fingerprints can be used to identify people," he replied evenly. "There's no harm in beginning to build a collection of them, ye ken, if I choose to spend my own time and resources on it?" The fact that his Scottish brogue had become more pronounced seemed to indicate his rising irritation.

Then, as if recalling I was still present and witness to this exchange, Grayling turned to me. "Miss Holmes, as you can see, I've not forgotten about the unfortunate Mrs. Yingling. Chloroform was found in her body, confirming our suspicions that she was, indeed, murdered. Poisoned. And at this time, it's my belief the murderer was an individual—most likely a man—approximately five feet, eight inches tall. His hair is medium brown and he—or she—is presumably of the upper class, and with a fairly athletic ability, for as you are aware the perpetrator entered or exited from the window. And the perpetrator was in Mayfair within twenty-four hours of the violent event taking place."

"Indeed." I confess, I was a bit taken aback by Grayling's certainty. He sounded uncomfortably like my uncle.

"And, of course, you would already be aware that he is right-handed." Now there was the most subtle note of triumph in his voice.

"Indeed," I replied. "But there are countless upper-class men with brown hair of that height in the city."

"I don't argue that. But I have a copy of the culprit's fingerprint, which, despite my partner's rude comments, could be matched to a suspect, should we identify him."

"Or her."

"Or her." Grayling nodded. "Precisely. And as poison is generally the tool of a woman, one must keep all options open. It would have been no trouble for even a slight woman to overcome the frail Mrs. Yingling with a rag soaked in chloroform."

Luckworth made a snorting sort of noise that would never have been accepted in polite company. "You can 'ave your fingerprints and measurements, 'Brose, but I'll stick with old-fashioned, handmaker ways. We'll see who finds the culprit first."

At that moment, an energetic rustling caught my attention. "Oh, no, Angus!"

The recalcitrant pup had sneaked Grayling's sandwich from the desk and was now tearing into its paper.

"Angus, ye blooming beast!" The ginger-haired detective lunged and managed to save most of his sandwich, but I suspected he'd find puppy bite-marks in the bread anyway. "*This* is for you, ye nogginhead." He picked up a bone from the floor and gave it to the pup. Angus sniffed at it, then crawled under the desk with his prize. He looked out at us with a woe-begone expression, then began to gnaw on his treat.

"Very well then, Inspector. I appreciate your information and would like to add some of my own." I went on to tell him what I'd learned about the dirt sample from Miss Ashton's front porch. "Therefore, the list of suspects is rather more limited than you might have believed."

"Thank you, Miss Holmes," he said. "That is very help-ful information. I shall take it under advisement and compare my measurements with the list of individuals who visited the Ashton household."

"Very well, then. I'll be on my way." I started toward the door.

"Miss Holmes."

I turned to discover Grayling in my wake. As always, I found it irritating to have to look so far up to meet his eyes. "Yes?"

"I'll escort you out." I lifted my brows in surprise, and he added quickly, "There are always unsavory characters being brought in here. I'd hate for you to encounter one."

"I see." I didn't, quite, but I wasn't about to make a scene with Luckworth as witness, despite the fact that the older inspector seemed quite involved with his ham and ched-dar sandwich. Angus, for his part, had emerged from exile under the desk. He was delighted with the shower of crumbs from the crusty bread.

"I trust you came through the activities of the other evening with no ill effects," said Grayling as we walked down the corridor together.

"None whatsoever."

"The injury on your arm?"

"A mere glancing blow. And you?"

"None at all, of course."

We walked several more paces in silence, then he added, "And I trust your party wasn't completely disrupted by your unexpected bathing in the river?"

"No. Not at all."

"I see you haven't given up consorting with that questionable young man," Grayling said. "Dylan Eckhert? An American and a likely thief."

I glanced at up him but held my tongue. Grayling knew Dylan as an intruder who'd attempted to break into the British Museum, and clearly remembered my part in releasing him from prison. He didn't know, of course, that Dylan was an American from the twenty-first century. "The charges against him were dropped."

"Aye, they were." His response was so bland as to imply his disappointment with that occurrence.

We'd reached the main entrance to the building, and I was prepared to walk outside and be on my way. "Thank you for your time, Inspector Grayling. And for the use of your coat."

He looked down at me and all at once I was reminded of that moment two nights ago, when his powerful hands pulled away my corset. Considering the fact that it was an extremely well-constructed garment, with slender leather thongs threaded through metal grommets stitched firmly into the boned satin, it must have taken great strength to rip it apart. My face heated and I was aware of a strange, rolling pitch in my lower belly.

"Miss Holmes." His voice carried an odd note. "I— er . . . what you did, chasing that thief, I thought was quite— heroic. Foolish, you understand, but heroic nonetheless."

I blinked, stunned and yet piqued at the same time. Before I could respond, he gave a brief bow. "Good day, Miss Holmes. Do attempt to keep yourself from any other foolish situations."

Then he spun on his heel and walked away.

# MISS STOKER

## An Unexpected Arrival

After speaking with Miss Ashton in her bedchamber, Mina went home. She claimed she needed to *knit*, of all things. I couldn't imagine anything more unlikely than cognoggin Mina Holmes making a sweater . . . except for Mina Holmes staking a vampire. I snickered, envisioning her lecturing the UnDead to death.

In Mina's absence, I was charged with watching over Miss Ashton. "I don't want her out of your sight," my partner ordered.

The only problem was I'd promised Florence I'd go shopping with her today.

She'd greeted me when I left in the morning. "The Opening Night Ball is on Sunday. That's only three days! And as much as I prefer to have custom-made gowns, *you're* going to have to settle for a ready-made ensemble, I fear, unless we get very lucky with Madame today."

I hadn't much choice but to agree to accompany Florence on the long-awaited shopping trip. But, as much as Mina Holmes might think otherwise, I'm not a fool. I was fully aware of the danger Miss Ashton was in, and that she couldn't be left unguarded.

Thus, as soon as I mentioned Willa Ashton's young, single cousin Herrell, with whom I'd walked through Vauxhall, Florence was delighted to include Miss Ashton in our excursion. So, I invited Willa to come shopping with us—and the girl agreed enthusiastically, despite her aunt's insistence she stay in bed.

Willa looked slightly better than she had earlier this morning but still had dark circles under her eyes. However, she was stylishly dressed, her hair coiffed and cream gloves spotless. She sparkled with excitement at the prospect of a day out.

We spent a pleasant afternoon shopping. Willa seemed to have forgotten her worries, and she and Florence got on well together. It was after six-thirty when we arrived back at the Ashton home, and Willa was kind enough to invite Florence and me in for a small supper.

Aunt Geraldine, who joined our meal, was perfectly lovely and charming. She regaled us with stories about her youth spent on the Continent, including summers in Rome and Greece and a short term of study at university in Paris. The clock was striking seven forty-five by the time we finished our meal. Mr. Herrell Ashton, however, made no appearance.

Mina wasn't due to arrive until eight-thirty. I couldn't think of any further reason to delay returning home with

Florence, and it was close enough to her arrival that I thought Willa would be safe if I left my post. I also hoped that if I kept my sister-in-law away from home late enough into the evening, she'd get ready for bed upon our return and I'd be able to sneak back out.

I was going hunting tonight.

However, I delayed as long as possible, even though Florence was making signals behind Willa's back for me to hurry. There was always the chance that the eligible Mr. Ashton might appear, which would delight my sister-in-law and could keep us there for another fifteen minutes to ensure Willa's safety. But that didn't happen.

We were standing on the front porch making plans for another shopping trip when a delivery carriage drove up behind my own vehicle and parked. I hardly noticed the tall delivery man as he carried his parcel to the servants' entrance at the rear of the house, for I was scanning the street in hopes of another carriage appearing. Namely that of Mina Holmes.

All at once a carriage came barreling around the corner. As it trundled down the street, passing the delivery wagon and my carriage, I heard a loud boom.

Something light and sparkling erupted in the air, and smoke billowed. Willa shrieked, Florence gasped, and I spun, looking around. An accident? Not blooming likely.

I dashed off the front porch, watching for anything that could be considered a threat. People came rushing out of nearby houses. The carriage had disappeared down the street, but a bulky item sat in the middle of the road, left behind by the speeding vehicle. Middy leapt from his seat in my carriage, and I joined him in the middle of the road. The large item was smoldering and looked like a bundle of clothing.

"Stand back! It might explode," I ordered.

But neighbors gathered in the yard and street. Middy and I, as well as one of the Ashton footmen, approached the bundle. The footman had brought a pitchfork, and I held my breath as he poked the dark object.

Nothing happened. He poked it again, using the pitchfork to open what appeared to be nothing more than a wad of cloaks and blankets.

It continued to smolder, and though I looked around, I neither saw nor felt evidence of a threat. No vampiric chill. No villainous figure lurking in the shadows. This would be just the sort of thing Pix would do to attract my attention. Hadn't he done so just last week in order to climb into my carriage?

But I wasn't taking any chances. The gawkers eased away, and I turned to Willa. "Let's go back inside for a moment."

The delivery carriage pulled out from behind my vehicle, and Middy waved as he took his place back in the driver's seat. Meanwhile, the helpful groom had poked the dark wad into a flat mass that smelled like smoke but no longer flamed.

I turned to Florence. "I left my gloves inside. I'll be right back. You can get settled in the carriage."

Still alert, I went back inside with Willa. Aunt Geraldine and the servants who'd come out to see the commotion followed us.

"I believe I left my gloves in the parlor," I said, walking quickly in that direction. I managed to check in every chamber on the way there. Nothing seemed off. When the gloves weren't found in the parlor, nor in the dining room, I said, "I must have brought them up to your chamber when you showed me your new earbobs, Willa."

She seemed startled at the idea, but after my impatient gesture, she led the way. As we approached, I sensed someone within. I stopped, holding out a hand to stop her beyond the door, and I peered into the room.

Just as I thought. It was the delivery boy. He stood at the window, looking out into the growing darkness. But he was too slight to be Pix.

"And what have we here?" I stepped into the chamber. Willa gasped behind me, and I shook off her grip. "Stay back," I warned just as the clock struck half-past eight.

When I heard the sound of the chimes, I stopped. Then I began to chuckle ruefully and gestured for Willa to join me inside the room.

The delivery boy, who was rather tall and slender, turned from the window. He swept off his cap and shucked his coat, then peeled off a false chin and pug nose.

"Good evening, Miss Ashton. Evaline. I trust you had an enjoyable supper?"

# MISS HOLMES

*Wherein Miss Holmes Becomes Chilled*

O nce Miss Ashton recovered from my unexpected appearance, she found the same humor in the situation as Miss Stoker did. They both plied me with questions.

"So it was just a pile of old blankets in the street?"

"I had to ensure everyone would run from the house at the same time, so I could remain inside, and unnoticed after my delivery. My uncle executed a similar plan when he was engaged in the Adler-Bohemian king case. It worked quite well, although the circumstances were very different."

"And you arranged for the man in the carriage to drop those blankets and set off a small explosion—"

"Just at the precise moment. I didn't know you'd be standing on the porch, but that simply made it all the more successful."

Evaline was fidgeting. "Florence is waiting in the carriage. I'm leaving. Good luck tonight."

"What do you have planned—" I began, but she slipped out before I could finish my sentence. I wondered what she had up her sleeve.

Nevertheless, there was nothing I could do about Evaline and her tendency to hare off on adventures without taking the necessary precautions, so I turned my attention to the more pressing matter of examining the bedchamber.

Once I assured myself Miss Ashton's room was free of any devices or mechanisms, I settled into a chair behind the dressing screen to wait.

I had instructed Willa to act normal as the remainder of the evening progressed. She was also to keep her maid from going behind the screen and—if possible—to keep her from the chamber as much as she could. It wasn't that I suspected the maid. I simply wanted to ensure that no one except Willa knew I was in the house.

I'd purchased more yarn during my travels today, and now I sat, needles clicking quietly, and contemplated. Grayling's description of the murder suspect in the Yingling situation both helped and hindered some of my theories. Unfortunately, the physical characteristics fit all the main suspects I'd been considering—Aunt Geraldine, Cousin Herrell, and the Nortons—either one or both of them. His information did, however, eliminate the black-haired, taller Mr. Treadwell, and the light-haired and shorter Miss Fenley.

I knitted faster, mulling over Grayling's final words to me. *Heroic. Foolish, but heroic.*

Was that meant to be some sort of apology? My needles flashed and clicked as I remembered the way he looked down at me, standing in the corridor at Scotland Yard.

I realized my ball of yarn was finished and I had a long, narrow swath of . . . something. So I dug out a second ball and kept knitting.

Tomorrow, I intended to visit Louisa Fenley again. I meant to confront her about her quackery and use that as leverage to wrest further information from her—namely, whether she'd been hired to fool Miss Ashton. I also believed Miss Fenley's skills could be of great use to me in my investigations.

"Good night, Mina," Willa murmured just loud enough for me to hear. She was finally ready for bed. "Thank you for being here."

I stepped out from behind the screen, still holding my yarn. The cat eyed me from her post on Willa's bed, blinking once. "Sleep well. If something happens, I urge you to simply act as you normally do. Don't call out to me or acknowledge my presence in any way."

"I won't." She turned out the lamp. I heard her rustling under the covers, and then silence.

I moved the dressing screen aside so I could see the moonlit window—which remained open to an unusually balmy summer night—and the closed door, and I could also watch Willa's bed. Then I settled back in my seat and continued with my knitting and my contemplations.

The house settled into silence around us. Sometime later, a clock struck midnight. And then half-past.

Herrell Ashton—*deeply in debt, currently controls the finances and could eventually inherit. Encourages Willa's séance experiments. Close friends with Dr. Norton. Easy access to household.*

Aunt Geraldine—*would inherit Willa's money. Easiest access to the household and séance chamber. Does not encourage Willa's spirit-talking.*

Amanda Norton and/or Dr. Norton—*A match between Amanda and James Treadwell was desirable. The doctor would be an excellent resource for committing Willa to a madhouse, thus getting the rival out of the way for a romance between Amanda and Mr. Treadwell.*

Was there a money issue for the Nortons? What was their financial situation like? Did Mr. Treadwell have wealth to bring to a match? I realized I needed to consult the *Kimball's*.

The clock struck two.

Willa sat up suddenly.

I immediately put down my knitting. I wasn't certain if she'd seen or heard something or had awakened for some other reason.

A sound caught my attention. A soft whirring, the faintest buzz. . . . I discerned a faint blue light emitting from the corner of the chamber.

Willa climbed out of bed and walked toward the blue glow, which grew brighter by the moment. She clearly wasn't aware of her surroundings, and I knew better than to wake someone who was engaged in the act of sleep-walking.

I crept behind her, careful not to touch her or move into her line of sight, but nearby for protection.

The blue light was coming from the spiritglass.

The sides had folded away to fully reveal the orb. What had once been dull and subdued was now bright and illuminated, emitting an eerie blue-green light. Willa picked up a paper from the table next to the spiritglass. Standing just behind her, I could see writing on the paper. *Glowing writing.*

Ghostly writing.

No . . . it was writing that could only be seen by the odd light of the spiritglass. I had to force myself to remain still and silent, but my fingers wanted nothing more than to snatch the note away from her. Willa shuffled through several papers on the table, papers that were from Miss Fenley's ghostly spirit writings. Or so the medium would have us believe. Now I had another reason to visit her tomorrow.

Then Willa made a huff of disappointment or frustration and turned. Still silent, she passed by me as she walked back to her bed. I'd been prepared to follow her if she left her bedchamber, but to my relief that wasn't necessary. She clambered back into bed and I caught a glimpse of her wide, vacant eyes, shining in the eerie blue light. The cat, who'd awakened during this episode but declined to move from his spot, glared at me as if it were my fault his sleep was disturbed.

As soon as Willa lay back down and settled into place, I moved silently to the table. The light continued to glow and

I was able to read the words written on the papers. An ugly shiver trailed down my spine as I read:

*You must help Robby by catching his spirit, Willa. Climb onto the high tower with his old fishing pole. Cast out for him and bring him home, tomorrow night when the clock strikes eight. Don't be frightened. I'll be there if you should fall.*

A second paper said:

*Come swimming with Robby in your shift, Willa, like when you were little. Bring the butterfly net so you can catch him and bring him with you. He'll be waiting for you in the street at the next stroke of five. Come and save him.*

The other papers were blank, likely explaining Willa's disappointment. No new "messages" from her brother.

I allowed the notes to settle back onto the table, but not before confirming they were the same ones Miss Fenley had written on during the séances.

Now the plot was becoming clearer. Someone had written on these papers in ink only visible under this light, and then Louisa Fenley used the papers during her séance. I could see even in the odd light that the black ink had been written over the invisible ink. And that the handwriting was completely different.

The question was: Did the medium know about the secret message, or was she an unwitting dupe?

My second question—how did Willa know to wake up at two o'clock?—was more easily answered. I'd been searching for the key to her mesmerization, and the clock striking two was obviously it.

I settled back in my chair and picked up my knitting. In spite of the late hour, I was still wide awake and my brain clicked along as quickly as my needles.

The blue light from the spiritglass faded after several moments, and the clock struck two-thirty. Three o'clock. Four.

The night was dead and dark. My needles shone for brief moments when caught by the slender bit of moon shining through the window. I was onto a third ball of yarn.

And then something in the room changed.

It grew chilly. Cold.

The curtains fluttered near the window, but the shift in the air wasn't coming from there. It was just . . . *here*. All around. My heart pounding, I put down my knitting and sat up straight, looking around.

My nose was cold, and when I gusted out a breath of nervous air, I could see the mist. My palms grew clammy. I looked over at Willa. She was still sleeping, but the cat was up and awake, its eyes wide. The moonlight outlined the hair rising all along the feline's spine.

Goose bumps had erupted over my arms and other extremities. My breath was coming in faster, white puffs. The cat hissed, his back arched. He was staring at something near the window.

I looked over and my mouth went completely dry. A glowing, amorphous cloud had formed at the window. It was tinged bright green, and as I watched, it billowed into the chamber, expanding into a column in front of the window.

Now it was *freezing* in the room.

I heard a sound from the bed, rustling among the sheets. Willa sat up. The cat hissed again next to her. Its green eyes reflected wide and angry in the dim light.

"Mother!"

I wouldn't have been able to speak even if I wanted to. I could only stare in disbelief. Willa slipped from the bed, fully awake and lucid—unlike earlier.

"You've come back!" She stood in front of the green gas, which had formed into a sort of cylinder shape.

Willa tilted her head as if to listen. Then after a moment she spoke earnestly. "I've been trying, Mother. But I can't find him. I'll keep trying, I promise. I'll bring him safely to you. I want you two to be together."

The green cloud spiraled into itself once more, this time, becoming smaller and smaller, and then wisped away into nothing. The tiny light remained for a moment longer, then winked out.

We were alone. The night was dark once again. The chamber returned to its normal temperature.

I realized I was holding my breath, and when I expelled it, I saw it was no longer white with frost.

"Did you see that?" Willa whispered. Until that moment, I hadn't been completely certain she was awake and aware. But her direct question, and the fact that her eyes clearly met mine, indicated her lucidity.

I nodded, not quite trusting my voice. When I stood, my knees were shaky and my fingers trembled. I went to the window, touching it, smoothing my fingers all around, hoping to find . . . something. Some sort of clue. But I had already examined it earlier. There was nothing there. No dirt, no warmth from a human body or mechanism, no disturbance.

Most telling of all: The four taut lines of invisible thread I'd strung across the opening were still in place.

Nothing solid had passed through that window. Whatever it was had been as insubstantial as air.

I must have dozed off in my chair in Miss Ashton's bedchamber, although after the events of the night, I wasn't certain how I'd ever quieted my mind enough to actually sleep.

But the bright sun streaming through her window woke me, and I straightened in my seat. A glance at Willa told me she still slumbered heavily.

I rose and stretched from many hours in the chair, then caught sight of the cat. He lounged on the bed, licking a paw as if nothing untoward had happened in this room.

But something had. Even I could no longer deny that something inexplicable, something otherworldly and Para-Natural had occurred.

The most telling fact was that the cat had reacted strongly to the green gaseous cloud. Common belief indicated animals were extremely sensitive to supernatural events and occurrences. This feline certainly had done so.

And then there was the indisputable fact that the room had gone ice-cold in a matter of seconds, and then returned to warmth just as quickly. I knew even physics didn't allow for such drastic swings in temperature. Even a machine couldn't cause such radical changes. One would feel the breeze. But last night . . . there'd been no such movement.

It just happened.

I swallowed hard. The thought that some supernatural, otherworldly *presence* had been here last night made me physically ill. Some entity that couldn't be explained by physics or logic or mathematics or science.

It was unbelievable.

It was disruptive . . . and a little frightening.

I collected my thoughts and exhaled long and slow. I'd mull over it later. Perhaps an explanation would occur to me then.

For now, I had to figure out how someone had mesmerized Willa Ashton, and who was trying to get rid of her. The first thing was to determine the origin of the curious instrument, and how it came to be in Willa's possession.

I wandered over to the spiritglass. It had spontaneously illuminated last night. Surely it had had some assistance, some hidden mechanism. A timer.

I admired its decorative lotus-flowerlike sides, noticing how they folded open to reveal the glass itself. The small orb, nestled among cogs and gears, was smooth and cool to the touch. It was this sphere that had shone with the blue light.

I picked up the sphere and realized for the first time it had been set upon a trio of three short metal spikes which appeared to affix the orb to its case. Perhaps those tiny metal flanges were the source of power for its illumination. Upon turning the sphere over, I noticed a design stamped on the bottom. Like the signature of the artist. No surprise the individual who'd created this fantastic device would have wanted to mark his—or her—work.

Bringing the spiritglass into the bright morning sun for closer examination, I caught my breath when I recognized the ornate *CB* marking on the bottom.

I had seen that identifying mark, and recently.

At the Charles Babbage display at the Oligary Building.

# Miss Stoker

## *To Kick Some Ash*

By the time Florence and I got home from Willa's house and I pretended to go to bed, it was nearly ten. Then I waited another hour before I felt sure my sister-in-law was asleep. Bram was at the Lyceum, of course, and wouldn't be home until at least two o'clock.

Thus, there was no one to notice when I climbed out my window and down the oak tree that shaded it.

Thanks to Pepper, who actually *did* know I was leaving, I was well equipped. Dressed in very wide trousers that looked like a skirt, I also wore a black feminine bodice that buttoned down the front. The decorative loops of satin at the hemline of the corsetlike top were large enough to hold stakes, a knife, and a small, ladylike pistol. I pulled on fingerless gloves and had my unruly hair pinned up in a smooth figure-eight bun. No stakes in my coiffure tonight, either, for they were all easy to reach at my waist.

At Pepper's insistence, I had another dagger slipped inside my tall boot, as well as a vial of salted holy water in the other. Over my bodice, I wore a large silver cross on a chain, and Pepper had also pinned two more in my hair.

*Vampires beware*, I thought as I alighted from a horseless taxi near Pristin Canal, two streets from the Pickled Nurse. *You're about to meet your end.*

Conscious of my invincibility, I walked boldly down the street, weaving among clusters of people on their way to a pub, dinner-house, or music hall.

I was stronger than any man and gifted with speed and skill. I had slain my first UnDead and proven my worthiness as a vampire hunter. I had a legacy to fulfill.

Woe to he who got in my way.

A chill filtered over the nape of my neck and I smiled grimly. UnDead nearby.

I sharpened my attention on each man and woman as I approached and passed them, measuring the sensation on the back of my neck.

The cool warning grew stronger as I neared a trio of men standing in front of an establishment called Ivey & Boles. A massive cogwork key dangled from the sign over their heads, which caused me to wonder if the place was a locksmith or some other metal-working business. The three talked and gestured, blocking the walkway to other passersby.

I slid a stake from one of the loops at my waist. One of the men had to be an UnDead, for the evil chill was growing fiercer and sharper as I approached. But they stood so close together, I couldn't tell which one.

As I drew nearer, I noticed a small, lithe shadow detach itself from the alley behind the trio. I thought nothing of it until one of the men clapped a hand to his long overcoat and spun. "Stop! Thief! Stop!"

He and his companions whirled, stumbling after the boy. But the small figure had already darted into the shadows and was immediately lost in the alley.

I could have chased the pickpocket and easily brought him to task, but I wasn't going to be distracted from my true mission. My destiny was a bigger, more dangerous prize than a street urchin who needed a silk handkerchief to sell for food.

The three men gave up their half-hearted chase after one of them tripped in the dark throughway and fell on his knees in a pool of sludge. They gathered on the street again as they turned out their pockets in turn. It appeared more than one of them had had his pocket lightened by the quick-fingered thief.

But now that I was right next to them, I realized my warning chill had evaporated.

*Blast it.* The prickling at the back of my neck had gone, and so had the UnDead.

Growling to myself, I continued along the street. Turning down the alley to Nickel's, I headed toward the Pickled Nurse. I felt an occasional chill during this patrol of sorts as I paced along the street in front of the pub, but

I was still too inexperienced to know whether it was really an UnDead. So I looked for glowing red eyes, but even that strategy didn't reveal any vampires.

By the time the clock struck two, I was frustrated. Either I was wrong about *La société* and vampires being in this area, or they simply weren't out and about tonight.

Nevertheless, I wasn't ready to return home. I was still spoiling for a fight. After all, that was what I was born to do. Not to sit back and contemplate clues, concoct theories, and make deductions. And *knit*.

No. I was meant to *do*. To seek out danger, to fight for life and safety, and to risk my own skin for others.

And so I headed to Spitalfields.

Though it was only a couple hours till dawn, Fenmen's End was loud, crowded, and as brightly lit as that establishment ever was. Which wasn't saying much.

I pushed open the doors and looked over the crowd, hoping to see Pix. Or at least Big Marv. Maybe he'd give me some grief for twisting his fingers, and I'd have an excuse for a good fight.

Of course, after Pix's appearance and disappearance in Vauxhall without a word to me, I could probably just as easily spar with him. I still didn't understand why he'd been so dark and cold that night. And I was annoyed that he'd vanished without a trace.

This time, I chose not to make a grand entrance and no one seemed to notice me. In the back, a group wagered over two men arm wrestling, but neither of the contestants was Pix. Several tables boasted dice or cards, and there was another where the patrons pressed in around a tiny wind-up dog that sprang up and then plopped into a small glass of golden liquid. The dog was removed and the patron drank to raucous cheering. It seemed to be some sort of game.

I made my way up to the far side of the bar. As usual, Bilbo was behind it and he recognized me right away.

"Where's Pix?"

"Dunno."

"Is he in his lair?"

Bilbo shrugged. "Oy'm not the bloke's keeper, missy."

A distinct chill filtered over the back of my neck. I whirled toward the entrance to see the man who'd just walked in. Tall, fair-skinned, pierce-eyed, and reeking of malevolence.

An UnDead.

This time, I had no doubt.

I was about to slide off my stool when I noticed Pix making his way across the pub. Where the blazes had he come from?

He went directly to the vampire and greeted him at the door. They seemed to know each other, or at least have some business, for the two launched into intent conversation.

"'Ere 'e be," said Bilbo helpfully.

"Don't tell him I'm here." I dove off my stool, then slipped around to the edge of the bar. "If you say a word, I'll break your fingers."

"Bleedin' darly-'eaded female." Bilbo stomped to the other end of the counter as I peered out from my hiding place.

Suddenly, Pix and the vampire turned and went out of the pub. Pix led the way, but the vampire seemed to be right on his heels. I didn't like that development. It felt wrong. Pix wasn't the sort to turn his back to anyone, let alone a man as evil as that vampire.

Pix was in danger. Perhaps he'd even been enthralled.

I scooted from behind the bar and threaded my way across the pub. I was just about to the door when a meaty hand landed on my shoulder. It was accompanied by a familiar, gad-awful stench.

"*You.*" Big Marv hadn't brushed his teeth or shaved, and he certainly hadn't bathed since I'd seen him last.

All at once, I was flying backward. I crashed into one of the building's support beams near the edge of the room. The stake fell from my grip and rolled across the floor. Pain radiated through my hip and along my arm where I'd landed, and the wind was knocked out of me.

I sprang to my feet, fumbling the knife out of my boot. Once I had a grip, I showed it to Marv. "You don't want to be touching me because I don't want to have to hurt you again. Pix won't like it."

He merely laughed, and the stench of his breath was nearly enough to have me on my knees.

I glanced toward the pub door, aching and a little out of breath, but mostly worried about Pix. I couldn't afford to be delayed.

Marv grabbed me by the front of my bodice, lifting me off the ground, and slammed me against the beam I'd just hit. All the air gushed from my lungs. My head whipped back and I saw stars. Now I was getting angry.

"Ye fleezy wench. I been waitin' t'see ye again. Ye owe me a good fancy there, as I bought ye a drink. An' t'night's goin' t'be it."

I brought the knife down, but he whipped up his paw-like hand and caught my wrist. Even with one bent and swollen finger, his sharp squeeze had me gasping. I dropped the knife.

"There's a goo' fancy. Now, I'm goin' t'take ye do—" His words ended in a feminine squeal as my pointed boot lashed out and up. Bull's-eye.

Big Marv dropped me, spinning away with an agonized scream, and I landed on my feet.

None of the patrons seemed to notice our altercation. I guessed it was a familiar occurrence in the likes of Fenmen's End. I snatched up my knife and stake as I dashed for the door.

Once in the night air, I paced up and down the street, willing the chill to return to the back of my neck. The rookery was nearly deserted. No one was fool enough to walk the streets of the stews alone in the very dead of night.

But blast it. Where the blazes was Pix?

They were gone, and that meant the UnDead had probably enthralled him, leading him off somewhere to tear into him with his fangs. The thought made my belly cramp.

*Where are they?*

At last the light fingers of a chill feathered over my neck, eerie and cold in the August night. I scented something deathly and old in the air. *This way.*

I listened to my innate sense, watching for the evil glow of red eyes. The prickling intensified as I made my way down the street, and I nearly walked past the dark, narrow alley . . . but I caught a glimpse of glowing red just in time.

My heart pounded as I shifted my grip on the stake. I could make out two shadowy figures, one with the unmistakable glow of red eyes, the other melding into the edge of darkness.

No time to waste. I hurried down the alley, taking no care to hide my presence. Distraction was the plan.

Distract, surprise, and attack.

The red eyes turned to me, and I was careful not to allow their power to catch my gaze. The UnDead's attention dropped to the massive silver cross on my chest. He reared back, his face a mask of shock and pain. Without sparing a glance for Pix, I lunged for the vampire.

Someone shouted—it might have been me—as I smashed into the UnDead. He stumbled backward and something flew from his fingers. I heard the dull *thunk* when it landed on cobblestones, and I rammed the stake up into his torso.

The vampire froze, his eyes burning coals and his fangs extended in an open mouth . . . then he exploded into ash.

Panting, I turned to Pix. He had just picked up something from the ground and slipped it into his pocket before I could see what it was. It was smaller than a pound note folded in half, and I noticed a slender cord before it disappeared into his coat.

"Are you hurt?" I asked. "Did he bite you?"

Then I saw his face. His expression was not the one of gratitude, or even surprise, that I had expected. Instead, his mouth twisted grimly and his eyes glittered dark.

"I don' know whether t'strangle ye or laugh at ye, Evaline." In his normal mellow tone, those words might have been laced with humor. But tonight, I could tell he was deadly serious.

I didn't know how to respond, so I launched into a diatribe of fury and fear. "Is that all the thanks I get? Saving your miserable life? You couldn't have hoped to fight him off. He might not have looked like much, but the UnDead—did you even *realize* he was a vampire?—they're strong, much stronger than men. He had you in his thrall, and he'd have drained you dry then left you for dead."

I drew in my breath to continue railing at him and realized he'd chosen to laugh at me. But it was a sharp, biting laugh. "Ah, then. Ye were worried on me, were ye, luv? I s'pose it's some cons'lation for interfering wi' me business."

"Your business? What do you mean your business?"

But Pix just shook his head, his mouth a thin, dark line in the drassy light as he began to walk out of the alley. "Wot're ye doin' 'ere in the rook'ry? Oy reckon the same as ye was doin' in and about the fightin'-club yesterday."

"How did you know I was at Nickel's?" We walked abreast down the passage.

Irritation still rolled off him and he shrugged. "An' ye didn' see me neither then, luv? Ye looked right a' me."

I mentally reviewed the scene at Nickel's. Then I stopped, my mouth falling open. "In the corner—that was you, hitting the punching bag." Oh, I definitely remembered him now. My stomach gave a quick little flip when I recalled how I'd admired his powerful, bare torso. How fast and hard he pummeled the man-sized bag.

"Aye."

"How did you know I was going to be there? Were you following me?"

Pix lifted his brows. "Per'aps I should ask ye the same question—for ye arrived after me, didn't ye, luv? An' why shouldn't a bloke be practicin' 'is side-jabs if 'e wants to?" He glanced over at me sidewise, his expression turning flinty. "Does yer beau know ye was checkin' up on 'im? Gabblin' into 'is affairs? Bloody 'ell, Evaline, a' least if yer gonna find a nobby bloke, can ye pick one who's nay up to 'is ears in debt?"

It took me a moment to realize what he meant. "Mr. Ashton is *not* my beau. He's a suspect in a murder investigation." Blast. I sounded like Mina. She must be rubbing off on me.

"'E's not yer beau, is 'e? Sure looked it to a one-eyed violin player."

"I was interrogating him for the investigation."

"While ye was 'anging onto 'is arm like ye couldna walk?" Pix scoffed. "Gawkin' up like 'e's a god? I didn't expect ye'd taken up wi' the likes o' that cove if ye knew 'e was a bad 'un. But I've been known t'be smack wrong."

There was a brittle note in his normally smooth voice. "Take up with? I wasn't—" I stopped and stared at him. I couldn't make out any of his features except the impression of eyes and mouth. A silvery gleam wove through the edges of his thick, dark hair. It made him look almost angelic.

I held back a snort. Pix. Angelic. Those two words didn't go together. "Is that why you're vexed with me?"

His low laugh was devoid of humor. "Vexed is too pretty a word t'describe 'ow I'm feelin' wi' ye, luv. Ye broke one a m'best cove's fingers, ye paraded ye'self into th' rookery like ye' 'ad no care fer yerself, causin' fights and disruptin' the place—"

"*You*," I said from between gritted teeth, "practically begged me to come find you when you interrupted us, playing that blooming violin."

"If'n I'd'a *wanted* ye to find me in Vauxhall, luv, ye would've," he said tightly. "But I didn't."

"What were you doing there anyway?"

"Now, luv . . . 'ow many times do I 'ave t'tell ye . . . there're some things ye jus' don' want t'know."

I wanted to stomp my foot. "You could use a music tutor. Your playing sounded like a cat squalling."

"Listen, luv. I don' need n'more crippled blokes. Ye leave a blind trail be'ind ye, Evaline, and ye take risks ye don' need to. Some day ye'll fin' yerself in a fine chancery. Stay away from m'rookery, luv."

"*That's* a likely chance."

He sighed. "Don' I know'at, ye darly female."

I shook my head. The man was impossible. "One thing I did find out in Smithfield is that *La société* has returned to London. But I haven't been able to determine where they meet, or where the vampires are living."

"Aye." Pix's voice was ironic. "An' if ye wouldn'na come flyin' in on me 'n' Fagley tonight wi' yer pointy stick, I'd'a squeezed the split from 'im and ye'd know all 'bout it."

"What?" I couldn't understand his slang half the time, but I was pretty sure he'd just called the vampire Fagley.

He stopped and looked at me, frustration oozing from him. "I've tol' ye, luv, I deal in information. It's m'business. An' ye came blastin' in on a very delicate predicament and spleefed it all t'hell."

"You *knew* he was a vampire." I couldn't help but feel a bit foolish . . . and aggravated.

"O' course I did. D'ye take me for a complete nobber, Evaline?" He shifted, moving the lapel of his overcoat to reveal a silver cross pinned to the inside.

Right. "What else do you know? Where they stay? Where *La société* is?"

"Not as much as I 'oped." He lifted a brow at me. "But I did d'scover the name o' the UnDead wot's leadin' the rest of 'em. Frenchman named Gadreau. 'E's got 'imself a mortal woman wot serves 'im. She 'as a pet spider wot she keeps in a cage. An' they frequents th' Pickled Nurse."

That I already knew. "And she's fond of Honey-Sweet pickles. But what's her name? Where do they stay? How can I find them? What else did you find out?"

Pix shook his head, his mouth still flat. "Yer gonna 'ave t'learn, Evaline Stoker, ye jus' can't rush in an' molly things up wi'out thinkin'. Th' fact is, I din't need savin', and ye darlied up me work tonight."

I bristled. "I'm a vampire hunter, and my job is to hunt vampires. I'm not going to stop and think about it—especially when I see a situation that looks threatening."

"Ye need t' take care, luv. Ye mi' be a mighty vampire-rozzer, but ye're still mortal. And ye still can be drained dry." His words were taut and his eyes glittered. "Or worst, turned UnDead yersel'. An' I'd 'ate that t'appen t' such a bang-up loidy as ye are. Once word gets out 'bout the female Venator, they'll be after puttin' a stop t'ye. And ye won' be safe nowhere." His voice had softened at the end of his speech.

I stilled as he reached up to brush my cheek, pushing a loose lock of hair from my face. His bare, elegant fingers tucked the curl behind my ear then skimmed lightly down the side of my neck.

"What . . . what was that thing he dropped back there?" He was standing so close . . . was he going to kiss me? Would I let him? "You picked it up and put it in your—"

"Ye don' wanna be worryin' 'bout that-there, luv," he said, easing closer to me. His lips had softened and twitched into a half-smile. The timbre of his voice had dropped. "An' I'm supposin' Oy should a' least be thankin' ye for savin' me . . . though ye really mollied m' work up instead."

"I didn't—"

But he leaned in and covered my mouth with his.

I didn't push him away. And I'm not ashamed to admit it.

When our lips touched, his were soft and gentle, pressing to mine and molding to them like a caressing hand. Heat and prickling shivers rushed through my body. Pix's arms had gone around me, and he pulled me close. I could feel the power in his embrace and the warmth of his torso. I knew I could break his hold at any moment. So I relaxed, kissing him back. I tasted a hint of ale and tobacco mixed with mint.

When he pulled away, the world was a little fuzzy. Kind of tilty. But I also had my hand in his pocket. I smoothly withdrew the item he'd placed in there as I stepped back, hiding it in the folds of my skirt.

"Well, then, there, luv." He straightened his coat sleeve. "Oy'm not sure 'oo was thankin' 'oo just then, but ye'll 'ear no complaints from the likes o' me."

"I'm fairly certain there shouldn't be any thanking at all," I said, once again adopting Mina's crisp, affronted tones. "In fact, I do believe an apology is in order."

He made a low, gritty sound that streaked down my spine. "O' course, luv. I'll accept yer apol'gy an' time ye want t'give it. So long's it's just like that."

And then, without another word, he slipped into the shadows and disappeared. The last thing I heard was his silky chuckle coming from the darkness.

But it was I, for once, who had the last laugh. I shoved the paper-wrapped item I'd pilfered into my pocket and headed for home.

# MISS HOLMES
## *Miss Holmes Makes an Error*

It was with some trepidation that I left Miss Ashton's home after spending the night there, but there was no help for it. I had preparations to make and clues to investigate. However, I fully intended to return by early afternoon and to remain with Willa until I'd put a halt to the evil plot surrounding her.

My first stop was home, to freshen up and repack my reticule. I slipped in and out without being trapped in conversation by Mrs. Raskill, taking enough time to send a message to Miss Stoker to meet me at Miss Adler's office.

We needed to reconnoiter and make plans for our next steps.

On my way to the Museum, I made a detour to Miss Louisa Fenley's séance parlor. Using the threat of exposure of her fraudulent activities, I induced her to show me some tricks of her trade. Although I left feeling pleased about that progress, my intention to find out who'd hired her to fool Miss Ashton met with a dead end. Miss Fenley hadn't been contacted by anyone to conduct séances for Willa Ashton. So the supposed referral from Mrs. Yingling had, in fact, been forged and manufactured by our villain.

Miss Fenley, however, did confess to taking advantage of the young woman's desperation and researching Willa's past in order to hold a realistic meeting.

"And how did you come by the papers you used?"

"The papers the spirits wrote on?" Miss Louisa was the very picture of ingenuousness.

"The ones on which *you* wrote. Let's be honest, shall we? You faked the messages—and I care not that you did so as much as I want to know *from where those papers came*."

She shrugged and I believed her when she said, "They're the same papers I use for all my spirit-writing." She showed me the drawer in which they were kept and I accepted that information as truth. Which meant that the papers with the glowing-in-the-dark message had been altered *after* they arrived at Miss Ashton's house.

This only confirmed my deductions that one of three people had the means with which to make such alterations.

One question I chose not to ask Miss Fenley was in regards to the strange and eerie message Espasia had delivered to Evaline in the voice of Mr. O'Gallegh.

I didn't want to know the answer to that query.

When I arrived at Miss Adler's office, I was pleased to find Dylan present. My mentor was not, and Miss Stoker had not yet arrived—which gave me the pleasure of a few moments of privacy with him. After all, I hadn't spoken to him since the night in the carriage when he kissed me.

But when I noticed Dylan's pasty complexion and its underlying gray tinge, the dark circles under his eyes, and the dullness in his gaze, I was horrified. He appeared worse than Miss Adler had.

I frowned. Maybe there was some sort of illness they both had contracted.

"Are you sick? What's happened? You look . . . terrible."

He waved off my concern. "I'm fine, Mina. All is well. I'm totally fine." His smile was bright and sincere, but I felt the rest of his appearance was cause for alarm.

"Truly, you look as if you should be in bed. Are you certain you feel all right?"

"Never better! Honest." He lifted a hand to brush his long blond hair from his eyes, and I noticed how thin his wrist seemed to be. Even the skin there was pasty and gray. There was blood on the inside of his sleeve, dots here and there all along the white cotton.

"What have you been doing? I'm sorry I haven't been here to see how you're faring." If it wouldn't have been so improper, I would have grabbed his arm and pulled back the sleeve.

"Oh, I've been busy. I just came back here to get some of my things. Everything is just fine, Mina. Don't you worry! Things are going really well."

Though enthusiastic, his voice sounded thick and slow, and I was growing even more worried. This was not the Dylan I knew. There was something wrong, something that made him different.

The office door burst open and Evaline swept in. "Do I have some news for you, Mina!"

"Do you indeed?" I intended to continue my conversation with Dylan, but he'd gathered up his things and, giving me an affectionate pat on the shoulder, hurried from the chamber before I could say another word.

"Later!" he called just as the door closed behind him.

I stared after him, torn between demanding more answers that he didn't seem willing to give, and knowing that Willa Ashton's life was on the line. I had to choose the more pressing problem, and turned to Miss Stoker—who'd been chattering on anyway.

"Gadreau? That's the vampire leader's name? He has a mortal mistress who has a pet spider and frequents the Pickled Nurse? Indeed. Excellent information, Evaline—at least, it would be if we were investigating the whereabouts of the UnDead instead of a disturbing plot to incarcerate—or kill—an innocent young woman." I could hardly conceal my frustration. In fact, I don't believe I concealed it at all. "Do you not even care to know what happened in Willa's chamber?"

"Of course I do." Evaline flumped into a chair. "Do *you* not even care to know how many UnDead I killed last night?"

"You needn't sound so . . . delighted about it."

"Whatever do you mean?"

"Of course you're a Venator, but you needn't be so gleeful about killing people. It's rather unbecoming, and a little startling."

Miss Stoker gaped at me. "Blooming fish! They're *not people*, Mina. They're UnDead. Vampires. Half-demon, immortal beings. Horrible creatures. They *drink blood* from mortals in order to stay alive. They *live* off the human race. And they'd as soon leave a person to bleed dry than kill them outright."

"I'm aware of all that. I *have* read *The Venators*." I sniffed and looked away. "Still. It seems wrong to feel that way. They were people at one time."

"I suppose you don't believe a murderer should hang, then, for his crimes?"

I spread my hands, unsure how we'd even come to this conversation. "I believe in the judicial system, but I certainly don't *celebrate* a hanging."

"I'm not *celebrating*—well, maybe I am a little. After all, it's my legacy to protect the mortal world from these creatures. And *they aren't people*, not any longer. There's no hope for them to ever . . . get better, or return to their normal, mortal self.

They're like that forever. And every vampire I stake is one less horrible creature that takes from people we know, draining the blood from people we love."

I went cold. A horrible, frightening thought lodged in my brain. *Draining the blood from people we love.*

The blood spots on the underside of Dylan's shirtsleeve. The pasty, gray tinge of his skin. The circles under his eyes.

*No. Surely that wasn't possible.*

*Don't be ridiculous. How would Dylan find a vampire anyway?*

I pushed the absurd thought from my mind. I could consider it and its implications later.

Miss Stoker was still glaring at me, but I lifted my nose and proceeded to inform her about the events from the night before—everything from the glowing spiritglass to the green amorphous cloud.

"How did Willa come to have the spiritglass anyway? Surely if we knew who gave it to her, we'd know who is behind all of this."

"I have asked her, and she simply doesn't recall where it came from, nor does she remember anyone particularly drawing her attention to it. One day she noticed it sitting on the table in the front hallway. On her first visit to Willa's house, Mrs. Yingling was the one who told her that it was an spiritglass to be used for communing with the spirits. If we only knew who'd set Mrs. Yingling up to do so . . ."

"Miss Norton! She was the one who introduced Willa to Mrs. Yingling."

"I'm pleased you recall that bit of information, Evaline. Yes, that's true. But it doesn't mean Miss Norton was the one who engaged the medium for the nefarious scheme. That could just as easily have come about after the introduction was made and the relationship between Willa and Mrs. Yingling was established. And so, for now, we must be on our way to visit Olympia Babbage. Surely she can shed some light on the spiritglass, for her grandfather's mark is on the bottom. If we can find out who commissioned it to light up via its timer-mechanism, I suspect we'll find our perpetrator."

A short time later, we were trundling through London traffic in Miss Stoker's carriage. It really was very convenient to have a partner with a vehicle at her disposal. It nearly made up for her impetuousness.

"So you think Charles Babbage designed the spirit-glass?" Miss Stoker seemed doubtful. "Hasn't he been dead for . . . a while?"

"Did you not observe such a marking on all of the notes and journal pages on display at the Oligary Building? Perhaps he left his—wait." I went still, my brain whirring into action. *Oh.* "I've made a mistake. It's—"

"Wha—*huh*? You've made a mistake? *You?* Wait." Evaline yanked open the window and stuck her head out, looked around, then drew herself back in. "The world isn't ending. Big Ben's Infinity Day Clock hasn't stopped. *You* can't have made a mistake. It's simply not . . . possible. It's a day just like any other day."

I was not amused by her antics. "Fine." I lifted my chin. "Then I suppose I shan't tell you what I just realized. And it's not a huge, great mistake. Just a minor one."

"Oh, well, then. You can tell me if it's only a *minor* one. I shan't think quite so poorly of you since it's only a *minor* mistake."

I pursed my lips and considered being obstinate and keeping my realization to myself. But that sort of circumspection is simply not in my nature. I have the compelling need to prove myself and educate others on the errors of their ways. So I succumbed.

"I thought the mark was the initials *C* and *B*. But it's a very detailed design, with many serifs and descenders and even some decorative colophons around it, and—"

"Yes, yes, I know. Blooming fish, Mina, get to the point. If it wasn't a *C* and *B*, what was it?"

"An *O* and a *B*."

"*O* and a *B* . . . *ah*! Olympia Babbage?"

I smiled benignly. "Miss Stoker, there is indeed hope for you."

Just then, we rolled up in front of the Babbage residence. Instead of a grand estate, it was a single-family house about the size of mine. However, the lot on which it sat was large enough that it could have contained two other buildings of comparable size. A barn sat near the back of the property.

Miss Stoker strode boldly toward the wrought iron railing that enclosed the yard. The gate swung open, its mechanism purring softly. The opening clicked closed behind us, and no sooner were we climbing the steps than we heard a distant chime inside the house.

No one answered our knock, but I already knew what to do next. "The barn. It would be a perfect workroom. I wager we'll find Miss Babbage inside."

We picked our way across the grass, which was clipped short but damp from the ever-present fog and drizzle. The building had several windows as well as random pipes that stuck out from the roof like fingers. As we approached I heard sounds coming from inside. Machinery—rumbling and growling, vibrating and rattling.

I peered through one of the windows, hoping to catch a glimpse of Miss Babbage.

While I didn't see her, it was clear the stable had been turned into a vast, cluttered workspace—even more vast and more cluttered than my laboratory. There were many lights strung up throughout the area and I was shocked to note that most of them were the clear electric bulbs that had been illegal for the past five years.

Half-built contraptions littered every surface—pieces of machinery and complicated inventions. Springs, coils, cogs, bolts, sheets of copper, aluminum, steel, wires, ropes, twine . . . and tools: metal snips, wrenches, pin-tuckers, and an ominous-looking metal pipe with a blue-orange flame dancing at one end. It sat in a metal holder attached to a large metal pole.

And there was no sign of Miss Babbage.

"Mina."

Miss Stoker's tense voice had me hurrying from the window. "What—"

I didn't need to finish the question. The door was splintered as if someone had broken through it—*into* the barn, rather than out of it.

"I can sense them," Evaline said. "Even now. I don't know how recently."

"Sense what?"

"Vampires. UnDead. They were here. And I'd guess they got what they came for."

Olympia Babbage.

# Miss Holmes

## Miss Holmes Takes a Drive

"Why would the UnDead want to take Olympia Babbage?" Miss Stoker said as we rode off in her carriage. "I have no blooming idea. But I'm certain they were there in her workroom. I might be new at this, but I have instincts. They leave a light, deathlike odor behind. The UnDead were there for certain, and recently. Likely just before dawn."

"Right." I wanted nothing more than to close my eyes and knit and think. There were so many pieces to this puzzle, I needed one of those wallboards like Grayling had to keep them all straight.

And now there was a connection between the Willa Ashton case and the UnDead: Olympia Babbage.

Coincidence? My uncle claimed that was impossible, but for once, I wasn't certain. What could the UnDead have to do with someone trying to murder a young woman?

"What is it?" Miss Stoker demanded, for I'd sat upright.

A shiver went down my spine and prickles needled the bottoms of my feet. *No. That's absurd. The Ankh . . . is out of the picture.*

But the Ankh wasn't dead. I was sure of it. And that was why I'd collected and kept all my notes about her.

The vampire Gadreau had a *mortal woman* who served him. Not that I could imagine the Ankh serving *anyone* . . . but *La société* seemed like the sort of thing in which that villainous woman would be involved. And many members of *La société* hoped to gain immortality through their connection to the UnDead. Immortality was certainly something to which the Ankh, who tried to harness the powers of a goddess, would aspire.

Then I deflated. No. It didn't seem quite right. The Ankh was a leader, not a servant. Still . . . I would review my casebook on the Ankh.

I refused to discuss my theories with Evaline, and she pouted the rest of the way back to the Museum. I was glad to quit her presence, for she was grating on my nerves. However aggravating she might be, I was nevertheless disappointed that Evaline was unable to assist me for the remainder of the day.

"I have to attend that dratted Opening Night Ball at the Lyceum tonight or Florence will draw and quarter me. And she's got the seamstress coming for last-minute adjustments to my gown, and a special woman doing our hair . . . I'm already late. I was supposed to be home by two!"

Her miserable expression was the only reason I forgave her for shirking her duty. "Very well then. I'll be with Miss Ashton today and tonight, but you shall have to relieve me first thing tomorrow. It's imperative she's not left alone any longer, but I have investigations to conduct. I am on my way there as soon as I speak with Miss Adler—if she's arrived yet." I alighted from the carriage and started up the steps to the Museum.

But according to the guard, Miss Adler hadn't been in her office for two days. A zap of uncertainty wriggled up my spine, but I had to put worry over my mentor aside for now.

Willa Ashton's life was in grave danger and that must be my focus.

Less than an hour later, I arrived once more at the Ashton residence.

I was immediately struck by a sense of disquiet, and it was with great foreboding that I employed the knocker at the front door.

The butler, Rightingham, answered, and I knew immediately something was wrong. His eyes were rimmed red and the tip of his nose pink.

"Miss Ashton!" I said it in more of a demand than a request, but I already knew the answer.

"She's gone. They come and took her away."

"No!" Uncaring of my rudeness, I pushed past him. "Where did they take her? Do you know? When? *Who*?"

"It was two men in a curtained carriage. They had the papers. Miss Geraldine, she cried and screamed and tried to fight them off, but there was nothing for it. He showed her the papers. Mr. Ashton, he wasn't here, and there was no one else. No one else to stop them."

"Where is Miss Geraldine now?"

"She went after Mr. Ashton, or to find someone—a magistrate or someone to help. I don't know when she'll be back."

Ill at my stomach and cold with fear, I was already running up the stairs to Willa's bedchamber. I didn't know why—perhaps it was to take one last chance to look for clues, to examine the spiritglass for anything that could betray the villain.

I had a suspicion, yes, I was fairly certain I at last knew who the perpetrator was . . . but I wanted to make certain. I grabbed the spiritglass and the sheaf of papers next to it, startling the cat from his perch on the chair. He hissed and thumped to the floor, his tail twitching in warning.

I ignored him, casting about the chamber. Nothing seemed to be out of place from earlier this morning. Then I smelled something pungent and unusual. I'd noticed it before, but now I sniffed again, lifting the papers to my nose for a better whiff.

Ah.

*Crickets. Pickpockets. UnDead. Smithfield. A floating key.*

My eyes widened and all at once, everything fell into place.

I rushed from Willa's chamber, pounding down the stairs like an army just as the front door knocker clacked. Rightingham and I got there at the same time, opening the door to an earnest-looking Mr. Treadwell.

"Is . . . erm . . . Miss Ashton at home?" the handsome young man asked the butler.

Oh, *no*. The poor man!

I hesitated, wanting to assure him I'd do everything in my power to save Willa, but time was of the essence. Instead, I thrust the papers, which I'd wrapped around the spiritglass, at him and said, "Whatever you do, keep these safe. I will send you further instructions. Do it *for Willa*."

Bewildered, he nevertheless took the objects and stuffed them in his coat pocket. Meanwhile, the butler struggled to control his grief whilst explaining that Miss Willa Ashton was not at home, and would not be for the foreseeable future.

To my great annoyance, the cab I'd engaged to bring me here had left, against my specific direction. Thus I was forced to walk out to the street and three blocks down in an effort to find another one. *Drat and blast!* Where was a taxi when you needed one? I needed my own dratted carriage.

Chafing at the delay, my stomach still upset and in knots—for I knew the clock was ticking—I hurried all the way back to the Ashtons', hoping Mr. Treadwell might still be there. I could beg a ride from him.

To my relief, a Two-Seat Charley was parked out front, presumably brought around for Mr. Treadwell now that he learned Willa wasn't there.

Puffing from my rapid walk, I approached the front steps just as the door flew open. Instead of Mr. Treadwell, however, I found myself confronted by Aunt Geraldine.

The usually perfectly groomed woman was a wild mess—her hair straggling, her eyes wide and desperate, her hands wringing her skirts.

"Miss Kluger!" I stepped out of the way so she wouldn't bowl me over.

"Miss Holmes, forgive me, but I haven't any time. It's Willa! They've taken her away, and I must try and stop them. I must save her!"

"She's not mad," I told her. "Willa isn't a lunatic. I can prove she's been manipulated into certain actions that cause her to appear to be—"

"Is this true?" She halted. "What you say, is this true?"

"You can trust my word. But I don't know where she's been taken."

"I do! Oh, will you come with me, Miss Holmes? You must tell them, prove it to them . . . before it's too late. Will you come with me?"

"Of course I'll go. But we mustn't delay. We must leave immediately. Is that your carriage?" I gestured to the Two-Seat Charley.

"Yes, oh, yes. I just returned from trying to find Herrell, but I couldn't. He seems to have disappeared! I didn't know what to do. I am so relieved you're here, and that you can help!"

I took a moment to scribble two messages, giving them to Rightingham to have delivered to Evaline and Mr. Treadwell, respectively. Then a footman helped me into the seat of the small, mechanized carriage. Miss Kluger climbed up next to me, and I was intrigued by the fact that she meant to drive it herself. Perhaps such a vehicle could be the solution to my transportation woes, and I wouldn't have to rely on Evaline any longer.

"Where are we going?" I asked as Miss Kluger navigated neatly through the busy streets. She was an expert driver, and again I considered how much more independent I would be if I should acquire my own form of transportation.

"There is a place in Smithfield where they've taken her."

"Ah. As I suspected. I trust it's near the locksmith Ivey & Boles?"

"You suspected? Is that so?" Her expression changed to a very cold smile. "And did you suspect that you would be joining her there as well, Miss Holmes?"

My heart skipped a beat. "In what way do you mean, Miss Kluger?"

"You seem to know an uncomfortable amount about my niece's situation. I think it would be best if you stayed with Willa at our purlieu in Smithfield. Then no one else will hear about your theories or proof that she was—how did you put it? Forced into doing things she didn't mean to?"

"I would never have stated it so inelegantly." My palms had gone slightly damp.

Aunt Geraldine merely smiled. "Have it your way, then, Miss Holmes. I had no idea you were so aware of what was happening. If I had, I'd have done something about it much sooner. I underestimated you, despite your family connections."

"Pity for you. And I suspect this won't be the last time you'll be outfoxed by a Holmes."

She laughed in a particularly nasty way. "I hardly consider myself outfoxed. Despite the conclusions you've drawn about my niece, you're not about to come out of this situation victorious. After all, you're trapped in my vehicle—oh, yes, I have the doors locked. There's no way out of here until I allow it."

"Apparently I hadn't considered that possible outcome."

"I should say not."

"But we are driving through the streets of London. I merely need to hail someone and call for help."

She scoffed. "London? No one will hear you. This city is an uncivilized place in comparison to my beloved Paris. I despised having to come back here when Willa's mother died. And these windows are tinted gray to keep out the sun—which we had plenty of in Paris, but not so much here. No one will see you."

"Very well, then. I'll trust your judgment on that at least. How much longer until we arrive at our destination?"

"As I am driving a circuitous route to ensure we aren't followed, and along less-traveled roads where it's unlikely we'd be noticed, I estimate perhaps another twenty minutes."

"Excellent. That should give us plenty of time to discuss precisely why you would go through so much trouble to make your niece go mad—or even die. My initial supposition of the motive was money."

"My, Miss Holmes. How fascinating."

But I wasn't finished. "Yet, I find money such a banal motive for what basically amounts to murder. And if you were a man, I might have been satisfied with that. But in this case, the perpetrator isn't a man, but a woman—which I'd suspected for some time. And women aren't quite as base and simplistic in their motives, are they?"

"Indeed. Miss Holmes, I do believe if the circumstances were different, I might actually like you."

"It was you who hired Mrs. Yingling and eventually killed her, wasn't it?"

"I should have known you'd figure that." Her voice wasn't grim so much as admiring. "Was that what put you on to me? I realized later I shouldn't have acted quite so rashly, but I was concerned that cloud-headed medium would reveal what she knew. And once I learned Her Royal Highness had set a Holmes on the case, I feared you might get your uncle involved."

"As you can see, it was not necessary for my uncle to become involved in one of my cases," I informed her. "What precisely did Mrs. Yingling know? That you'd hired her to help make Willa believe she was going mad, all the while driving her to become more and more dependent upon the séances?"

"Of course. And the beauty of it is, now that Mrs. Yingling is dead, I will regain the title of the little cottage in Sussex where she planned to retire and where I intend to relocate shortly. It's an excellent plan, if I do say so." Miss Kluger shifted the vehicle and turned down a dim, narrow street.

"And what about Olympia Babbage? Did she know too much as well, and have you had her snuffed out, too?"

"Once again, your astuteness astounds me. But no. Miss Babbage is too valuable to be removed from the equation. She has many diverse skills that would be a shame to destroy. However, like you shall shortly be, she is in our custody and we shall keep her until she is no longer useful."

I was relieved that the young female inventor hadn't met the same fate as Mrs. Yingling. "What I'm most curious about is how you mesmerized Willa in the first place, and why. Why not just leave her be?"

"That was a grave error on my part, and one I regretted from the moment it happened. The first time I mesmerized Willa—which was simply when I visited her chamber in the middle of the night and used a golden ball on a string—she wasn't completely, as we describe it, amused. Enthralled, hypnotized—whatever you wish to call it. In a very malleable state of mind."

"And so she remembered what happened whilst she was amused . . . but as a dream. A dream where she visited Robby and saw that he was still alive. But it wasn't really a dream. You took her there. And that was your mistake."

"Yes. I had no idea how powerful Willa's mind was, to fight my considerable ability to amuse a person. When she began to remember that 'dream,' I knew it was only a matter of time until she realized it wasn't a dream—"

"And that she really had been in Smithfield, near a sign with a very big, so-called *floating* key—that is, Ivey & Boles. Their storefront is quite distinctive. When she mentioned seeing a large cogwork key in her dream, that caused me to realize she might not actually have been dreaming."

"Just so. You *are* quite brilliant, Miss Holmes. But it's a shame you didn't realize it was *I* who was the perpetrator before you got into this vehicle."

"Perhaps it *was* a miscalculation on my part. But I am also curious as to why—and how—you caused her mother to visit Willa in the first place, in her chamber. I assume you're unaware I witnessed one such visitation last night. I confess, I haven't been able to determine precisely how you conducted that particular sensation. It was quite . . . authentic."

"That's because I didn't. I can't take credit for that, Miss Holmes. Those spiritual manifestations are real, and they are part of the reason I was forced to act as I have."

"You believe the ghost of Marta Ashton is actually visiting her daughter?"

"I have no doubt of it. For that's what has caused Willa to be so certain Robby is still alive."

"Is he?" That was one thing I hadn't quite figured out yet.

Aunt Geraldine gave me an enigmatic smile. "If Marta hadn't been speaking to her from the spirit world, then Willa would never have pursued the belief that Robby was still alive, and she would have thought nothing of her so-called dream. It would have all died down, and I wouldn't have been required to arrange for her to be manipulated by a medium in order to confuse the issue. Those visitations are authentic."

"The question of the authenticity of Mrs. Ashton's visitations is, apparently, the first of two things on which we must disagree, Miss Kluger."

"What, pray tell, Miss Holmes, is the second?"

"That you have been outfoxed by a Holmes for the second time." With that, I withdrew the Steam-Stream gun from my voluminous skirts and pointed it at her. "Wouldn't you agree, Miss Kluger?"

# ᴹɪss Holmes
## *Welcome to* La Société

"I suspected you for quite some time, Miss Kluger." I adjusted my weapon so it pressed into the side of her torso. "But it wasn't until I smelled the pickle juice on the papers in Willa's bedchamber that I realized it was you behind all of this villainy."

"Pickle juice?"

"You're quite fond of the Honey-Sweets in particular, aren't you? That information, combined with the crickets I kept noticing inside an otherwise pristine house, finally made the pieces click together. Crickets are the preferred food of spider pets, are they not?"

Miss Kluger shifted the vehicle and braked, driving into a spot beneath a dark, heavy overhang. "You are quite clever, aren't you?"

"I am a Holmes," I replied modestly.

"And here we are."

"And so I shall meet Gadreau now? Your partner—and, I must assume, your lover? The ringleader of this entire operation, and the current leader of *La société*. Is he expecting us?"

"He's certainly not expecting *you*." Miss Kluger's tones had become irritated. "But I had to seize the opportunity to remove you when I found you at the house. You are, as you said, a Holmes."

"I am."

My companion turned off her vehicle. I turned my attention to the dirt-blackened brick wall looming above us. Clearly, there was a rear or hidden entrance, for the alley was deserted and there appeared to be no other sign of life. The only door was a heavy metal-and-cogged one of sturdy wood.

I maneuvered myself across the seat to follow my captive out of the vehicle once she opened the door. I was prepared for her to slam it closed on me, so I positioned my foot as a blockade . . . but either she didn't think of it, or didn't bother to try.

"Just to be clear . . ." I hauled myself out of the vehicle. This was a difficult prospect when maneuvering heavy skirts while training a gun on one's companion. "I only wish to retrieve Willa, and her brother Robby—who I've deduced is still alive—and then I shall leave you to your revolting, blood-drinking *société*."

"Is that so?"

"I have no qualms about using this weapon, and I can assure you, the steam that will shoot from it will sear your skin painfully. It's unlikely you'd expire from the injury, but you'll be hurting for some time. I want Willa and Robby. Oh, and Olympia Babbage as well. Then I shall be on my way."

I sincerely hoped I was wrong about my other, deep-rooted fear. That there might be yet another person I would have to rescue. *No.* I shook my head. He wouldn't.

Miss Kluger muttered something I took to be a reluctant assent, and I followed her to the door. My heart thudded and I drew in a deep breath as I pulled a heavy necklace from behind my bodice.

I had been prepared for everything so far. My deductions had been spot-on. I severely hoped that wouldn't change.

She spun three of the cogs in the brass framework that embraced the door. I heard the clicks and automatically counted them, noting the direction she turned each one. It was rather like opening a safe, and focusing on such a mundane thing helped calm my nerves.

The cogs and gears released with a soft groan, then parted in the center of the door. My prisoner pushed it open and I followed her into a dark foyer.

The door closed behind us and I gripped the Steam-Stream gun more tightly. I hoped I hadn't made a grievous error. And I hoped Miss Stoker would act on my message. *Posthaste.* The soiree at the Lyceum would have to wait.

Lives were at stake.

Including mine.

I kept the gun pressed into Miss Kluger's back as she opened a door at the opposite side of the foyer. At once we were admitted to a spacious room.

My first impression was one of *red.* And heat. Cloying heat. And a heavy, metallic scent. *Blood.*

The walls were covered with expensive red fabric— velvet, silk, cotton, tapestry—and paintings. I recognized a Rembrandt and what I was certain was a da Vinci, not to mention a number of others. The furnishings were heavy and ornate, made of mahogany, wrought iron, and bamboo. The place would be quite cozy and luxurious if I didn't know this was the lair of an UnDead. A fire burned in a large fireplace on one wall.

I found it enlightening that vampires wanted heat but could not tolerate sunlight.

Sofas and settees piled with silky pillows littered the chamber. Several bottles of wine and trays of food filled a table on one wall. And sitting in a large, thronelike chair was a man—presumably the Parisian vampire Gadreau. He was surrounded by a group of children—his gang of pickpockets.

Well then. I was going to have to rescue all of them, wasn't I? I prodded Miss Kluger nearer.

"*Bonjour, ma chère.* I see you've brought us a visitor." Gadreau didn't rise from his seat, but gestured with a slender, effeminate hand. He spoke English with an accent. "And who might you be?"

"Miss Mina Holmes."

We were close enough now that I could see the gleam of his fangs, protruding from beneath his upper lip. A striking man, attractive in an aristocratic way, he appeared to be about thirty years old. However, since he was a vampire, I knew he had to be older in actual years.

"Ah, Miss Holmes. Welcome."

"I'm here for Willa Ashton. And Robby, her brother." I scanned the group of boys while keeping an eye on Miss Kluger. Fortunately, I recognized Robby straightaway from his sister's pictures and drew in a relieved breath. He was here, and alive.

Gadreau's attention had settled on my chest. "I see you've come armed. So to speak."

He referred to the silver cross I'd hung around my neck. "I always come prepared."

"Indeed. And you seem to be in possession of someone most important to me." He gestured to Miss Kluger. "And so if I give you Willa, and Robby—"

"And Miss Babbage."

"Mademoiselle Babbage as well?"

"Yes. I'll not leave without them. And the rest of these poor boys. I cannot in good conscience leave them to your evil ways."

"But truly, Mademoiselle Holmes. You are very strict. How am I to live if I do not have my boys? My little—what do the English call them? My little snakesmen are indispensible to me."

"I'm certain they are. Your band of pickpockets has garnered quite a reputation here in London as having the fastest and lightest of fingers. I'm certain the credit is all yours, enthralling them and training them as you have—after you abducted them. Or was it Miss Kluger who provided them for you?"

"But of course. I cannot go out in the daylight in search of those best suited for my work. *Oui*, my darling Geraldine has always had a talent for finding those with slick, elegant fingers and sharp eyes."

I turned to Miss Kluger in outrage. "Your own nephew? You would have sentenced him to work for an UnDead? Is it not bad enough that you have committed yourself to a life with him, but your innocent nephew as well?"

"It was Robby's own fault." She drew up and away from me. "He saw me walking through here—it was the night he'd followed Herrell to his boxing club. Herrell sent him home, and while he was riding in a cab, Robby saw me. He followed me and Gadreau, and by the time I noticed—"

"By that time, I'd seen the fine young man, and he'd seen us. We couldn't allow him to return home and tell tales. Besides. I'd always wanted a son." Gadreau smiled affectionately at Robby, who returned the favor. "We UnDead cannot breed, you know."

"And so you kept him captive here."

"At first he protested, but after a time, he became comfortable with his new life—as they all do. And then we introduced him to the joys of *La société*. The only problem was that he missed his sister Willa. He wanted to say goodbye to her."

"And so you amused her and brought her to see her brother." I turned back to Miss Kluger. "But it didn't work out as you'd planned, and she remembered the visit. And then you were in a pickle."

Gadreau, at least, appreciated my attempt at humor. His lips curved and his eyes glinted with humor. "Indeed."

"Perhaps you could enlighten me. What does an UnDead want with a gang of pickpockets? And food and wine and artwork. You subsist on blood, not bread."

"Ah. But just because one is immortal doesn't mean one doesn't appreciate comfort and beauty, or has lost one's taste." He swept his arm around the chamber. "My slick snakesmen and their quick fingers allow me—and my beloved Geraldine—to live quite comfortably. And though I may not *need* bread and cheese to survive, I am still a Frenchman and I still can appreciate the taste of a good Bordeaux. Aside from that, my boys must eat as well."

"I see." I couldn't suppress a little shiver, for at that moment I understood yet another purpose for the gang of boys: a ready supply of fresh, young blood for their master. "But how do you keep them from running away after you abduct them?"

"It helps that Geraldine and I have our own particular way of—heh—*amusing* them in order to gain their compliance."

"You mean enthralling them?"

Gadreau inclined his head in acknowledgment. "These youngsters come to enjoy their game of chance, of picking pockets and learning their way through the streets."

"Was that one of your snakesmen at New Vauxhall Gardens, on the opening night? Ah, yes, I recognize the boy—there you are."

"Indeed. Poor Ferdy came back empty-handed that night, didn't you, boy?" Gadreau returned his attention to me. "And so now here we are—you with your silver cross and lethal weapon, and your demands. It's quite a list, now, isn't it? Are you quite certain you don't wish to search the back rooms to see if there is anyone else you might wish to negotiate for?"

I didn't care for the way his irises had turned more pink than red, and the sudden malevolent tone that crept into his voice. "I'm here to rescue Willa and Robby and Miss Babbage—and whoever else I can. I'm sorry about your gang of thieves, but I'm afraid I must take them with me. They will want to return to their parents once they are out from under your thrall."

"All of them. Indeed. But I'm afraid that's not practical, Miss Holmes. Taking them all with you."

"I can easily find a carriage large enough, or we shall walk to the Underground—"

Gadreau chuckled gently. "Ah, no, mademoiselle. You misunderstand me. You see, it's not practical at all—for many of them . . . they do not do well in the sunlight."

As if on cue, several of the boys looked up at me with glowing red eyes and long, lethal fangs.

I was so taken off guard I failed to notice Miss Kluger was edging away until she lunged to the side. Before I could recover, something heavy and flowing dropped on me, hot and suffocating. I struggled to drag myself out of the cloying material while fumbling in my deep pocket for the vial of holy water. . . .

But the next thing I knew, I was pummeled to the ground, tightly enveloped in the heavy fabric . . . and smothered into darkness.

# MISS STOKER

## *Wherein Our Heroine Has a Rude Awakening*

Moonlight streamed into my bedchamber through the window . . . where a dark figure was climbing in.

I bolted upright and was out of bed by the time Pix's feet were on the floor. Tonight he was hatless and garbed in close, black clothing. But he wore the false sideburns once again and his collar was turned up high to obscure his face. For some reason, that really aggravated me. He was always hiding, stealing about, and covering himself.

"What in the blooming fish are you doing here?"

I thought I knew the answer. But the square, palm-sized device I'd slipped from his overcoat last night was well hidden. And not in my bedchamber. I had unwrapped it from its papers, but I still had no idea what the flat, metal object with metal grommets and curling wires was. A cognog like Mina might have an idea, but I was at a loss. So I sure as Pete wasn't going to let him steal it back.

For a moment Pix just stood there. The light glowed from behind him so all I could see was his shape. But I realized I was half-illuminated by the moon and stars—and that my figure was outlined beneath the loose cotton night rail I wore. Blast it. I moved into the shadows, but my insides were fluttering and my palms grew damp.

All I could think was that he'd kissed me last night. And now he was here in my bedchamber.

"Did ye 'ave a fine time a' th' Lyceum tonight? Chattin' and dancin' wi' the charmin' Mr. Dancy, were ye?"

"How did you—never mind. Yes, it was fine. And I'm exhausted. I need to sleep because Mina insists I take over for her at Willa Ashton's house first thing in the morning."

I glanced at the package that had arrived from her, via Mr. Treadwell of all people, earlier today. I'd been too busy getting my hair done to unwrap it or read the separate note Mina sent. Florence was Attila the Hun when we were preparing for a social engagement like the soiree.

"What do you want?" I demanded again.

"I thought ye'd be wantin' a gander at this." He tossed something onto the edge of my bed.

It was a scrap of butcher paper, like the one from the Pickled Nurse. It even smelled like pickles. "And so?"

"Look at it."

I had to come into a beam of moonlight to see the fragment. My hair prickled when I recognized the simple sketch on it. A long-legged spider. "Where did you get it?"

His expression was hidden in the shadows, but his stance was stiff and removed. "It was tossed in m'violin case at New Vauxhall. By your *paramour* . . . or someone 'oo was wi' ye an' 'im."

"Ashton is *La société*?"

Pix shifted, easing away from the window toward my dressing table. Not even the flash of a teasing grin. But his attention never left me. "Ashton or 'ooever else was at the gathering at Vauxhall."

"Are you saying there was a *La société* meeting the same night of the grand opening? At the Gardens?"

I'd spent hours combing the place, searching for UnDead. How had I missed them? I looked sharply at Pix. "How do you know this? Right. That paper was an invitation for you, wasn't it?"

He shrugged, his silhouette outlined by the cool moonlight. "Ye know better'n t'ask certain questions, luv." He was next to my dressing table now, out of the moonlight and into the shadows . . . but he made no move to come closer to me.

I looked back down at the butcher paper, wondering what it all meant. I'd show Mina tomorrow. Surely she'd have a theory—or two. And, as usual, Pix was noncommittal and ambiguous. Blast him.

"Why do you always wear a disguise? And why do you have to sneak around so much?" I burst out. "Who or what are you hiding from?"

He became very still. "What makes ye think—"

"Blast it, Pix. Do you think I'm a complete cloud-head? You can come around regularly and take me off to your hide-away and steal kisses from me, but you can't even tell me your real name. Or let me see your face in a good light. Your *real* face. And you sure as Pete can stop using that fake accent around me too."

"Fake accent? Oy, luv, me accent isn't fake." But his voice was a little tight. "Exaggerated at times, mind, but not fake."

Well, that was some progress. "I don't even know what you look like. For real."

"An' it matters to ye, does it, Evaline, luv? Wot a bloke looks like?"

"If he's going to kiss me, then, yes, it does matter."

He reached up to his face and peeled away one of his sideburns. And then, still silent, holding my gaze, he did the same on the other side, tucking them both into his pockets. Then he tore off eyebrows—thick, dark ones I hadn't even realized were false—and, finally, a small piece of rubber that was attached to the end of his nose. The pieces of his disguise were all simple and subtle, but together, they greatly altered his appearance.

Pix pushed his thick, dark hair out of his face and stepped into a beam of moonlight. I caught my breath. I'd thought he was handsome before, but now . . . "Thank you" was all I said.

He nodded, still looking at me, then eased back so his face was in shadow once more.

Struggling for something cool and witty to say, I noticed a faint light out of the corner of my eye. The small package from Mr. Treadwell sat on my chest of drawers. A subtle blue light glowed from beneath its wrappings.

I wasted no time pulling the papers away. Inside was the spiritglass. It was closed up into the shape of a small brass pentagon, but the light filtered through the cracks. I must have pushed a button or released a lever, for it opened in my hand to reveal the small blue sphere. It glowed enough to throw shadows around the room.

"Where did ye nick that?" Pix moved toward me for the first time tonight. He was replacing his false eyebrows.

"Mina sent it to me." I shuffled through the items on my bureau and found her message from earlier today. Or, rather, yesterday, I thought as the clock struck half-past one.

*Willa has been taken. I know the identity of the perpetrator but dare not put it in writing. You should also have received a package from Mr. Treadwell. It will contain important evidence. If you hear no further word, the worst has happened and I've gone after her. The hideaway of* La société *is in Smithfield, near Ivey & Boles. For obvious reasons, I shall need your particular support. Contact Grayling and ref: Yingling case.*

"Blast." There'd been no other message from Mina—unless it was in the foyer on the front table. I hurried down on silent feet to check and found the surface empty.

When I returned to my chamber, Pix was reapplying the rubber piece to his nose while reading Mina's note. Not a bit of guilt crossed his face, the blooming snoop. I wondered how many of my drawers he'd combed through whilst I was gone—looking for the object I'd lifted from his pocket.

"You won't find your curious device in here." I yanked my wardrobe doors open as quietly as I could. My boy breeches were tucked in the back, as were a pair of comfortable, worn boots that had hollow heels. I dragged them out along with a black shirt and coat. "I've hidden it where even a slick-fingered thief can't find it."

"Yer no' s'bad yerself, luv. I didn't granny ye diggin' in me pockets. Granted, I was a bit mollied at th' time. But ye'd best return it. It's not somethin' the likes o' ye want in yer possession." The accent was back in full force, the disguise replaced, and the fragile connection between us broken.

"Right. Of course. More secrets." I dove behind the dressing screen. "Don't look." I tucked the divider around so it made a half circle and blocked me from his view. I could see over the top if I stood on my toes. "In fact, you can leave. Go. Get out of my chamber." My voice was muffled during this last bit as I shrugged the black shirt over my shift and a self-lacing corset.

I bent down to yank the breeches on, then the boots. I expected him to be gone when I straightened back up, but he wasn't.

"I told you to leave. And I'm not giving it back—whatever it is. Not till I find out what it is." I finger-combed my sagging hair into a thick, wild handful, then braided it and tucked the plait inside my shirt. Still ignoring Pix, I pulled out the trunk from beneath my bed and armed myself with stakes, holy water, a knife, and a silver cross. Too blasted bad I didn't have Mina's Steam-Stream gun.

"Good-bye, Pix. I've got work to do." I vaulted out onto the oak's branch.

By the time I reached the ground, he was there too. Surprise, surprise. "This way," he said.

Parked in a shadowy corner between two buildings was a small vehicle hidden by a fabric cover that resembled bricks. Not quite a cycle, not at all a carriage. It had two large wheels on either side of an enclosed platform on which the driver would stand—or two people if you crowded enough. The steering device was a large circle, like in an automobile. When Pix bent to shift a lever, I saw the distinct flash of a spark.

Electric, then. Was he *trying* to get us arrested?

"Get on." He shoved a pair of goggles at me.

"Don't you want to know where I'm going?"

"Oi know where yer goin', luv. T' check on Miss 'Olmes and make sure she's in 'er bed, safe and sound."

He gave me a little shove and I stepped onto the platform, settling the goggles into place. He followed, closing the door behind us.

Gad, he was close. It was tight in the small space. A vehicle definitely designed only for one.

We started off with a jerk. I expected us to trundle along the street, but to my surprise, he turned down a dark alley. The only illumination was a small glow from the base of the vehicle. How could he see where we were going?

We drove between two very narrow buildings, and directly toward a brick wall. I stiffened when he made no move to slow, but to my surprise, the wall opened. Then we were going down into darkness. The sewers?

It definitely smelled like the sewers. Musty, crusty, and *ugh*.

As soon as the doors closed behind us, the vehicle stopped. There was a gentle click followed by a spark off the tail of the cart. Something rumbled gently beneath my feet and the whole contraption rose as if something inflated beneath us. Pix moved his arm near my waist and a light came on. It beamed into the tunnel ahead, illuminating a thick, glistening river of . . . I'm not sure what. I didn't want to know.

"Through the *sewers*?"

He chuckled, his mouth very close to my ear. "If them blokes the toshers can do't, why not us? Now 'old on, luv." He shifted again and I heard a soft whirr as a clear shield rose from the front and sides of the vehicle. He pulled a lever, turned something, and the faint rumble turned into a pleasant roar as the transport leapt forward.

We sped through the tunnel. At first I was afraid the sludge would splash up all over, but the shield protected us, and there were hardly any splashes anyway. We zoomed along on top of the water. The ride was surprisingly smooth, and the unpleasant smells from the sewers were lost in the breeze. I couldn't imagine a faster form of transportation—except maybe Inspector Grayling's steamcycle.

We came out of the sewers and the vehicle lowered back to the ground. The wheels turned beneath us as Pix zigzagged through dark alleys and courtyards instead of streets.

When we arrived in front of Mina's house, I jumped out before he even stopped. The building was dark. That was no surprise, for it was nearly two o'clock in the morning.

I hesitated, unwilling to knock and possibly waken the household (although as far as I knew, it was just Mina and occasionally her father; Mrs. Raskill lived in a separate apartment next door).

Before I could decide what to do, Pix was next to me. He bent at the door and I saw the flash of something slender and metal in his hands. His wrists moved sharply and neatly, and the door swung open.

"After ye, luv."

I'd only been in Mina's house once before. It took me a moment to orient myself, and I checked the laboratory first. She wasn't there.

I came back out into the main area and slipped past the kitchen and through the living space. It took mere seconds to check the bedchambers—both were empty.

If Mina wasn't here, she had definitely gone after Willa.

Ready to leave, I turned to speak to Pix and saw the golden filter of the streetlamp buffeting over the fireplace mantel. Something there caught my eye. I froze in surprise, then walked over. Surely I was mistaken.

No. I wasn't. I picked up the photo, staring, unable to believe my eyes.

Very well, then. That answered one question that had been nagging at me for a while.

Now I had even more reason to find Mina.

# MISS STOKER

## *The Point of No Return*

We walked over to Pix's vehicle, parked under a gaslight.

"I don't even know where *La société* is." Desperation made my voice high and tight. "I searched all around last night, but I couldn't find the vampires in Smithfield. How can I help Mina if I can't find her?"

"That, luv, is where I can 'elp ye out. Despite yer mollyin' things up, I managed t' smooth thin's over wi' me business associates."

"You know where they are? Take me there. Hurry! There are lives at stake."

Pix looked at me. His expression was filled with remorse, yet I saw determination in his gaze. "Aye, and it'll cost ye, luv. I must 'ave that packet."

I couldn't believe it. "What the bloody Pete is it? Why is it so damned important?"

He shook his head. "Evaline. Ye can't be involved in it. For yer own safety. An' that's the last I'll say on it. Now, ye gi' me the packet and I'll take ye where ye wanna go. Or ye can waste the night wandering' through Smithfiel', looking fer wot ye canna find."

I had no choice other than to agree. Fortunately, my house was on the way to Smithfield. I handed the palm-sized object to Pix with a glare.

He slipped it in his pocket. "I feel much better now, luv. Ye'll thank me someday."

I doubted it, but at that point it didn't matter. We were off to Smithfield, where I hoped I wasn't going to be too late.

By the time we arrived in the dark alley, I could see the faintest light in the eastern sky. My neck was frigid. There was no doubt of the presence of UnDead. This certainty was something that had been missing when I patrolled the streets of Smithfield.

Pix approached a heavy cog-and-gearworked door. I gripped my stake and waited. He leaned in, listening closely as he turned cog and gear in a variety of directions while I chafed at the delay.

Finally, the cagework loosened and the door opened a crack. I turned to him. "There's no need for you to go inside. I told you, I can do this. Vampires are my specialty. You stay out here and—"

"An' ye get all bent up when I tell *ye* t'stay out o' danger." His eyes were dark and furious and matched his tight voice. "Don' be a bloody *mug*, Evaline. Ye 'ave a knack fer makin' me see the red as of late, don' ye?"

With that, he shoved past me into the dark building.

Fine. If he wanted to face a troop of UnDead, that was his blooming choice.

I slipped in behind him, hefting a stake in my hand. Pix was a dark shadow ahead of me as he moved along like a shadow himself. And why was I reduced to following him? Whatever happened to ladies first?

A door opened next to me and I hardly had to think about it: My arm pistoned back as the vampire emerged, then slammed forward before he even knew what happened. *Poof.*

I grinned as Pix turned around. I dusted ash off my arm as he glanced over me in the dim light. Obviously he was still angry, for he turned and continued on his way. Then I heard low, urgent voices from behind a door and I stopped.

". . . Willa!" came through the wall.

I must have made a sound because Pix was at my side in an instant. I noticed he had something in his hand too: a stake. Well, at least he'd come properly armed.

I eased the door open and found myself face to face with Mina Holmes and Olympia Babbage.

"About dratted time." Mina yanked me into the chamber. "I've been here for hours, waiting for you. It's worse than I thought, Evaline. Most of the boys—all the missing boys, including Robby—*they're* vampires now. Most all of them have been turned. The rest they use to feed on, and to steal, until they decide to make them UnDead. It's a band of vampire pickpockets!"

"What happened to you?" Blood stained her neck and I could see two puncture wounds there.

"They accosted me and tied me up, then one of the little buggers thought I'd be a good snack. Fortunately, I now know how to escape from binding ropes—thanks to Miss Fenley—and once I was free, I surprised my attackers with a splash of holy water. I escaped in the melee and was able to find where they were keeping Miss Babbage. We've been hiding out waiting for you."

"Right." I couldn't hold back a smile of admiration. "Nicely done."

"Now we have to locate Willa and get her out of here." But Mina's voice sounded wobbly and her eyes glassy.

"I have some salted holy water." I bent to dig in my boot.

"Later. We must find Willa and escape as soon as possible."

"It's nearly dawn. The sunrise will make it that much easier."

I turned to Pix, who had been speaking intently with Miss Babbage. "You know each other?"

He looked mildly uncomfortable. "Aye. We 'ave . . . business."

"Business" again. It took only a moment for it to make sense. All the electric lights in her workshop, just like the ones in his place . . . the gadget he wore on his wrist to open the door to his apartments . . . the floating-driving motorcar . . . They were a match made in heaven. I wondered if he called the pretty blonde "luv" too.

And kissed her in the shadows.

"What are you waiting for?" Mina gave me a shake.

I pulled free. "Follow me. I'll lead the way."

I slipped into the hall without a backward glance at Pix. The others followed. I heard a soft murmur behind me, then Mina tugged my arm. "This way. We don't want to go toward the main parlor or they'll see us. And I didn't get to check the rest of the place. There might be . . . um . . . there could be someone else here. Whom we need to extricate."

The hideout was much larger than it seemed from the exterior. *La société* must have taken over the entire building. The corridor we walked was short and narrow, with five doors. Mina listened at each one, then opened it to check inside.

Inside the fourth door, she gasped. I pushed in past her, stake at the ready, to see a woman in a crumpled heap on a small bed. A bit of light shone through a barred window. It gave us enough illumination to see the dark mass of the woman's hair spilling around her.

She was sleeping or worse, for she had no reaction to our presence. Her breathing was so shallow so as to be hardly noticeable, and when Mina checked a wrist for her pulse, she shook her head grimly.

I recognized the woman wasn't an UnDead, but when my companion pushed the hair from the victim's face, neither of us were prepared for the sight.

"*Miss Adler?*"

Suddenly there was a small light in Mina's hand, casting a direct glow over our mentor's pinched, slack features.

"Is she dead?" I whispered.

"Pulse is very faint, and she's hardly breathing. She's bad. And . . . look." Mina held the small illuminator so I could see the marks on Miss Adler's neck and shoulder. They were raw and fairly new, with blood still oozing from them.

My companion handed me the light as she lifted the woman's limp hand. Bloodstains marked her sleeve, and there was another set of marks on the inside of her arm. They were older. Much older.

"*Evaline.*" Mina turned Miss Adler's wrist for me to see more clearly. On the inside, where the skin was the most delicate and thin, was the unmistakable image of a seven-legged spider.

*La société.*

"She always wears gloves, or that wide-banded watch. She took care that no one should ever see it. And it's not new." Mina went back into action. "She needs help, desperately. And I'm not sure . . . it may be too late already. She's lost an inordinate amount of blood. Observe her skin."

Miss Adler had a pasty gray pallor and her breathing was shallow and rough. Even during our examination, she'd neither moved nor opened her eyes.

"They've drained her dry." Then another, even worse realization struck me. "Oh, gad, *Mina.* They might not have only fed on her. They might have—"

"They might have *turned* her," she finished for me. "That's how you turn a mortal to an UnDead. The vampire drinks all the blood, feeds on the human until they are . . . comatose from loss of blood. And then the UnDead offers his own blood for the victim to drink, to feed on."

"I *know*." My voice was fierce and low. Pix had come to stand next to me and for some reason, I wanted to touch him.

"Is there any way to know whether she's been turned?" Mina asked.

I shook my head. "Not until she wakens. If she does."

"The fact is, in her state, I suspect she'll either die from the loss of blood, or she'll awaken as an UnDead. She's lost too much blood to survive."

"Yes. Either way . . . we have to get her out of here. We can't leave her."

I turned to Pix. "You need to take her. Please. Take her to safety while I find Willa. You and Olympia get Miss Adler. . . ."

For once, he didn't argue, though temper flared in his eyes.

"You go too, Mina."

"Not bloody likely," my partner said angrily. "I'm not leaving here without Willa. And . . . there might be others."

But I hardly heard her, for Pix took me by the arm and yanked me aside, away from the others.

"Evaline Stoker." His teeth were clenched so hard he could hardly get the words out. "Ye are th' most infuriatin' female . . ."

"You know I'm right. She's got to have help—"

"That woman is beyond 'elp, an' ye know it. But I'll do as ye ask—I'll get the Adler woman and Olympia out into the sun, where they'll be safe—well, unless Adler's been turned—but then I'll be back." He glanced at the small window. "'Ere. That's the best way. Opens right into the dawn."

I wasn't certain I could do it. . . . I grasped two of the bars and began to pull. I knew I was strong, but I didn't know if I had enough. I felt the iron rods give, just a little . . . or maybe it was my imagination. Still, I pulled.

"Move." Pix shoved me out of the way. I swung back toward him, but he held up a hand. "Jus' wait." A small light flared in his hands. "*Move*," he said more fiercely, lobbing the light at the window.

*Boom!*

A cloud of smoke exploded into the chamber as Pix shoved me toward the hallway door. I stumbled out into the corridor, looking back to see that not only were the bars gone, but the window had gotten significantly larger. Fresh air, tinged with the gray of dawn, streamed into the room. Mina bumped into me as she staggered into the hall.

With a smooth movement, Pix hoisted Miss Adler over his shoulder. Olympia stood by, blinking owlishly, the pale light of dawn filtering over her pale blond hair.

She was probably wishing for a piece of paper to make notes.

Hearing shouts in the distance, I bolted the chamber door to give Pix a few more seconds to escape. Then I rushed down the hall, checking every door to see if Willa was behind it. I had no idea where I was or the layout of the building, and after a short time, I was completely confused.

"This way," Mina hissed, grabbing my arm. She yanked me down a hallway that seemed familiar. Despite her pale face and the renewed shine of blood at her neck, she seemed clear-minded. She led me around a corner, and we found ourselves facing the open door of a parlor. It was a large warm, red space with low gas lamps and a roaring fire on one wall. The chamber was empty and oddly silent.

"Where did they all go?" Mina whispered. "They were all here hours ago. The place has become deserted."

"I don't know, but if we're going to find Willa—" I stopped, for I heard a noise behind me.

Mina turned. "Willa!"

Her throat and dress were covered with blood. She looked pale, but there was lucidity in her eyes. As bad as she appeared, she looked much better than poor Miss Adler.

She flew toward Mina. "Oh, thank heavens you're here. They brought me here, and I thought—"

"You're going to be all right. We're taking you home now."

"No!" The defiant order resounded in the empty chamber.

I turned to see a group of boys, ranging in ages from nine to fourteen. They stood in a cluster, with one boy in front. He had honey-blond hair and a handsome face. He must have been Robby Ashton, boy vampire.

"You'll not take Willa," he said. "You'll not take her from me!"

"Come now, Willa," Mina was saying. Her expression was anxious, and she gripped the girl's arm tightly. "You need to come with us. Everything's going to be just fine."

"Robby needs to come home. I promised Mother I'd help him—"

"You promised your mother you'd help him get to her, to find her. To find your mother so they can rest in peace together." Mina's voice was odd: slow, steady, and very careful. As if she walked some dangerous line. "Robby can't come home with you, Willa. . . ."

The group of boys had moved into the chamber, forming a half-circle at the entrance. They were a motley crew . . . and from the blazingly cold chill at the back of my neck, it also seemed Mina was correct: All or most of them were UnDead.

"Take her out of here," I ordered Mina, watching the gang carefully. They might have been boys of ten or eleven, but each was more dangerous than a grown man with a weapon.

I was facing an army. I gripped a stake in my hand and pulled the silver cross out from behind my shirt.

"No!" Robby's voice was shrill and agonized, and he reared back a little. His companions edged closer around him, despite the deterrent of my cross. Some of them flared red eyes and revealed fangs. Others, the ones who were still mortal, brandished knives.

Still watching the boys, I eased down to pull two vials from my boot. "Mina." I tossed one to her. "Now get her out of here. I'll take care of this."

I gave her credit: She did her best. Mina tried to pull Willa with her, but the other woman dug her heels in. "I can't leave him. I can't leave Robby!"

"You *must*! Do you not see?" Mina struggled with her, but the blond girl fought back, crying. "He's no longer your brother. He's lost to you."

"Willa stays with me! I'm not going to let her leave again," Robby roared. His eyes flared red, and his lips curled back to show long, lethal fangs.

In one swift move, the boy flew across the room toward Willa and Mina.

I vaulted forward, stake in hand, and crashed into him in midair. We tumbled to the floor, his sharp nails clawing at me viciously, his mouth in a horrible rictus of fury and desperation.

"You can't have her! She's my sister!" He was filled with horrible strength, violent and desperate—a match even for me. He drew blood from my face, my throat, and I fought to keep hold of the stake, crushed between Robby's torso and mine. We rolled on the ground as Willa screamed and cried for him and Mina held her back. The other boys gathered around, randomly kicking me as I twisted and rolled with the lunatic boy.

From the corner of my eye, I saw Mina's arm move sharply toward the crowd. A rush of water sparkled through the air, then splashed onto them. Without pause, she did it a second time and more holy water sprinkled onto their sensitive skin.

Robby slammed his head into mine, smashing into my cheek. The pain gave me a rush of furious strength and I bucked and twisted, whipping his head against the ground.

I pulled free and leapt to my feet. Robby surged up after me, mouth stretched with malevolence. But it was too late. Before he was even upright, I had the stake ready and drove it home as he lunged, right through his heart.

Robby screamed, high and terrified . . . then exploded into ash.

I staggered away, savage satisfaction blasting through me as I looked around for the next victim. What was that— two so far today? One yesterday in Spitalfields—

An agonized shriek tore through the stillness. "*Nooooo!*"

Suddenly, Willa was on me, tearing at me, pulling at my hair, pounding on me. "You killed my *brother*! *You killed him! You killed Robby!*"

Somehow Mina pulled her off me and I staggered to my feet, shocked and confused. "Willa, I—"

"You killed my brother!" she screamed again. Her shrieks were turning into sobs, echoing through the cavernous entryway as she continued to pummel and scratch at me. "*How could you kill my brother?*"

I heard voices in the distance, pounding feet and shouts. I readied myself with my stake, stepping away, but I was shaky and unsettled.

What was wrong with her? Didn't she understand? Robby wasn't her brother anymore. He was an UnDead!

A door at the opposite side of the parlor burst open. Pix stood there, and behind him, I could see the entrance where he'd unlocked the door, and, beyond, the outside courtyard. The bare light of dawn spilled over the cobblestones.

"Willa, please." Mina struggled to hold her back from me.

Pix helped Mina drag a hostile, sobbing Willa out into the safety of sunlight.

I turned to face the rest of the UnDead members of the pickpocket gang, who were just recovering from their bout with holy water. The four mortal ones edged toward the wall, watching with wide eyes.

They surged toward me like rats attacking a piece of meat. Three, four, five, maybe six of them. It was eerie and terrifying to be fighting boys, so desperate and evil. I swung my stake, stabbing one in his slender torso, then turning to meet another. It was horrible, killing these young boys—boys who should have been playing and going to school instead of drinking blood and being turned to ash.

They came, one after the other, pulling at my legs, tumbling me to the ground. Three pounced on me and I jammed the stake up into the nearest one as another kicked me in the head. Ash blasted into my nose and mouth. Coughing, I twisted, trying to rise, but now there were three more of them on me, their weight and furious nails and teeth holding me prisoner as I bucked and kicked.

A shadow rose over us, and then one boy froze. He burst into ash as another one screamed and reared away. I freed my arm, shoving the stake up into him.

Then it was silent. I looked up at Pix, who stood over me. His expression was inscrutable. The air was heavy with the stink of evil and death, along with foul ash. Fragments of it still filtered through the air.

My eyes stung. I shook the loose hair from my face and hauled myself to my feet, turning away from Pix.

I stood silent, breathing heavily, looking around at what remained of a dozen young boys.

Confused. Shocked. Disturbed.

My hands shook. My belly lurched. *What had I done?*

A hand touched my shoulder.

"Don't say a blasted word," I snapped at Mina. The sting in my eyes was tears.

"Evaline," Mina began.

"Stop," I hissed. "For once, just *stop*." I blinked rapidly and turned before anyone could see.

She didn't understand. She couldn't.

None of them could. Ever.

# MISS HOLMES

## *Aftermath*

I t was a terrible, horrifying task to drag Willa Ashton from what had been *La société*'s lair.

She was inconsolable, and no matter how much I tried to reason with her, she couldn't accept the death of her brother. I had to forcibly keep her from attacking Evaline more than once after that. That disreputable Pix made himself useful by herding out the four boys who hadn't been turned UnDead, keeping close watch on them. None of them appeared to want to escape. I could only assume whatever thrall or mesmerization had been inflicted on them had not worn off.

I also took one last sweep through the hideout to see if I could find Dylan—or any other member of *La société* who needed to be retrieved. I hadn't really expected to find him there, but nor had I expected to see Miss Adler either. Still, I was beyond relieved when there was no sign of my friend.

By the time we managed to get Willa and the rest of the pickpocket gang out into the daylight, it was well past dawn and the courtyard was filling with curious bystanders and the authorities. But for once, London was greeted with a bright yellow sun that cast a warm glow over the dark, drab buildings of Smithfield.

Pix—who, I must admit, had been instrumental in the entire process of our escape—disappeared at the whine of police caddies approaching. I would have done so myself, for now that Willa was safe I was desperate to find out Miss Adler's condition—except that one of the Met officers who arrived on the scene was none other than my ginger-haired nemesis.

"Good morning, Inspector Grayling."

"Ah. Miss Holmes. I should have expected it. Wherever there are dead bodies, fires, pickpockets, or explosions, you always seem to appear. I received a cryptic and nearly illegible message from your friend Miss Stoker which I interpreted as a request for assistance. What is it you've gotten yourself involved in this time?" He looked down at me from that excessive height. "Was it you who caused the explosion?"

"Of course not. But I'm happy to report, I've solved the Yingling case—as well as put a stop to that particularly adept pickpocket ring. The culprit is Miss Geraldine Kluger, who has been attempting to discredit her niece, Willa Ashton, so she could be committed to a lunatic asylum. She was also instrumental in abducting a number of boys and forcing them to act as a pickpocket gang."

Although I explained in great detail about our escapades, I declined to tell Grayling about the UnDead element of the case. He struck me as the sort of man who would scoff at the very thought of vampires running about his London.

"And so," I finished, "as I saw no sign of Miss Kluger during my final search of the hideaway, I suggest you put out an arrest warrant for her. She is driving a Two-Seat Charley."

"Right then. Admirable work, Miss Holmes. Between your experiences and the evidence we collected at the crime scene, once the Yard apprehends Geraldine Kluger, one can expect her to be incarcerated for a long time." He handed me a handkerchief.

I took it and raised a brow. "Inspector?"

"You appear to have met with some . . . mishap of your own." He gestured to my neck.

*Oh.* I immediately dabbed at the blood encrusted on my neck, thankful I'd already applied salted holy water to stop the bleeding and encourage healing.

"Let us be thankful there weren't any two-story windows for you to try and tumble from" were Grayling's last words as he turned to his official business. "Or rivers to fall into."

I might have had a witty response, but at the moment I was much too worried about Miss Adler. Instead, I grabbed Evaline and said, "Pix said Olympia took Miss Adler to the hospital. We must get there immediately, for in the event she *does* awaken . . ." I stopped, for I didn't want to put it into words.

Evaline looked at me with expressionless eyes. "Yes. I'll take care of it. *If* she awakens, I know what must be done."

# Miss Holmes

*Many Questions and One Answer*

"I was young. And impressionable. I was in Paris! And *La société* . . . that's what they do. They prey on impressionable, naive people—especially young ones."

A very thin and pale Miss Adler was speaking to us in her office one week after the events at the *La société* hideout. But, miraculously, she was alive—*mortal* and alive.

And it was all thanks to Dylan.

Not even certain where he was or what he'd been doing—though I was terribly relieved *not* to have found him in *La société*—as we left Smithfield that morning, I sent word to Dylan that Miss Adler was gravely ill, suggesting he come at once.

I was sure he'd want to see her one last time. I sent one message through the Museum and another to Dr. Watson, not knowing whether Dylan had been spending time with my uncle's partner. I didn't know any other way to reach him so urgently.

When Dylan arrived at the hospital, he rushed up to me. "What's happened to her?"

To my relief, he looked less gray and pasty than he had the last time I saw him. I couldn't help but glance at his shirt sleeve when he took off his coat—and it was pristine and white. No bloodstains.

"Vampire bites. They drained her blood. If she survives, it's because she's been turned UnDead," Evaline explained.

"She's lost too much blood." I felt exceedingly weary and lightheaded myself. "She's hardly breathing and her pulse is very weak."

"I can save her."

I stared at him. "What do you mean?"

"*I can save her.*" Before I could react, Dylan was shouting for nurses and Dr. Lister and several others for assistance.

"What is going on?" I demanded, trying to quell my rising hope.

"Blood transfusions, Mina," he said rapidly. "I'm a universal donor. I can give blood to anyone." He brandished Prince Albert's pin, now on his coat lapel. "This helped—it made them all listen to me, and I've been testing out the procedure for a week now. I've been working with Dr. Lister and Dr. Watson. Mina, I can give Irene *my* blood."

I shook my head. I was still feeling weakness from my own loss of blood, for I didn't understand at all what he meant.

As it turned out, it didn't matter whether I understood or not. Whatever Dylan did—and he promised to explain it all to me in depth later—it saved Miss Adler's life.

He was a hero again. I looked at him across the office and he caught my eye, giving me a smile that made my stomach flutter. How foolish had I been to think he'd fallen in with *La société*?

But now that Miss Adler was alive and recovering, she had things to tell us. Things we needed to know, and things perhaps she should have been forthcoming about sooner.

I glanced at Evaline. She seemed almost herself, although I detected some brittleness about her since everything related to the spiritglass case had ended. I could only surmise it had to do with that ugly scene with Willa after Evaline killed Robby.

Incidentally, there'd been an announcement in the *Times* that Miss Willa Ashton and Mr. James Treadwell were to be wed, and her guardian, Herrell Ashton, was giving her away. I suspected neither Evaline nor I would be invited to the nuptials, and although I didn't care at all about the social event, I felt as if Miss Ashton should at least acknowledge the fact that, without Evaline and myself, there wouldn't be any nuptials.

Obviously, with Miss Geraldine Kluger out of the picture, Willa no longer needed to worry about being committed to a lunatic asylum. The whole story was in the papers—at least, the censored part I'd given to Grayling—and so everyone, including the Nortons, knew poor Willa Ashton had been manipulated by her aunt. Miss Kluger's motive was put out to be greed—she wanted control of her niece and nephew's money, and she forced a group of boys to play pickpocket for her as well.

I returned my attention to Miss Adler with difficulty and apprehension. Although I'd been brimming with questions since learning she bore the mark of *La société*, I found myself surprisingly reluctant to hear her story.

Whatever else I deduced, it was clear Irene Adler had, at least at one point, been a willing member of *La société*. What wasn't clear, and what I was strangely reluctant to ask, was how she'd come to be at Gadreau's lair a week ago. Willingly or unwillingly. I wasn't certain I wanted to know.

"There was a *La société* meeting on the night of the grand opening of New Vauxhall Gardens. And I'm certain I saw you there at the Gardens, Miss Adler. Were you at the meeting?" Evaline let her voice trail off, but she was watching our mentor closely.

For the first time since I'd known her, Miss Adler appeared utterly uncomfortable. "I . . . did attend. For a variety of reasons. I wanted to find out why they were in London. I knew of Gadreau, of course—he's been a powerful vampire for more than two decades. I needed to know what brought him to London from Paris."

"Presumably it was his mortal lover, Geraldine Kluger, the certified spinster. She came back because her sister, Willa's mother, died, and she was going to take care of the children. Robby and Willa."

"Fine job she did taking care of them," Evaline muttered.

I nodded. "Aunt Geraldine did it all to keep her lover happy, comfortable, and safe. It was all for love—a powerful motivator, if I do say so. And in fact, I did, did I not? Early on in the investigation?"

"As I recall, you were speaking of Miss Norton as a possible suspect, because she was in love with Mr. Treadwell," Evaline pointed out.

I sniffed and turned to Miss Adler. "Even after all that, you didn't see fit to tell us you were a member of the group?"

"No. And I made a mistake. But . . . it's not something I'm proud of. It was a foolish thing I did, getting involved with *La société* many years ago when I was living in Paris. I had some friends, and we . . ." Her voice trailed off and her eyes shifted down. "It was a mistake of youth." Then she looked up at us with a clear gaze. "I hope you can forgive me for not being completely forthcoming. I didn't realize it would become such a dangerous concern."

"*La société* and the UnDead are always my concern," Evaline said flatly. "And always will be."

"Of course you're right, Evaline. Please accept my apologies, again. Sincerely. I'll be bringing Her Royal Highness Princess Alexandra up to date on everything that's occurred— including that you and Mina have aborted *La société*'s return— and I'll highly recommend you to her once more."

"But what were you doing there that night?" I pressed. "Why were you there with Gadreau and Miss Kluger? And nearly dead? Were they trying to kill you?"

For the first time, I had the disconcerting experience of seeing Miss Adler appear chagrined. "When one is a member of *La société*, one knows how to communicate with other members. As you may have suspected, the Pickled Nurse was a location where messages could be delivered and received, and one night I managed to gain entrance to the purlieu. I thought I could do my own detective work, and report back to you. But my true purpose was discovered and Gadreau and his boys . . . they took the opportunity to express their displeasure with my infiltration." She reached over to touch Dylan's hand. "If it hadn't been for you, I'd be dead. For I would never have drunk the blood of an UnDead, and I was nearly dry. And you two, Mina and Evaline. If you hadn't searched thoroughly enough . . . You all saved my life."

I looked away when I noticed the uncharacteristic glistening in her eyes. Evaline cleared her throat and Dylan shifted in his seat.

"Very well then." Miss Adler tucked her handkerchief away and turned to me. "As far as Scotland Yard is concerned, the case with Mrs. Yingling is closed?"

I nodded. "Yes. I heard from Inspector Grayling that, thanks to my information—including a description of Miss Kluger's Two-Seat Charley—they were able to apprehend her. She's in custody and will stand trial for kidnapping and attempted murder. Unfortunately, during the scuffle of removing her from her vehicle—which has tinted gray windows—Gadreau tried to escape. As you might recall, it was a very sunny day, and . . . well, I do not believe he got very far." I smiled grimly.

"The vampire burned up?" Dylan asked, his eyes lit with humor. "You mean, he doesn't sparkle in the sunlight?"

I shook my head and rolled my eyes with affection. I had no idea why he was under the impression that UnDead glittered in the sunlight, but he was always making jests like that. "I haven't heard from Grayling precisely what the police thought about Gadreau's sudden disappearance, and I'm certainly not about to ask. Let them investigate that mystery if they so choose."

"And so all of the Para-Natural happenings have been fully explained?" Miss Adler said.

I did not respond.

That was the one thing that niggled at me, the one thing I couldn't accept. There was no physical or rational explanation for the green amorphous visitations of Marta Ashton . . . as well as the odd messages for Evaline.

The only other interpretation was that they had, in fact, been real spiritual manifestations.

I'd mulled over the possibility for days, trying to find a more palatable explanation for those occurrences.

But over and over, I returned to Uncle Sherlock's philosophy: When even the impossible has been eliminated, whatever remains, regardless of how improbable, must be the truth.

And yet the truth was one I could not accept. Or, at least, I did not *wish* to accept it.

Visiting spirits? Ghosts? Speaking through mediums and dreams?

I didn't like the realization that there were things of this world that cannot be explained through logic and deduction. It made me feel unsettled and inadequate.

It made me feel as if I could never be wholly certain of everything I understood about the world, ever again.

After Miss Adler left to rest and Dylan returned to hospital—where he'd been spending a good amount of time—Evaline offered me a ride home in her carriage.

"I've been meaning to speak to you about something for over a week now," she said once we started off. "But I wanted to think about it first."

"What is it?" She looked very serious. Maybe she was going to bow out of our partnership in order to hunt vampires full-time. If there were any left in London—we didn't really know. And we wouldn't until one showed up again.

Evaline shifted on the carriage seat, her pretty face serious. "Where did you get the book *The Venator*?"

Her question took me by surprise. "It's my father's, I would guess. Or I suppose it could be Uncle Sherlock's. I found it in our library at home. I discovered it one day—I've read every volume in there. It was tucked in the back behind another book, and it appeared interesting."

She was still looking at me strangely. "I don't think it's your father's."

"What do you mean?" I felt an odd sensation inside me. What was wrong with her? But my heart was pounding, my insides were in an upheaval. There was something unsettling about the way she was staring at me.

"Why do you have a picture of my mentor, Siri, on the shelf above your fireplace?"

I stared at her and the whole space seemed to tilt and then right itself. "That's not your mentor," I said stupidly. "That's my mother, Desirée."

# ACKNOWLEDGMENTS

As before, the number of people to whom I owe gratitude for their support for *The Spiritglass Charade*, and the entire realm of the Stoker & Holmes series, is amazing.

I'm always thankful for the never-ending work by Maura Kye-Casella, her support for my ideas, and her willing ear.

Kelli Chipponeri is an editor extraordinaire and constantly blows me away with her attention to detail, creativity, and determination to make these books the absolute best they can be. They are so much better for her efforts, and for that I'm truly grateful. Her assistant Ariel Richardson is a huge, behind-the-scenes rock of support and surely knows the books as well as Kelli!

The entire design, marketing, and publicity crew at Chronicle Books continues to stun me with their ideas, responsiveness, and tireless hours spent on this series—especially Kim Lauber, Ali Presley, Lara Starr, Amber Morley, Jen Tolo Pierce, and Kelsey Jones. I couldn't be more pleased and proud to be part of the Chronicle Books family.

I'm indebted to my foodie friends Gary and Darlene March, MaryAlice and Dennis Galloway, and Renee Chodkowski for helping me "stock" the bar at the Pickled Nurse—I look forward to trying all of your creative pickle flavors at some future gathering.

A big thanks to my dear friend and colleague Mara Jacobs for doing a last-minute read of an early version of this manuscript, and for the subsequent discussion over our favorite cheesccake at Tomato Bros.

A special hug and so much love to Darlene March for being there for me in the last year, in so many ways, and for helping me always delve ever deeper.

LeeAnn Louis-Prescott, Jana DeLeon, Liz Kelly, Erin Wolfe, and my mother, Joyce, have all helped me along the journey with this book through love, support, and other creative processes—and I adore you all. Thanks to my other writer friends for listening: Trish Milburn, Kate Cross, Holli Bertram, and Deb Holland.

And finally, I am blessed to have such a supportive, loving husband and children, especially during those crazy weeks approaching deadline. You have no idea how much your love, sense of humor, and intelligence affects my creativity. Thank you, and my love always.

# Miss Stoker

## An Astonishing Request

*You killed him. You killed my brother!*

I woke with a start and my eyes bolted open.

My heart was pounding and the sheets covering my skin were damp. Darkness pressed into me. I fought to shake off the dream, but awful visions of blood and darkness, fangs and glowing red eyes, still danced in my mind.

*You killed my brother!* The shrieking accusation echoed in my head. *How could you kill him?*

I flung off the bedcovers and stumbled to the window with shaky knees. Silvery moonlight filtered over the tree looming just outside, but there was no flash of evil red eyes to be seen.

As I drew in deep breaths of dank, gloomy London air, my pulse slowed. Surrounding me was the constant undercurrent of steam—the breath of our city, flowing and hissing like that of a massive being.

In the distance, Big Ben's round face glowed dully behind strands of heavy night clouds. Pikes, pipes, and the pitches of rooftops, along with the unmistakable spire of the Oligary Building, jutted upward in an infinite black jumble.

I'd done the right thing, staking the vampire.

I was a vampire hunter. That was my calling, my legacy. I couldn't second-guess my duty.

But Willa Ashton's accusations and her enraged expression still haunted me, both during the day and in my nightmares. *You killed Robby! You murdered my brother!*

A shadow across the street, sleek and catlike, caught my attention. All thoughts of Miss Ashton and her brother fled, along with the last bit of sleepiness.

I recognized that shadow.

It took only a moment to whip off my nightdress and yank on a pair of boots, a chemise, and a short, simple gown (in that order). I was still buckling my new front-fastening over-corset when I climbed out the window.

While I dressed, I'd watched the shadow slip across the empty road and into the darkness spawned by our neighbor's hedge. So when I landed on the ground, light and soundless, I knew where he would be waiting.

But before I could open my mouth, a dusky voice spoke in my ear, "That was a righ' quick change o' duds, luv. Unless ye were sleepin' in yer boots."

I managed to control my startled reaction. How did he move so fast? "Perhaps someday you'll learn not to underestimate me, Pix."

He laughed softly, and the sound traveled down my spine as if he'd traced it with a finger. "Evaline, luv, yer the one person I would never underestimate."

My knees felt trembly again, and I decided it would be best to put some distance between myself and the disreputable, annoying, *sneaky* pickpocket. "What are you doing here?"

"Thought ye migh' want some company on yer patrols." Pix remained in the shadow of the tree, but I could still make out the pale shape of his eyes, a sliver of light along one side of his jaw, and the messy cloud of dark hair. I'd also come to know him well enough to recognize the exaggerated nonchalance in his voice.

"Is that so?" I asked, realizing I sounded uncomfortably like my cohort, Mina Holmes. If she were here, she'd probably already have deduced how Pix had gotten to my neighborhood, why he was present, and what he'd last eaten. I pushed away the thoughts of my know-it-all partner—who claimed her unnatural ability was merely a practice of observation and deduction—and shifted to get a better look at him. "How many nights have you been lurking here, waiting for me to go out?"

I felt a little exposed, and I don't mean because I was hardly dressed (at least by my sister-in-law's standards).

The truth was, despite the fact that three weeks ago I'd slain nearly a dozen vampires in the space of seven days, I *hadn't* been out on the streets, looking for more UnDead. Not since that awful episode with Willa Ashton. And if Pix had been watching and waiting for me each night, he would know I had been shirking my duty.

I pushed away a niggle of guilt.

"Now, luv, don' yet get yer corset lacings all mollied up. I jus' happened t'be in th' vicinity and thought I might find ye climbin' down yer tree."

A Night-Illuminator trundled by, burping steam and sending a small circle of golden yellow light around in its wake. Pix and I shifted as one, moving out of the edge of its glow.

"I haven't seen any UnDead since that night in Smithfield," I said, which, strictly speaking, was the truth—mainly because I hadn't been looking for them. I was certain there weren't any left in the city anyway. Or so I'd been telling myself. "Have you?"

"Nay, luv. Nary a red eye nor a fang t'be seen—at least in Whitechapel and thereabouts."

I relaxed slightly. After all, it had been Pix who'd warned me the vampires had returned to London for the first time in decades. "So what brings you to this 'vicinity'"—I'd noticed the inconsistency of his Cockney before—"that made it convenient for you to be calling on me?"

His shadowed expression changed, and for a moment, I thought he wasn't going to answer. His lips flattened, his gaze shifted away . . . then came to focus, sharp and dark, on me. "I need yer 'elp, Evaline."

I blinked and closed my mouth, which had fallen open. Then I grinned. "Of course you do. So . . . what's the problem? You said you haven't seen any vampires around, so it can't be my stake you need. . . . Is Big Marv giving you a difficult time? You need someone to put him in his place again? Break another finger? Or—wait, I know—you want me to be your arm-wrestling champion for some big competition. No worry, there, Pix, *luv.* . . . I'm happy to stand in for you." I could hardly control my glee. "Or are you looking for pointers about your wardrobe? You could stand to replace that overcoat. It's a bit shabby, and there are some fine Betrovian wool—"

"Evaline." His voice shook, as if he too were fighting to keep from laughing. "Be still. And I do believe that's the first time ye've ever called me luv." He ducked closer to me as he spoke, and the last few words wafted over my cheek. His breath was warm and pleasantly scented with tobacco and some other pungent spice that Mina Holmes could probably identify, but I couldn't. Pix's hand—ungloved as usual—brushed against mine, and I wasn't certain whether it was an accident.

"Oh, you needn't read anything into it—that's how I address all the young men I know."

"Including your Mr. Dancy?"

"Of course," I responded—even though I'd hardly given a thought to the handsome, charming, and well-dressed Mr. Richard Dancy in weeks. "Now, about that overcoat . . ."

"We can discuss overcoats and sundries later, luv. Righ' now I'm on to more pressin' concerns." He hesitated, and I got the impression he was steeling himself to make his big request—whatever it was. "I need ye t'find out somethin'."

My interest faded. "I'm not the one who *finds out* things, Pix. I'm the one who *does* things. I'm sure Mina would be delighted to assist you, after she lectured your ears off—*are* those your real ears, or are you wearing fake ones again?—about her techniques and observation skills and how she's as brilliant as her Uncle Sherlock, which I think is stretching things quite a bit."

"I've a new customer," Pix said. "A partic'larly large and lucrative client, and I need to find out who—"

"Customer? For what?" I had a fairly good idea what he was talking about, despite my question. I still didn't know what that small, palm-sized device was I'd pickpocketed from him a few weeks ago, but I'd come to the conclusion it wasn't the only one of its kind.

Approximately the size of a pound note folded in half, the object had been flat and sleek, with an intricate array of copper, bronze, and silver wheels, cogs, and dials on one slender end. It also had two small, stiff wires protruding from it. I couldn't begin to guess what it was or what it did, and I hadn't had the chance to ask Mina to take a look at it before Pix blackmailed me into giving it back. But I was fairly certain the little machine had something to do with what he called his "affairs."

"Evaline." His voice had gone sharp. "I've tol' ye before, there are things ye don' need t'know."

"Right then. How can I find out who your new customer is—that's what you want from me, isn't it?—if you won't tell me what they are buying." That was a reasonable question.

Something crinkled softly, and he pressed a paper into my hand. I was bringing it up to examine in the drassy light when he stiffened.

"Hush." He shoved me into the darkest shadow—and though *I* hadn't heard anything, I closed my mouth and listened.

Nothing. I heard nothing but the normal, mechanical sounds of the city at night, saw nothing but the random golden circles of gas lamp streetlights, felt nothing but the normal shift in the air . . . and the strong, silent power of his grip.

After a moment I started to speak, but Pix lifted a hand sharply.

Then, without a word, he curled his fingers around my arm and tugged me after him. I pulled easily out of his grip, but continued to follow as he darted from the shadows of tree to hedge to alley to fenceline.

"Look." He pointed abruptly into the sky.

Several blocks away in the narrow space between buildings, brushing past the sky-anchors that floated above a fog-enveloped cluster of roofs, was a slender, elegant vessel, cruising through the sky. Of a long, elliptical shape, it had a bulge at the bottom and batlike wings on the sides.

It was an airship, the likes of which I'd only seen once before: the night I met Pix.

I was aware of a sense of déjà-vu, standing in the darkness with his lean, muscular body brushing against mine, looking up at the eerie object as it made its way silently through the sky.

A beam of light winked on from the airship. The pale stream aimed straight down, riding over the peak of a roof, bumping down the side of the building, and then up the side of the next building as the ship continued to glide over the city. Another beam flashed out, scoring over more buildings in the same choppy way. The ship was coming closer, and the very sight made all the hair on my body prickle and lift as if I'd been dunked into an icy river.

Pix's breathing had become more shallow. His normal easy stance tensed.

"What is it?" I asked. I'd done so before, several times, with no response—so I had little hope he'd actually answer. "Is it the same one we saw . . . before? At the British Museum?"

His chin brushed my forehead. "Aye. I'd hoped they'd gone, but no."

"They? Who?" I realized he hadn't dropped the 'h' in 'hoped,' but for once I was smart enough not to be distracted. I was more interested in finding out about the airship than calling him on his inconsistent accent.

"They're watching the city. All of us. Stay out of the light, Evaline," he said, his words warm against my hair. "Mark m'words, luv, things are about to be changin'." He groped for my hand, and the paper crinkled as he closed my fingers around it. "I gander this might 'elp. Find out what ye can, and let me know. Ye know where t'find me."

And with that, he melted into the shadows.